AF278741

The Gods Wait

Part One

The Age of Aquarius

1: A Sawmill Discotheque

Pascal Adanoma sat down to go to sleep, where he thought about baseballs teleporting around a baseball diamond in layers of energy levels. It was dark in his room. He lived alone. He didn't make his bed every morning, and sometimes he didn't shower before lab. His biggest secret, however, was that his socks didn't match that day. He had many secrets.

He rolled around in a twist of blankets, sweating slightly, a pillow between his legs. He had fits of restless legs, and sometimes he got so tied up in his blankets that he violently squirmed free of them completely. He thought about falling asleep: baseballs in the field, stealing hydrochloric acid and collecting enough to explode a two-liter filled with aluminum foil, but then Doctor Allan Hatch would be furious with him. Doctor Allan Hatch had told him not to steal supplies from the lab, and Pascal worried that he wouldn't be able to spend as much time in the lab as a result.

His eyes carefully avoided the display of his clock. If he looked now, he'd get anxiety over how little sleep he was going to get. He has to wake up sooner than he'll get his rest.

Across the world from Pascal, his unknowing brother Richard Adanoma fell asleep on the couch, but not because his wife was mad at him. He couldn't sleep, so he decided to watch TV in the living room. He turned on a daily sports show at first and started browsing by the second rerun, eventually dropping the remote because he couldn't find anything. An infomercial , a soft blender-selling serenade, sounded him to sleep. Richard sold ladders.

Pascal fell asleep. Richard dreamed of a maple-roasted pig lending him some sweets from its rib. The pig smiled. Richard woke up. Pascal slept. Richard got up and went to the refrigerator. He ate leftovers. Pascal dreamed about the cult of the Nintendo 64. His thumbs twitched without his notice. Richard thought about popping the bubbles cooking into his eggs.

The city was small. Pascal avoided the rush by using back roads, and his fifteen-minute commute turns into a half-hour. Richard was the rush. Richard's socks matched. He got them for Christmas. Pascal drove a nineteen ninety-four rust wagon, mostly rust colored. Richard drove a two-thousand thirteen sedan. It was convenient for him and offered a semblance of luxury. Pascal always ate fast food in the parking lot of the restaurant. Pascal also bought an extra dollar-menu double cheeseburger to take into the lab and snack on if he finds an opportunity. Richard left work to eat lunch. Pascal left no traces; he cleaned up his station as he went, and no one ever saw him use the restroom. Richard frequently commented on how the burger he had for lunch made him gassy.

Richard made cold calls. Richard drove into a university and talked to a couple of good-ol' boys, facilities engineers. Richard asked for their inventory; it read:

- Thirty step stools – in maintenance closets, in supply rooms, some A/V equipment was stored on a high shelf, one became a permanent step at a loading dock behind the cafeteria. They were sturdy enough to hold at least two men.

- Five A-frame ladders – two Bauen industrial burnt orange eight-foot ladders; very mobile and convenient for changing out lights, two twelve-footers for painting odd jobs, gutter sweeping, and trimming the tall bushes at the entrance to the university, and one four-foot ladder that seemed to have found a new home at the theatre department. Richard would use this; the thespians knew the ladder wouldn't find its way back for some time.

- Two extension ladders – used to trim trees and clean the windows of the more impressive buildings, one fourteen-foot and one twenty-eight-foot. The twenty-eight-footer was a Type 1AA ladder, which meant each step can safely hold three hundred and seventy-five pounds. This was more than they needed, but they'd had jobs that required some strange payloads. One time, they had to carry an armchair off a roof after a party was busted. The fourteen-footer had one broken shoe, which was an obvious workplace safety violation.

Pascal used a step stool to reach an unopened box of pipettes from the storage. He thought they would be none the wiser.

...

Nine hours by plane away, in a city so bright that it blinds the souls and eyes of generations, there's a dark holy room playing deafening bass and beat, something post-industrial, a sawmill discotheque, strobes, ambiguity in both dress and sobriety, smokes of all flavors and drinks of all colors, musk: it's the sixth hour of the Sabbath, and here the Lord is being celebrated. There are, after all, several degrees of public or more-or-less private sex being had—in the corners, at the booths, on the floors—latex or cloth sometimes in the way—the drifting attention span of the lazy father at Mass—sweaty flesh slapping like cold cuts on display, salting in its own brine. Heiko, normally adept on the cement, slips and falls on a wet spot, spilling two cups of water. He's not used to disgrace, especially the type that is noticed during communion, and an unfortunate squeal escapes him as he falls, desperately grabbing for anything to soften the impact. He smacks his chin against the damp floor. Doctors say that sensitivity to light is a symptom of a concussion, but doctors aren't as religious as these people.

As a boy growing up somewhere near Wilhelmshaven, his mother used to wake him up, "Bubchen, sei schnell, sonst du die süßen Wolken morgens verpasst." The sweet clouds of morning time. It made the world look like a fairy tale gleaming with a glaze of confectioner's sugary syrup. He was never up early to fish, like his brother, but rather to eat a bit of last night's dessert that he tucked away in his dessert sock and watch the fog rest easy on the lake, what seemed like some supernatural essence. The stuff of gods, Heiko would never think as he nibbled on stale Franzbrötchen. His brother would have already come to the lake, hooked several desperately-flopping creatures and returned home to the realist's appreciation of his mother, which is not to say that she didn't love Heiko. She loved Heiko like she loved poetry; she was prepared to starve for either, and either would cause starvation.

The clouds were settling over his cognition, now clouds with urgent figures propping him up, shuffling fingers, headlights, someone is yelling in an apartment down the street, why was his phone coming through with so much static? Mist clung to everything he saw. Effy is here; he rested easy seeing her face emerging from the lake. Effy.

Blumen hab' ich mir bestellt,

Blühe wieder, bunte Welt.

Kleine Brötchen für kleine Jungen,

Keine Brötchen für keine Jungen.

Another figure as well but soft-sweet things whispered in inattentive ears. "Heiko, your birthday!"

He smiled like a chubby little boy, satisfied with finishing his piece of sock cake, a smile splitting his head in two, "You don't...get...get anything."

"Heiko, please, what is your birthday?" The concerned tone didn't bother him—it reminded him instead of his aunts and uncles asking him why he wasn't better with his hands.

"I just want...to squeeze you!" His posture adjusted, back arching, as if he tried to raise his arms to reach the source of the soft sound.

Sometimes they'd drink the sweetest red wine from Turkey they could find, Merlot grapes from the Anatolia, or so Ihsan told them. Simpler times found them giggling at the naked old men in the quieter spaces of the Tiergarten on Saturday afternoons. The honest sun would set and their red mouths would blend in the night. Effy never let herself get caught up, however.

"I only kiss boys; I never touch them," she'd once revealed to him when he suggested going to the park in an off-moment for her. Her nature was his necktie. She was good at keeping him inconsistent, sometimes feeling some tinge of something that could almost be the hotness of belly that is regret. She didn't really talk to other boys.

The naked old men had a brutal honesty about them, lying there in the park. There they were in full, simply there. Some of them drove to get there, some walked, living close enough to do so, and some took the U-Bahn. Across the spread of them, it could've been bet on that there were at least two accountants, several unemployed men, some of which undoubtedly being the philosopher-architects of the city, one loving father and four drunks, several spliffs or roaches thereof, at least an erection obscured only by posture , and plenty of lingering East German vernacular. What a changing time, and here they were, being humans in an animal garden.

The two sat there, cross-legged, in the sun. Heiko had his shirt off and tied around his head, as one does in such a free place. "I'll be one of them one day," Heiko smiled at Effy revealing pink-stained teeth and a drunken, asymmetrical but unconcerned gaze.

"Hopefully that one there with the nice butt."

He rolled forward onto his stomach and pulled his pants down. "Could I pull it off?"

"Stop," she laughed, "I'm leaving if you're taking off your pants."

"Don't leave; I'll get drunk, and I don't want to have to nap before tonight."

"It's not my problem if you get drunk. And what's tonight?"

"Ihsan's friend is in town."

"Oh. Did you get me some," she asked, knowing exactly what he was implying.

"That's not my problem," he replied content with himself, "but I did. You can thank me tonight."

"Oh, *shut up*. I'll kiss your cheek if you're lucky," she liked to remind herself.

Heiko would be content to meditate on this possibility as if he hadn't just abused his afternoon kissing her in the park anyway. It wasn't about the experience, the feelings and sensory action and reaction, but about the anticipation and the afterglow. She was prettier in his mind's eye. She didn't sweat; she glistened. She certainly tasted of Merlot ten minutes ago, but she would taste of righteous wine, the sort of booze that God gave you to celebrate your vitality. She was full in her body, but she was ripe in his spirit.

It was like the difference between seeing a fish in the lake and then seeing them flop about on the land—the elegance of their movement and the sheen of their chromatic scales under the water, their dumb mouths and eyes and stiff bodies bouncing around all in futility, or the kind of way they cheat their fate by taking a lucky bounce back into the water, which he had seen happen a few times to his brother's frustration.

The taste of her flesh was very real, and there were moments when she seemed like she had a dumb mouth and dumber eyes and flopped about, sometimes taking lucky bounces back into his fantastic Effy, but much of the time he left her in the water altogether. He was not a fisherman; he was more poetic than that in this great city. He may have been a fisherman in some alternative life, some bloke sticking worms into hook to get fish onto line to get meat into belly or coin into purse, thinking about nothing other than the obscured probabilities of the fishes' judgments on decency in real estate.

Instead, he thought about cats, or the various marketing schemes by which one gets dosed with ideology in this day and age. When they were on their way into the park, Heiko had noticed a banner on a street parallel to the park's border that featured a sign: "Say no to racism." It had a link below it, a strong assumption that someone would actually type out a link, and multicolored Ampelmännchen, the ones that were normally red, reaching hands out at their sides and hands overlapping. He'd seen the slogan on digital banners towards drunk hooligans during football matches, but they couldn't read, and there weren't any Ampelmännchen on the banners, what with their larger-than-Berlin approach to racism.

There were highlights of red in the people in his life—beards, scars, shirts, and hands—but never a fully red person. Effy had a streak of red in her hair at the moment, but that was liable to change at short notice. His mother had once had red eyes after his brother got caught kissing a troubled neighbor girl, or at least he remembered her eyes being red. Her voice seemed to be red at the time as well, billowing straight out of the kitchen as Heiko snickered over a piece of sweet bread sitting underneath the window outside. The young Heiko very much enjoyed his mother's and brother's strife.

Red, yellow, brown, blue, and white Ampelmännchen in a line, together in time forever. Stuck, printed on a banner. They couldn't hold sweet bread because they were stuck with each others' hands, a fatalism-in-dependency that recalled a spray-painted picture of two men kissing and something about tödliche Liebe. Heiko wasn't sure where he saw it. Fat stick figures—the physical icon of a Twitter movement or the product of a board of black ties collaborating over a graph of expected target audience coverage fed by tax dollars and faulty non-profits.

There's red people, and then there's cat people. Heiko saw more cats than he could count dart through the same alleys by his apartment day by day, occasionally with some paltry treat still struggling in their effective mouths. Cats governed Berlin block by block: rights of passage to buildings, property rights for the dumpsters, even necessary and sufficient conditions in the finer clauses of treaties and alliances. The color of a cat didn't matter; what was important was the bureaucratic sway a feline had. You simply don't step on a cat's toe. They hiss and show their fangs and scratch wildly. It was always an unpleasant experience, Heiko thought, reflecting on the various stray cats that governed Wilhelmshaven. On one particular instance, his brother had overused a fishing spot and the cats had caught on to the whole thing. Carl, an orange kitty, and Brock, a gray one, met up early that morning to discuss the plan. They gathered their resources, which was not an easy task for cats; they are generally independent and would only collude for the most savory and bountiful of heists. The Duo called for a PPFA meeting to address the masses. Exactly according to the plan, the cats attacked him as soon as he pulled a fish above the water. The embarrassing display of a human ran off in a fit of fear and rage, and the cats divvied up their portions. His brother had not told anyone the reason why he came home empty-handed, which he seldom did, and he didn't know that Heiko witnessed it all. Heiko's brother, simply put, was a dog person.

It all played into a philosophy of his about the cities—that the rule of law surrounding a city forced a lot of people to revert back to a sort of savagery, that the city is in itself a sort of infertile crescent for humanity, breeding cutthroats and liars where there isn't enough of anything. There exists, in Berlin and countless other cities, an unending growl of activity. Some districts don't sleep. Some streets don't wake. To his knowledge, Berlin wasn't the worst of the ranching world. In moments of despair, he would even compare any adversity he faced to the idea of living in China, something far removed and culturally inaccessible that he often caught strange factoids of when he browsed the internet. He would never grow to recognize his bias.

"Saturday's going to be abgefuckt," he said, snapping out of a daze, and he remembered seeing the wrinkled men kissing at the East Side Gallery, "Effy, do you remember the painting of the two men kissing at the gallery?"

"I remember the cartoon faces that seemed to drag on forever, especially the goofy ones with the big lips. I would like to see those again, actually, early this morning or late tonight."

"It's a plan, as long as this stuff is good."

"We'll have fun regardless. Just the idea of it puts one in the mood to dance."

"Where do you want to go?"

"*Prince Charlie's*, of course!"

"You've read my mind," Heiko said, sipping on a glass of wine, observing the naked men some distance in front of them, chatting away at each other with a variety of poses and dispositions.

Carl and Brock had been a recurring theme in the life of young Heiko. Brock was something of a Judas, having once abused the family's lodging and warm spirits during a low point in his life, only to abandon the family and hit the road seeking fresh pussy. He didn't make it far before being hissed at by a younger Carl, who was spry and vicious at the time, not yet the charismatic general that he would grow to become. Carl had, of course, deathly scared Brock, who promptly shot up a tree, not previously knowing he could have done so. Carl masqueraded around the base of the tree for five hours straight, meowing occasionally to draw attention from the locals, letting them know that he was holding Brock hostage. After much consideration, Brock decided to bolt from the tree in the direction of his old house. He saw the kitchen window open, and jumped from the tree, landing gracefully and flying off with Carl close behind, his ears pinned back, fangs out, eyes wide and narrowed, looking like a snake. Brock was beginning to lose ground as he approached the window until at last he leaped gracefully up and through the window. Carl sat at the base of the window, unsure of what to do, until Brock came triumphantly around the house holding a quarter of a gutted fish in his mouth.

The two returned to their township treading along gracefully with tails fixed in the air, each with a healthy chunk of flesh in their mouths. They sat at the base of the tree and nibbled with lazy cat-eyelids and gentle purrs until other kitties gradually gained the bravery to approach, relying on a social understanding between them, a sort of *you go, no you go* approach to the duo. Carl and Brock generously shared at least a lick with everyone who showed up, tasty bites for the prettier or the fiercer of the cats, and it was this way that they formed what became known as the Provincial Potential Feline Alliance (PPFA), a unit that assembled under no ordinary circumstances and generally maintained its fervent individualism, with Carl and Brock as the faces of the polycephalic body, though no one knew at the time that Carl was quietly the true decision-maker.

They had a knack for managing resources, a very rare talent in cats, as demonstrated by various heists, burglaries, and assaults they had staged on the larger neighborhood around them. Needless to say, the PPFA had earned a reputation, and the local populace began to grow wary of the various abandoned sheds, coops, and barns that littered the landscape, hubs of cat clan activity. Both Carl and Brock lived peacefully off of the bounties they earned and the tributes they got. Carl was beginning to carry a gut as a result, and Brock could generally only be seen out when he was chasing down pretty kitty tail. It was the natural atrophy of power yet nearing no critical point. They kept their secrets close to their fluffy chests, and the abundance of fish under their authority kept the rest of the kitties honest.

Heiko was lost again in dream about the pleasantries of drinking wine with Effy at the East Side Gallery, and he forgot that he was drinking wine with Effy at the Tiergarten.

Carl and Brock eventually left the openness of the tree. First of all, the other cats were getting too comfortable and close, often pressing for their shares and being curious kitties about the sizes of their shares, and they also were becoming too involved in the planning. Secondly, there was no protection offered by the tree nor any space for granaries. Lastly, the entirety of the Catfish Affair had torn at their diarchic system; through no fault of planning, the young, all too eager son of an apolitical passionate momma cat was dragged under water by a thirty-pound catfish and never seen again, and the diarchs had crossed each other for the first time in public blame. Barney, a rather slimy creature with comically asymmetrical face markings, had publicly berated the leadership, the first time they had been openly skeptical. The secret of the generous window to the kitchen with the fish inside was the only thing keeping the duo in a lazy power. Carl found an abandoned coop that was near the mouth of the stream that the birds favored for fishing, and Brock took a barn upstream, a bigger castle and safe from the catfish attacks. The secret that kept both of them in power was then contested; it was the deadlock of power, a prospect of mutual destruction that would hopefully limit their potential of expropriation. The PPFA at large was dissolved into Carl's faction, the Probable Feline Alliance (PFA), a state-socialist monarchy that prided itself on autocracy only for the benefit of its individual members, a popular concept for cat society, and Brock's faction, Brock's Pragmatic Feline Army (Brock's PFA), a benevolent republican dictatorship founded on the basis of acting effectively and only on behalf of its individual members, a popular concept for cat society. There was a third party, the Provincial Potential Former Alliance (PPFA II), started by Barney, who'd grown to be a voice of tradition among the kitties. This organization was headed by the Senate, led by the slime himself, and settled for a quasi-nomadic lifestyle as they were too populous to inhabit one place for too long before being chased off by dogs or becoming a local attraction for young boys to throw stones at. They were moderately ineffective in battle as well, having established themselves on a tradition of comfort, which ironically made them have to be much more active to get by. They survived off of a roundish boy who sometimes left socks with sweet bread around a house as well as the collective of beggars they had parading around the various savory-smelling buildings in a row on a stone street. It was tradition, after all. At the moment, the Senate was splitting up half-chewed scraps of raw chicken, stale bread, and a tin of worms that had been stolen from a loud boy. The PFA had been planning a grand heist of the window for some time, which involved scouts and a chain of communication that would corral the loosely-assembled task force, the Poaching Fleet Array, to strike immediately upon advisory of Carl. The movement was to be started immediately, and it would be followed up by the predatory feline assault of Brock's PFA, an action only made safe by its own improbability given that Brock would think he had a Protective Fixture of Assets keeping him safe from Carl's PFA. Little would he know that the P.F.A of Brock's PFA against the predatory feline assault had been betrayed by Carl's Poaching Fleet Array. Brock, unbeknownst to Carl, had been planning an invasion of the window as well. He was not going to use any scouts at the house for fear of being watched by Carl, so he gathered his standing army, his PFA, at this point a reputably strong group of cats, to launch a full-scale, one-and-done assault on the house. Brock had used scouts to see that the young human they often attacked had caught several fish and was on his way back to the house with a bounty, and they could get both the fresh fish and the contents of the house garbage and pantry as well. Brock led his troops from the point of an all-out charge, the pugnacious frontal assault, just as the scouts had told the messengers to tell the advisers to tell Carl to begin the operation. Carl gave the word, and the Poaching Fleet Array, comprised of a slight majority of the PFA's population, was mobilized. Unfortunately, the PPFA II was, at this moment, begging for sweet bread from the plump human underneath the outside of the window. The boy got up and ran as two petrifying formations of assailants charged him directly. Carl and Brock, thinking Barney had discovered their secret, directed troops at the PPFA II and, also seeing each others' armies, at their rivals. It was bloody and vicious. Hisses and squeals rose in a violent choir of cat violence, cats swarming about each other in blurs of furs and batting claws. The PPFA II was slaughtered and routed by the more cruel of the soldiers, its constituents seen scattered, ears back, eyes wide, trailing red. The Senate was quickly killed without dignity and torn into shreds, God-fearing cats who had never taken the time to deal with the more immediate threats of their world. The PFA's PFA slowly began to overtake Brock's PFA's PFA, Carl himself sinking his teeth into backs, sides, and necks, the only advantage being cruelty. A woman's shriek split the scene, and the human who had brought the fish out emerged from an upstairs window with a slingshot, the sweet-bread one next to him watching with delightful agony. A clever rock landed precisely on the side of Carl's head, splitting it wide open, and he was killed with his eyes open, stonily gazing at Brock. Brock called out for a mass retreat, seeing that, of all groups present, they'd been collectively decimated. Cat against human now, all party boundaries were lost, as rocks fell injured cats left and right. The cats fled to their homes, and Brock, seeing the opportunity for a fresh start, brought out the remainder of his granary, now enough to easily feed the small remaining population, to the nomadic PPFA II and the coop that housed the former body that was the PFA. He announced plans to form a new, democratic society, called the Partnership of Parliamentary Feline Authority and began an era of peace, known as the *Pax Feles in Aeternum*, a short-lived golden age of kitty culture.

The afternoon drew to a close and the two parted ways underground, Heiko saying goodbye vicariously through the digitized voice, "einsteigen bitte!"

"Zurückbleiben bitte!" And she was off, a spirit never closer or further, or so it seemed. She had a grace of being totally unaffected, and that may have been her only charm. Heiko was left alone to stare into the core of a motley dog at the foot of a beggar. It was common among the cigarette-butt collectors to fancy themselves dog people in hopes that it would inspire something like sympathy, but the various PFA's shared little with them. The truth of the matter was that the spark in the eyes of these dogs would just as soon be lost their masters', and the image of them together, pathetic and his best friend, desperation, inspired thoughts of contagious disease. They were much smellier and took up more space on the U-bahn. The relationship was an ineffective diarchy or an apathetic dictatorship. No one locked eyes with the man, but Heiko looked at the dog.

Emerging from the underground, a symbolic gesture that always brought a deep breath into Heiko's lungs, he was met by the smell of döner and the noise of Turkish knives clanging and scraping each other in the carving of a great meat tower. Heiko would regularly indulge in a dürüm, a convenient snack and the pinnacle of handheld flavor, and he contented himself with the fact that they had some form of vegetables, his only consistent source thereof. The very best of them would be perfectly crafted to offer the same bite of cucumber sauce, cucumber, chicken (or turkey if he was really feeling himself that day), and leafy greens, and the juices of the meat would be trapped in the bread, saturated salty. Fleshy flesh, like a consumable Effy. Today, like yesterday and the day before, he would treat himself, quietly ordering from the same shop he went to everyday unless he was feeling shameful enough about his habit to walk down the street to another vendor. The problem with that was that he didn't trust their consistency as much, and the usual vendor recognized him and would occasionally treat him to any number of home-cooked Turkish treats; these restaurants were basically extensions of a family's dining room, and one could often find a group of ten or fifteen Turks dining together as the only people in the shop. At least three times in his life, he prided himself on being drunk-confident and charismatic enough to have been extended an invitation to their little feast.

He was always surprised that he never saw Ihsan here. Ihsan worked at a convenience shop right around the corner. In his naivete, he wondered if Ihsan had some sort of allegiance or turf. He couldn't believe that each of these stores was sustainable anyway. He was always the only one in there that didn't look like family, and he gave them only three euros for his meal on every visit.

He received his treat and scurried off down the street to his building, unlocking the gigantic front door, walking through the alley, up the first and second flight of steps, and quietly keying into his own flat. He hated that his floor-mates might hear when he's home, which was never the case in his childhood. Heiko locked the door behind him and felt a giddy excitement in being safe and sound, as was the case every day, and having his food accounted for. Settling down at his computer, he immediately opened up his favorite or second favorite outlet, an anonymous imageboard with the tightly-moderated theme of literature. He was first greeted by a grotesque picture of an large black spider, which he immediately assumed was some attempt at developing a signature, a common but not too common thing—to post a consistently-themed image along with every text post. This was, of course, an affront to the entire philosophy of anonymity. The post read as follows:

"I don't get why someone would buy into Nietzsche without going to the logical conclusion of his philosophies, i.e. Stirner. Please share your Nietzschean arguments here."

He paused, mid-bite, clicked to reply, attached an image of a smug frog, and typed a close variant of one of the first phrases he had learned in English:

"kill yourself, spiderfaggot :^)"

There's a certain type of film in your mouth after a street-food nap, a sort of dry-grease coating, and a distinct lack of satisfaction, just like the dissatisfaction when you refresh the page and find that no one was visibly upset enough to reply to your post. That's how he lost—his opinion dropped into the void. In a dim-lit room, in an apartment with high ceilings and a window looking over an alley with a small courtyard filled with bikes, on a block that was filled to the brim with poor student-artists and poorer Turks distributing paprika-flavored crisps, condoms, and towers of meat, in a district that suffered from a lack of industry and as a result had no offices and an abundance of convenience stores, in a city that never slept, in a country that only wept, Heiko was feeling discontent.

...

Ptolemy's favorite feat, the slaying and inherent taming of a lion with a sort of question-mark-for-tail, was reincarnated shortly before all this, insurmountable distances away and through some magic coincidence of light and perspective that seems to stir spirit into even the most positivist of us, like looking out over a waterfall and taking in the masses of fluid dynamics with gravity crossed, unfathomable generations of evolved biology in stepped tiers of interacting ecological systems, and the massive tectonic movements that would have to have taken place to have resulted in such a sight; the endgame of which, the spirituality of it all, for the positivist, is the dream of someday being able to derive *pure* information out of it all, plug it into a simulation, and run it back once more, heaven or hell, and maybe even being able to inject consciousness into it, eventually creating another simulation therein and injecting consciousness again, another level, further and further.

There was no cataclysm, however, no clash of planets and no rebirth. Heiko hit his head, though, which could be interpreted many ways.

Responding to the backlight of his phone breaking the clean serenity of the dark, he pulled a hand up from its sleeping sleepy position hanging from the side of his bed, not yet feeling any of it and realizing that he wouldn't have the dexterity to yet grasp the phone. He rolled over onto his back and let his arm rest at his side until it woke up, it having a mind of its own. He could tell by the blurred projection on the wall what kind of notification it was. It was an anonymous messaging application that he had rigged to send him a message when one of his secret addresses received an email, a service he custom-installed to his secret mailbox.

Guo Qu lived a quarter of a lifetime waiting for such a message, the other quarters reserved for Hollywood, wishing he had learned to play Mahjong, and spicy peppercorn masochism in that order. He was very excited to see the latest West-funded and -inspired blockbuster, translated roughly as *The Thirteen Hairbands and The Beautiful American*, which was about a series of BDSM action orgies between a popular American actor's doppelganger and thirteen virgins (and, in later scenes, rather sullied young women) in between sequences of Zach Damon cutting the heads off of the invading Japanese eunuchs in Nanjing, led by a villain who has one son. It was to be released tomorrow, the latest from the esteemed director Zhang Li, who had been credited for heart-throbbers such as *Pool Man No Husband*, *Pen and Paper Soldier Wife*, and *Beautiful Land Two Whore*, as well as thrillers like *Ten Bullet One Pirate Alcohol* and *Fast Car Watch Out Lamppost: Lawsuit*, the latter of which being a particularly good meta-analysis of American film culture. The thrillers took a sort of noir approach and were empathized with slow jazz soundtracks. Seeing the film would probably have to wait given the opportunity he was about to check.

Sure enough, a simple job, but time-consuming. Keylogging, some light cross-referencing to learn about the mark, and a clever distribution through emails. Included in the description were several links to be sent to the correct addresses per his research: *Old Man Young Girl Fart Sniffing*, *Cuck Watches Wife Take Tyrone-asaurus Cock*, *Creep Salting Customers' Food Cumpilation*, and *KKK And Black Teen: Leather and The Pump*. The last one included the address within the email. Guo wondered what this person had done to deserve this slandering. The bill was sourced to an American with an American as a target, which was his normal business, but it usually wasn't this vindictive, instead email address collection or credit card sweeps en masse. He hadn't pictured the Americans to be vulnerable enough to need to exact this sort of revenge. They never were in the pictures, anyway. This was either a very strong or a very weak person. There was a cold professionalism in the instructions that seemed to indicate some internet-worldliness, as if this was like bartering with the weekday market vendors over Earth beans at the base of Guo Qu's building.

If he got to the pedantic tasks quickly, he could probably get enough done before the movie to take a break for its showing. He hoped only that it would recall some of the traits of his all-time favorite film, *Sand Man Sing Song*, a rock operetta shot in first-person from the point-of-view of Sand Man, who was never seen in the film but sang exquisitely. The part was given to a half-Australian Chinese who excelled at Han folk music covers played with an oboe ensemble behind him. His opposite, Daniel Victory, the only orange face seen as the antagonist of a Zhang Li film, was played and voiced by a spray-tanned Turk, Bahman Baris, who was notorious for his partying and generosity in substances. The most famous scene of the film was shot in the Mexican parts of the Sonoran desert for tax reasons and had accrued some popularity there. Sand Man, our one true perspective, was atop a medium-sized hill in prayer, andante, sing-songing a few choice words with his deity, the name of which had been formed with a play on words to literally translate as "Relief Aid," but Relief Aid had not yet imparted his eternal wisdom when Daniel Victory showed up with a jazz band in a helicopter during Sand Man's quieting ritardando. This was the part that Guo Qu loved—the climax of the film. Sand Man picked up the volume and tone of his melody, and a righteous battle of song broke out between the smooth jazz and the suddenly-oboed classic Han music, all in English with Chinese characters subtitled to make it seem traditionally exotic.

Sand Man (in forte, chorus):

Relief Aid, here is he!

Orange-faced man, here is he!

Look at his group, no solid ground!

His seven orifices aren't connected.

Daniel Victory (smooth):

A sharp stick points out, smooooth cat,

Let jazz protect you from this cow.

Sand Man (verse, mezzo piano):

His spear not can pierce his shield!

Or his shield not can pierce his sword!

Relief Aid, please shut Daniel mouth,

Like bottle, fortuitous bottle.

Daniel Victory (smoother):

He play qin to nine cow, one hair,

Face as crude opium sex,

Or is that me, smoooooth cat?

The last Daniel Victory line had such a strong impact on its audience, the sort of uncertainty as our evil orange either recognizes his own evilness in opposing such a morally righteous person as Sand Man and quasi-repents, admits that he knows he and his culture are evil and wishes to glorify it as trendy and attractive, or discovers his own insurmountable insignificance even within his own world, ultimately deflating his titanic persona into a groveling jazz-cat on a helicopter. The Chinese public seemed to project their own interpretation of the line depending on their opinion of Americans.

The song's literal English translation had made for a few viral videos on the internet, all of the traditional expressions lost on them and lost as well on Chinese viewers who had a better command of the language than the search-engine translation application that the film's script was designed with, but that didn't take away too much from the entire film. The sort of pop-politico-philosophical ambiguities presented could not be diminished. Will the general populace be worse off in gradually descending to the level of Daniel Victory, embracing hedonistic ideals and loose tempo? Or will they ultimately side with the righteous fascist, Sand Man, and his ethno-centric approach to the changing times?

Guo Qu ultimately found himself a self-governing technocrat among the rabble. He was alright because he didn't shop in fancy super-grocers and he exclusively undermined the American system for a living. He would also never give up spicy peppercorn and couldn't for the life of him enjoy the use of peanut butter, the ultimate gastro-cultural imperialist. It was purely unconscious for him, being a 'good' Chinaman. On one hand, he was going to ruin an American man's life for a few dollars today. On the other hand, he was going to ruin an American man's life for a a decent amount of Renminbi today. Regardless, *The Thirteen Hairbands and The Beautiful American* was on his mind this morning more than the contrasting dialectical approaches to analyzing his nationalistic tendencies.

He got up after some deliberation and sought the staling bag of spicy and numbing fish flavored potato chips that he had left open at his desk the night before. The slightest stale gave the chips a full body, making them almost seem to be more than just a sliver of potato and oil: a healthy, well-rounded breakfast that left your tongue without feeling. He sat down and mentally cracked his knuckles. Dave Stevenson, only child, husband of Kate, Kate—one sister, niece, Alyssa, banks of information on Alyssa. Vibrant social media usage and hashtagging all negro-Judaic movements. Kate and Alyssa for sure. New friend—Cierra Wallace, employee? Negro, non-Judaic. Dark. No reference to the KKK, but sure, why not? Search professional directories—formerly "Sal's Greasy Treats", now "Linole-yum," owned by a group, Stevens and Sons, managed by Doug Stevens, Wallace Stevenson, and Dave Douglas, three greasy white faces with greasy slicked hair and the same tie playing off the same pattern in the same jackets with the same white-shirt background. Stevens and Sons recently acquired by Peachfield

Chemical, too much going on there, not being paid enough to breach corporate networks. That makes four links to varying profiles. Closing in on Dave Stevenson, *were all their names like this?* The movie tonight was going to be so much fun. If only his job was more respectable, he'd have more friends to go with.

...

Cierra Wallace was feeling particularly dark this afternoon. Breakfast found her at the receiving end of the normal overweight charms of the good ol' boys in the freight industry, her regulars at the restaurant, and she was good about giving them just a bit less than they wanted.

"Was everything alright, y'all?"

She was answered with a chorus of burps, the sound of taut leather writhing at the creases of their bellies as they shifted for their wallets, and one attempt at a kind smile that was interrupted by gas sneaking up, "better than it was *BRRUUP* yesterday."

"And y'all want it split three ways?"

The uglier two of the three representatives of J.F. Trucks giggled, like they did everyday, and the heads of FastWay Logistics and Hairtertel Shipping nodded, suppressing gas and leaning forward to try and adjust for the trajectories of noxious fumes escaping up their esophagi. Thoroughly despicable humans, she thought, but they tipped well, probably hoping that one day they'd find her somewhere outside of this shithole and live out some light raceplay fantasy on her, much to her obscured appreciation. Her fantasy was to find some acid and drop it into their eggs, but she only thought of this at work and never remembered to look up if the drug would be broken down before it entered their systems.

The breakfast rush ended, and she was cleaning up and prepping her service station for lunch when her boss, Dave Stevenson, tried to pull the nonchalant maneuver of 'popping in to see how you're doing.' He even gave her an insultingly gentle punch on the arm, "hey Cierra! How are *you* doing today?"

His smile was as wide as the vacuum behind his eyes. "Oh, I'm doing *great*, Dave, thanks for asking. How are *you*?"

"I'm fantastic. Did you see that fight that went viral outside the Kendrick concert? My goodness, that was the funniest thing I'd seen all day. Hey, I've gotta get outta here before my mother-in-law stops by, but I'll be back to see you later. Keep grooving!"

She smiled at him hollowly, knowing that he couldn't help himself. She loathed him for it, and loathed him more for his assumption that she would have taken part in what he knew as "Black Twitter," a medium that he perused specifically trying to close the distance to her, sometimes hum-singing patches of lyrics involving some kind of Goblins or Jewish lawyers. She did not, however, browse Black Twitter, and the mere mention of Kendrick brought up her uncle, ex-member of the Euro-famed jazz duo, *The Wallace Brothers*, who had always tried to get her into African-American music when she was a child. She had always rejected it and later rejected her uncle because of it.

Dave was simpler than all that. He was nothing more than a restaurant manager, as if he had studied cheesy lines and some strange gait in the womb and emerged with an application, handing it to the doctor; his unglowing mother surely expressed a disappointed sigh as she saw her khaki-wearing Oxford blue-shirted newborn son promptly asking the nurses how their shift was going. He occasionally wore socks with his boating shoes, which she knew was a taboo among his people. Acidity towards Dave festered in her mind after his quick, unthinking comment.

She just didn't understand why he would even try with her. She avoided giving him an excuse to manage her. She worked hard and honestly, coming from no surplus of income and disgusted from seeing the very slightest excess (not in education, insight, or art, but in bread on the table) resulting in the J.F. boys getting sweat stains on the bellies of their shirts during breakfast. The tips they left this morning put her around fourteen hundred in cash stashed in several empty deodorant sticks in her bedroom closet, right next to another empty stick that stashed her weed, which, for her, was something of an inherited tradition, possibly her only one. What wasn't a cultural tradition for her was that she was extremely well-read in philosophy; she had just finished *Der Einzige und seine Eigentum*, an egoist piece by a contemporary of other old white men with others' heads up their asses. In fact, she had recently been referred to a literary forum that, as she understood it, specialized in the field. She planned on posting there when she got off work, and she was excited about it.

The cash that she had saved was for a rainy day, hers or maybe someone who deserved a rainy day, or maybe both. Regardless, it was getting to the volume where it would be sufficient in any of the number of methods she had considered over the course of collecting it. It was strange to her that she'd be back to square one after it was gone—back to being an evenings-only part-time student at an unfortunate community college and a mornings-and-afternoons waitress at an unglorified diner.

Lunch was fast approaching, and the rush began to take her mind off of things, soon being replaced by the smell and delicate appeal of the ham-and-cheese sandwich, grilled buttery to golden perfection, something precise enough to captivate all from the Redwoods to the analytic janitors of ivy-leagues. Fat and flesh, a beautiful combination that left any proper man drooling, with a savory treat made from oldened bovine nectar, a real statement on the state of the food chain, and the refined grains used were far removed from the base primitivism of European breads.

She would serve up a healthy baker's dozen of these every noon, each smelling worse than before, to different breeds of appetites. The lunch patrons belonged much more to motorized scooters, wheelchairs, tanks of oxygen, voids of eyebrows, and all the things that inspired a healthy appetite in any proper cynic. She felt quite powerful in handing a heart attack to grasping maws or placing it in front of eyes that were hopelessly locked onto the plastic table cloth between a paper napkin, pre-loaded with cafeteria forks, knives, and spoons, and the sickly left hand of the mouth, a beautifully-framed narrative for the tasteful cuisine.

Her work weeks were spent looking forward to Thursday, which today happened to be, when the local old folks home would manage to drag its members to a lunch that they couldn't see or taste. She liked to imagine that they used stretchers to get the sacks out of bed and wheeled them straight into the bus, and maybe the bus even had rows of wheelchairs instead of seats, an empty hall when no one was inside. They'd probably have to start the process around eight in the morning to wait for the lift to go up and down twenty times and to wait for some hag to put her teeth in and some pervert to put his pants on and stop telling the male nurse about the "itch he couldn't reach between his leggies." Then, they'd get to the dive at about eleven and spend another hour taking down loads of wheelchairs full of empty eyes.

Her favorite patrons were Clyde, the benevolent but loose-boweled; Barry, the miserly Jew with a wrinkled tattoo of the outline of Valkyrie wings; Hal and Kenneth, who would hear something about what some toothless beauty did yesterday, then spend the entirety of their time asking each other '*do what*' and juggling bits of misinformation between them; and the so-called Spice Girls: five old women, Jade, Carol, Gloria, Kay, and Bets, who prided themselves on their quick wit as it related to referencing '80s pop culture that they were too old to enjoy at the time but fancied themselves as 'with it' because of. They had, of course, never heard the Spice Girls, nor did they know they were a music group, but a few of them had heard their granddaughters talking about them ten years ago and assigned it some cultural relevance and edge in their eyes. Between the five of them, they were hip enough to have broken two, leaving the Spice Girls rather sedate at the moment.

The group was being attended to by a few men dressed in white, wheeling them in and politely asking, "Mrs. Singletree, how are you doing on this beautiful day?" Their shiny smiles were beautiful, the snowy cap of a crisp mountain of aesthetic, Cierra thought.

The tables were always pushed together so that the group ate a perpetual Last Supper together, never knowing which members would be gone by the next Thursday, and here they were, centered around a wrinkly Jew with the peaks of wings poking out the back of his shirt collar. The kitchen had several preconstructed ham-and-cheese's for the occasion, an extra green bean casserole was in the oven at the moment, a whole vat of cole slaw had been scrapped up, and they had baked an extra pecan pie this morning. Cierra personally brought a flask with a few shots of whiskey, which she snuck into the coffees of Hal and Kenneth, who'd struck up a deal to give her large tips in return for her feeding them contraband. She usually made about ten dollars from doing the transaction, and she had been doing it for about fifteen weeks now, a healthy slosh fund growing in the deodorant stick.

"Oh, my, they make chairs so low to the ground these days," Jade, one of the more able-hipped of the Spice Girls, was complaining to her posse as she put her hand on the back of the chair and squared up for a controlled fall. Her dark blue knit pants were riding up into the regions that God had abandoned some thirty years earlier, and Clyde, across the table, was grinning widely.

"I didn't know you were so flexible, honey," Clyde suggested.

Kay, still standing, attached to her walker, turned her entire body to Clyde in an immobile, skeptical stance, "Oh, please, you like it tighter than that." All of the Spice Girls had engaged Clyde in intercourse of sorts, something that a bystander would hardly even describe as erotic, for they moved so slowly that they looked somewhere between napping and the afterlife, and their cheeks were rosy enough to look made-up by a mortician, though lacking the decency in apparel.

Clyde, thinking that she was making a comment about his diaper-related problem, took offense. "I'm tighter than you are sweetie," he said, satisfied with his quick wit.

Bets chimed in from her wheelchair, "Oh cram it, old-timer, no one wants what you're selling." Her voice contained within it the rasp of your average helium smoker.

"I'LL HAVE A COFFEE," Kenneth abruptly shouted, from across the table, thinking he had spaced out and almost missed ordering when he heard 'wants' and 'what.' He then realized that the waitress was nowhere to be found and looked generally confused.

Hal, thinking he too had spaced out, shouted, "ME TOO, CAN YOU ADD SUGAR FOR ME?" That was the code word.

"YOU DON'T TAKE SUGAR."

"I KNOW THAT YOU OLD KOOK—IT'S THE WORD!"

Cierra, from her server station some safe distance from the commotion, was quietly giggling at the apocalypse that was this weekly trip. Clyde, by this time, had stood up to prove his virility. It was quite a statement for their type to get up when they didn't have to—it proved that they could and that they had the wherewithal to actually execute the maneuver. Barry, next to Clyde, smacked his lips in the same way he compulsively did. "Clyde! Save it for tonight!"

Carol, another wheelchairer, embittered from having just acquired the freedom post-hip-fracture to be seen and interacted with normally, said acidly, "No coffee for Clyde, he needs to cool out."

Never missing the opportunity to talk about anuses, Jade, who had long ago abandoned any sense and sensibility, piped in, "besides that, he let loose like a balloon filled with warm stew the last time he drank coffee."

Carol and the rest laughed at Clyde, "Dear, you just got FACED."

One of the beautiful, tall assistants, a black one who was helping Kay sit down at the opposite end of the table, snapped at Jade, "JADE! We agreed, no talk about anything below the belt at lunch!"

Jade, always proud to make the staff allude to genitals, replied, "quit buggin' out, buppie, I'm sure you're doing well down there."

Barry, having stayed mostly collected about the madness unfolding around him and feeling a tinge of jealousy as he and Jade were having an on-again bout of anal sex recently, dignified the table with a pound of his fist, "That will simply do, all. I want to order my sandwich and I'm certain that we've been scaring off our lovely server."

Cierra took that as her queue and began the process of negotiating the same menu with every member of the meal, just as she did every week, and, after some fifteen minutes of hard-pressed eye-squinting decision making, the table was accomplished in ordering the same meals for the same appetites as before. The origin was an abstraction to her, their original thought and decision long lost but replicated just so every week. The cole slaw stained the plates the same, and the ham-and-cheeses were plated just so, and the same flickering light above her server station gave her the same tempo in pouring the same shots of whiskey into the same mugs of coffee, and she was looking forward only to another evening spent listening to the placid ramblings of Señor Flanker, a moderate gut anglo with a rigid adherence to the beautiful prose of his idol, Petrov Perez.

Flanker was somewhere between a D-list academic and an answering machine, and his praise of the ethnically-ambiguous Perez left Cierra no choice but to call him Señor. The professor took it well, thinking it made him somehow closer to his hero, whom he'd only every interacted with through the oral copy/pasting of Perez' textbook, *Gretel's Birds and Hansel's Bees: A General Approach to Ecology, Recontextualized in German Fairytales*, for the entirety of the class: four stoners sitting in the back row, a few barred out and eyes-closed adding and dropping the class at points that seemed much too late to do so, two housewives who must've annoyed their husbands until they were sent to this concentration campus, and Cierra, who had been defiantly reading egoist philosophy in the open during lectures for the last two weeks. Upon being questioned for her choice in literature, she told the Señor that she wanted only to pick the brains of the German identity behind these tantalizing studies in mythical ecology. "Ah, Sarah, always ahead of the game! Anyway, it is quite pragmatic, in our academic interpretation, to assume that these sort of hybrids, the Frog King for example, *der Froschkönig zum Beispiel* to you, Cierra, were more intricately designed anatomically, and somewhere along the linguistic development or minimalization of the stories we lost that. Take Kuk, for example, the Egyptian frog-head. If we're to superimpose this sort of altmodisch design upon our more modern tale, or should I say, New High German tale... we would get a much more interesting cross of dietary requirements and a much more complicated ecological system in place as a result. So, let's all treat ourselves and suspend our disbelief for a moment to consider the possibilities."

Kuk, the Pepe of yesteryear, seemed ever-relevant, the smug airs of the dark god in his native and your foreign place, knowing all that you can't and being a goddamn frog in the meanwhile, which seemed, to Cierra, to be nothing more than a freeing concept—to be goddamned, just like her, born into a skin she didn't want to live with, being stuck in the dark but not knowing much about it. It was the modern realization of the Egyptian cosmogony: a frog on the internet that clearly knows something you don't, and you can't begin to tell what's happening on the other side of the pixels, where some invisible logician smites you with wordplay and access to Wikipedia, throwing spooks in your spokes until you fall over, unless, that is, you gain the strength to crush the creatures in your wheels. That was her ideal. She wanted not to have been born differently but to live differently in the very spite of probability, of the world at large, and of her pupal state. She was bitter about herself at present because she hadn't yet the superiority complex to dismiss everyone else and all existing structures, and, in this way, she felt herself an untermensch in the grip of ressentiment and cozied up in the shell-plastic chair listening to the Señor rant about the essentialist approach to the traits of the Seven Dwarves and how their environment would've been shaped more directly by Grumpy than Sleepy, though it could never be said that Sleepy wasn't equally responsible for the conditions at present, for, despite his inactivity, he had a decent footprint, and what should be done with Sneezy? "Let's not get ahead of ourselves for now."

At some point between idealism and egoism, Flanker shut up, and Cierra had the sense to pack up and go home, an ungated community of low-income apartments at the crossroads of Budweiser and Olde English. She didn't wave hello at the normal committee of country-listeners on folding chairs as she parked her car and walked past them. She was on a mission to validate her reactions to Stirner.

She had been referred to an anonymous image board, the Board, that supposedly housed many fanatics for the philosophies of Stirner, possibly the only intellectual safe haven for such beliefs. Vaguely knowing what it meant to be on an anonymous image board, she thought she would try to jest with her own identity with a clever picture attached. A black widow on her carefully-crafted web would do, hopefully guiding an assumption of a fierce femininity behind the post and a break from the average. She knew the Board to be asexual, but not in the tolerant sense; it was safely assumed that every member was male, and she had seen several viral instances of women being targeted after revealing their femininity, a Faustian annihilation.

Carefully crafting her post to only draw serious replies and having seen the brevity of other posts on the site, she wrote:

"I don't get why someone would buy into Nietzsche without going to the logical conclusion of his philosophies, i.e. Stirner. Please share your Nietzschean arguments here."

She patiently waited as the thread refreshed, a timer ticking down to every automatic data recall. Ten seconds, nothing. Twenty seconds, nothing. The longer no one contributed to the thread, the more likely that no one would end up seeing it—the death of an idea.

But then, a reply. Instantly. From nothing to something, and the something had a picture of that goddamn frog, that smug face that tore at her inferiority. The post read:

"kill yourself, spiderfaggot :^)"

Blind rage. Blind rage at the disconnection with the world that stared her down and her own inability to cope with it; these three words reminding her that she was not strong enough to overcome the displacement, and that she couldn't even further her own understanding of this weakness because this smug frog wouldn't even contribute to the conversation, as if the entity behind it was all-knowing enough to legitimate such an personal attack.

The page refreshed again, and another post showed up, text green with satire.

"Daily reminder that Nietzsche was a syphilitic who probably fucked his horse, and Stirner?

>literally who?"

Her lack of direction crashed down on her. It was a lost cause, all of it: her studying, her working to overcome, her sitting through ridiculous lectures by a remarkably obscure pseudointellectual, her serving whiskey to elders and having witnessed Clyde shit himself that one time, which wasn't even funny at the time. It seemed there was nothing she could do to move past it as if she was perpetually suffering to no discernible change in her situation, and that son of a bitch Dave had reminded her of all of this. He was always closer than he needed to be, a micromanager when neither micro- nor macro-management was required. She closed her internet browser, not wanting to see what else would pop up.

How could she genuinely make a change? How could tomorrow have no chance to be like today, or yesterday, or the day before, or any definite time before that? Her funds came to mind. She had a certain power in her access to the internet and a pile of cash, but what could she make of it? There are a number of legitimate routes, all requiring some ingenuity and wittiness, but most only have a tangible effect within the arena of the internet, one of its biggest shortcomings. She needed something that would travel from her computer to her reality. She needed to break with victimhood at large, to make something for herself, and, from her perspective, there was only one way to do so: to make a victim of someone else, the subsitution of the object of a miserable sentence. What does someone do to break the cycle? Something to someone else. She'd read about it everywhere and had a loose concept of Haves and Have-nots as it applied to having white skin and a penis, but she was going to fuck someone regardless of her background.

Revenge. It came to her from the disposition of Kuk and the smirk of Pepe, something she could do to be a dark deity, knowledgeable in an uncertain time. Being as internet savvy as she was, she had heard of and explored a program that allowed access to the deepweb, where she found she could trade virtual currency for anything. She set to exploring for a while, looking for something that would tickle her fancy, and then she found it. She knew it would right the wrongs of her day, and how beautifully it would happen.

Black men with bandannas and banners, squinched faces of wire-frame glasses and politico-dyke hair and thin necks, not a Hispanic in sight other than one sexually-ambiguous pink-haired one holding a sign, *me tiro al perro*, hashtags on street corners. Megaphone footage, "KEEP YOUR HATE SPEECH OFF MY CAMPUS," hashtagging shitlord on videos of racist professors, looking for evidence of the world-wide WASP conspiracy, comments about appropriating hairstyles and asking if its okay to wear something for Halloween, screencapped text messages from drunken fathers being Nazis to innocent daughters, screencapped messages from drunken #boyswillbeboys to innocent girlfriends, women are amazing, women are beautiful, women are strong, men are predictable, men are problematic, let my daughter be naked at school #boyswillbeboys, ethical problems associated with raising male children, images of women in the media, Olympic women being objectified, lots of sex, worrying about curves, being chastised for being fat...

Alyssa secretly hated fat people. She could never post anything with a trace of allusion to this, knowing that some fifteen to seventeen percent of her fifteen thousand followers also followed fat pride blogs. It disgusted her, and she occasionally enjoyed going on binges of watching fat people eat online, the pleasure in their faces, the best ones having buttered rolls on their foreheads, chins, and, of course, in their mouths, dozens of buns on their proud buns, not a breast to be found anywhere, pig skin on their pig skin, their worldview limited by the very fat closing in around their eyes, and you don't see them smile except when they're opening a full jar of mayonaisse. The best of the reviews are produced well enough to warrant the host waddling around the kitchen instead of a stationary camera at the table. It was only good fun to see knees and elbows disappear like little pins had been stuck into the fat at halfway points up and down limbs, pins stuck in to keep some semblance of form, almost like how a clown ties balloons together and they pinch in at every knot. "FattyRants" was her favorite, a channel she subscribed to on one of her ghost accounts, BlackhawkLover1 (though she hated blackhawks), and, at this point, itprimarily featured a man who complained about his weekly hospital visits, all the anxieties associated with waddling through bureaucracy, huffing and puffing and trying to blow the whole house down, having gaggles of nurses fail take his shirt or pants off, seeing their faces turn sour when they lift up his upper-left-middle chest flap trying to get a pulse and are met with last week's scent plus one week of fermentation. His continued health problems had led to the hospital getting a specially-designed bed, lower to the ground and two and a half times wider, in a specially designed room to fit the mechanism it housed that moved the bed up and down. Fatty rants about being judged by people and having to contact clothing manufacturers and custom order his clothes, but he also rejoices in the latest fast food craze. He's got anywhere from an hour to three years to live, and he wants you to hear his voice. He never had a chance. His only friend growing up was Mac, and he believes in fatalism-in-loyalty.

Her phone dinged with a notification, new e-mail from a "d.stevenson," surely her uncle. It contained a shortened link, which she didn't trust but the same curiosity that makes her watch Fatty made her click. Petrifiying fear and satisfaction and a sick validation: *Old Man Young Girl Fart Sniffing*, her worst and best fears confirmed, images of a younger Alyssa staying at her aunt-and-uncles', Dave-and-Katie's, Kate having gone shopping, Alyssa, at five years old, finally becoming embarrassed about her bodily functions, has to use the restroom, and Dave, the once-innocent but always suspicious, the white face that can't obscure its deeply perverse nature, goes in the bathroom after she comes out, "pee-yew, did you make stinkers in there?" Horror, shock and awe as the truth came out, a type of trauma that she'll be able to feel forever. She felt sick and touched herself to make sure she's still in control, but she didn't feel like she was, probably having been creeped on and the subject of all sorts of sick perversions that got her uncle off. It was all coming together, that he only used the main bathroom, Aunt Katie being the sole user of the master bathroom, that they used to invite her and her friends over to the pool on fine summer days and feed them all sorts of delicious foods. He probably had cameras everywhere. There were probably videos of her all over the internet. She was going to have to do some extensive fetish research, a sick pain that she had to endure to get to the bottom of this.

Why would he send this to her? What depravity, what indecency and commitment thereof led him to break and admit his fetish? Should she publish it to her blog or call Aunt Katie first? This might even warrant a video. It does.

She scurried off to the bathroom, invigorated, more alive than when watching Fatty. Maybe she could even break the habit, maybe she could be someone else's internet guilty pleasure, maybe she already was, and she began to do her makeup only to make herself cry in front of the mirror, ruining the lines she had just drawn on her eyes. Questions that she was more curious about than anything else kept her tears coming. *How could he? How could he? What's wrong with him? How could he do that to Katie? What has he done to her? That poor, strong woman, staying in a marriage with him. How could she stay with him? How could anyone stay with him?* And those curiosities, as they do, gave way to insecurities. *How could anyone stay with anyone? I can't even stay with Fatty. My blog isn't even that big. Fatty is doing so much better than me.* And those insecurities to ploys. *Can I go viral? Can I gain ten thousand follows just from this video?* Tears were flowing down to the corners of her smile. She was wearing jeans and a violet bell-sleeve blouse, off-the-shoulder, having planned to go to the mall, but she changed into her pajama pants and an ugly t-shirt. She fluffed her hair up.

The camera was set up. She sat at her desk, sunk her posture, started recording, and got to work on the tears again, looking off-camera and distant. Sounding sullen, she began, "hey all, Alyssa here, Destroyer_of_Cishet, I have something serious to talk about today," She looked camera-left again, wiping a tear from her eye and further smudging her makeup, "I just learned that I was sexually abused for years as a child, I had entirely blocked out the details as victims of sexual abuse often do," she looked directly in the camera, "I don't know why I'm telling you this, I just don't know what to do, I feel so violated, so weak, such a victim, and I don't know what to do. It was my uncle. Apparently he has some sick fetish—I can't even describe it, like some pedo-scat thing that involves innocent children, but apparently he recorded me going to the bathroom in his house, which I did every weekend of every summer for so long," she couldn't look straight at the camera, "I don't know if I'm reaching out, or what I want to get out of this, or if I should upload this. I know nothing will ever be the same, but everything that I've learned from years of being an activist has told me not to take blame for making his crimes public. The worst part is his boyish smile when he used to embarrass me by asking if I just 'made a stinker.' I would've never guessed how sinister he was behind that innocent face. I wanted to love him. I just wanted him to love me. I used to love spending time with him, and he just used me, and the worst part is this creep had the nerve to send me this twisted video, I don't even know how he found my email address, of this senile-looking pervert sniffing some girl's ass who was squatted over him, and she was—" she sobbed, "—she was—she was *farting* on him, and I put it all together right away, all the years of abuse, that son of a bitch, Uncle Dave, you son of a bitch. Uncle Dave, you piece of shit. Uncle Dave another part of the problem, another outing of the true nature of men, of boys. I feel horrible. I'm sorry I had to share. I was breaking apart on the inside. I'll probably be quiet online for a while. Me and my family are going to be going through some things. Thanks for listening. Goodbye."

She hashtagged every cause she could think of: #HeForXir, a movement to remove the male gender distinction on government records, #ProbablyAllWomen, a movement that selectively chose female racecar drivers as its spokespeople, #BlackPeopleAreStillHere, featuring prominent non-culturally-prominent blacks in professional attire (from dental hygienists in purple to sage bass players jazzing about anime, also in purple), #CryingOfLot12, a reaction to the controversial impound auction's listing of an illegally-parked car, whose owner had dodged years of parking tickets, seized during an impromptu abortion, #8StacksForThoseBoysTheyTookCareOfTheBoy, a crowdfunding movement to pay for the group of Jewish lawyers primarily responsible for the acquittal of Tec 9 SMG Murder Killer, charged with indiscriminantly shooting in a gun range, #ShoesForTheStarving, a viral nonprofit who 'brought fly-ass sneakers to broke jokers,' #SayNoToRacism, and other relevant campaigns.

This and a few relevant cross posts and ghost-sharing would ripen, an investment that does better without being touched. With any luck, other prominent members of the community would take it upon themselves to find, rout, and neuter Uncle Dave, the dark face behind the white skin of the Caucasian male, the inner depraved savage, the raw human. *Was he on meds? Was he off his meds? What kind of meds did he need?* Did she need to leak his information, or would they be resourceful enough to find him on their own? They didn't share a last name, but the internet is pretty clever.

After making those few slight touches to her own campaign, she decided she must retire herself as to not create too many footprints. For now, she could give in to her distraction. *Fatty Rants about the King Rib Sandwich Being Removed from the Menu*, a fresh upload. In a dim-lit room, blinds half-closed and masking the early afternoon rays trying to brighten her mood, those pigs, in an outfit that she threw together for pity, in a tab of the internet she brought up for self-preservation, a fat man was cradling a sandwich, the last sandwich of its kind for at least ten weeks, like a holy grail: repurposed, recolored beef,mechanically molded into delicate contours with fake grill marks, brown sauce saturating the bun, which had a semblance of transparency in its greater depressions resulting from greasy fat fingers. Its bright yellow wrapper, which he was holding the bottom of the sandwich with, framed it delicately, the sliced bread of this generation, our generation having continued the perpetual furtherance of amenity that its parents taught it, and their parents taught them, and their parents taught them, for there's no shortage of good parenting as it applies to ease-of-access. Fatty was giving the King Rib his normal score out of ten saucy fingers and the millimeters his eye slits opened in excitement, a 9.3 strength-of-association score with the sandwich's potential to increase societal healthcare costs and kill off undesirables over the course of a shrinking lifetime, a real milestone in the way of engineered foods. It wasn't a perfect system, but it was a good rule of sausage thumb. Tragically, the sandwich's fatality score (an entirely separate measure from its saucy-fingers-out-of-ten score) would have to be divided by at least two because it was only available in waves of indulgence, a simple but clever marketing scheme.

That was one of the highest scores she had seen, and it fueled his indignance that the sandwich was going away. Alyssa would have to mark her calendar for the day it returned, and she daydreamed a bit about how excited he would be, snapping out and rewinding the video to see what she missed. *Slurp slip slop slap*, was it his tongue smacking or maybe the sweaty clapping of his neck rolls and his head bounced in ecstasy?

"Doesn't King Mac know how much money they could make if the King Rib was year round? It's stupid. It's plain bad business, and, if it weren't for the Original Mac, I would probably prefer Debbie's Thirder-Pounder, with it's eight point five rating, price point being a big advantage but sauce falling somewhere short, too much mustard on the musto-mayo spectrum."

FattyRants, a new brand of celebrity athlete, was sponsored by an expensive cardiologist in Los Angeles. His confounding survival of each day was the only commercial advertisement Dr. Pincock needed, and his sponsorship was considered charity, cutting him a number of tax benefits. On all the legal work around the sponsorship, FattyRants was known as Jacob Waal, but his real identity got a few hundred thousand views per weekly video. More importantly, his content was chopped and screwed into parody videos and compilations of neck jiggles that cumulatively made millions of views every week. FattyRants was safe-for-work porn for skinny people, or not-safe-for-work gospel services for his supportive obese audience who were likely to seek the medical services of the esteemed doctor.

For Alyssa, he was not even safe-for-work. He was the only porn she was ashamed of viewing. She was a part of a movement of sexual revolution, after all, of what started as her own volition but had quickly transformed into a inverse fascism of culture, the ideal and superior being the inferior, the most victimized, the most obscure, superior, and she imagined she was taking steps in the right direction by having been sexually assaulted. It was, in this way, that she would forever be indebted to Uncle Dave, who gave himself, selflessly, for her bettering, the contemporary Jesus figure running a dive restaurant into the ground after he would surely be fired for pedophilia. Why did he do it? Why did he relinquish everything? Was this some symptom of a deep discontent rather than some perversion coming to light?

The only thing in common that her domain had with the evil anonymous image board was that the Board had a fixation with baiting out pedophiles and reporting them, followed by scandalous news coverage of their intentions. The Board had a sort of selflessness in its anonymity, a daunting enemy that could mobilize at any point on any number of enemies and invisibly so, and she figured that they would be an automatic instrument of hers following this video. There was, no doubt, a certain element of intelligence behind the Board, resources beyond what they appeared to have based on the sheer number of frog memes pasted on the front page and the crippling social anxieties they faced, not even having the courage to post online with any identity at all.

There was a brief moment where Alyssa thought that the Board may have had some doing catching her uncle, who was probably a pedophile at large caught only through his heroic niece outing him. They could have found him out in a larger web of crimes and reported him to her, knowing she had the public face to deal with him. That is how they worked, she thought, programmed by the media's painting of the Board to be a collage of movie references. They work invisibly, otherwise they compromise their power, but, inversely, that's how their culture is also so toxic at its surface level. She had spent a cumulative five minutes on the Board in her life, and the sheer volume of *niggers*, *faggots*, and *cuck*s had turned her off for life. They were an invisible hand of dedicated minds with unknown abilities and further unknown motives. They could choose to involve her in their greater plan, but she would never choose them. Flashes of news clips played in her mind:

"Hacker 'Anonymous' busts yet another child pornography ring."

"The political activist group 'Anonymous' leaked bulk email data from intelligence agencies."

"Who is 'Anonymous' and what does it want?"

"Faceless 'Anonymous' confounds the rest of the internet with its invisible hand."

She was just a mouthpiece for a truly anonymous contributor.

As always, the question was *who is anonymous.* After all, if Dave really just confessed to his crimes, he could have easily used any other medium, a more personal text message, any form of more anonymous communication. The decision to use an email was strange given that he shouldn't have had her email address. Could he have outed himself to the Board and let them do the rest? Or did Aunt Katie do so? There was no telling how deep the conspiracy went.

...

Dr. Pincock, an esteemed cardiologist to many has-been Hollywood actors, troves of passing-grade actors with enough money left to keep themselves alive in style, was locked in traffic on his normal route from northern Santa Clarita to Burbank, where his office was located, thanking his decision to only be dependent on one freeway, the official pavement of the Golden State, eight quiet lanes and a void of webs of on-ramps and the hell that comes with them. His office was less than a mile off the freeway, not far north of the zoo, and he liked to think of it as his own zoo, any number of jellyfish, whales, or fat cats occupying rooms waiting for his presence, and he walked freely like the prettiest girl at the ball, randomly choosing doors to pick up the clipboard for and enter to the chagrin of his subjects. One patient, an ex-sitcom star with a cocaine addiction resulting in and from various heart problems, was convinced that he needed the blood of a jungle cat and was paying an exorbitant amount to research the feasibility of such a thing. Another patient, an ex-boxer who had once bitten the ear off a tiger, actually had a bit of the blood the other was looking for, and his stomach had developed a bacterial infection that ultimately resulted in a chronic shortness of breath, which Pincock had treated with a survey of steroids that increased red blood cell count, resulting further in a stroke that left the poor athlete with a terrible speech impediment.

The Doctor walked by a closed door, glancing at the clipboard, and recognized the name immediately, a new patient that he heard was coming in soon. Peter Aldridge was an EDM producer who wore a famous owl mask during every show, known to neon circles as "Fowlst," who had developed heart palpitations upon listening to his own music. This was to be the Doctor's introduction to the rising generation of cardiac problems associated with the epidemic use of MDMA, bass-heavy music, and synchronized light shows. Aldridge had been raised with a background in classical American music, namely having been the trained monkey-child behind a viral early-internet alternate-lyric fiddle cover of *The Devil Went Down to Georgia*, and he had traded it all in for a vapor aesthetic and a surplus of eighteen year-old club sluts who wanted only to be rhythmically fucked by an owl. *Knock knock, crrrr-reeeee*; he needed to get someone to fix the door.

"Mr. Aldridge, yes, I've been awaiting your visit."

"I heard you can fix me."

"I can certainly try. I read all of your paperwork; it's a concerning palpitation associated with an auditory stimulus, no?"

"Yes, it's quite problematic, happens often with the drop."

"Ah, yes, 'the drop,' and, of course, in your profession, that's quite an obstacle."

"I've actually not played a show in a long time. Between you and me, I've been hiring others to wear the mask and go dance like they're mixing music for the last few days."

"Have you experimented with different types of music?"

"Well, yes. I've been watching bluegrass concerts," the patient seemed apprehensive.

"...And?"

"...and I've been trying to incorporate the fiddle back in."

"And you're not comfortable with this?"

"I don't want my parents to feel like I was born that way."

"Mr. Aldridge, with all due respect, the decision to pursue treatment is very serious. I want you to know that."

"Doc, we both know that these palpitations are about to be a serious problem."

The Doctor paused. "That is something to consider."

"So what are you going to do for me?"

It was just like that that Dr. Pincock contacted a few universities known for research in drugs that faced similar physiological problems. *What could bring Aldridge to a new association with his music?* He was trapped in the past.

To the Doctor, this was something more than the potential for a new client base—this was a revolution of medicine. There had been centuries of isolating reactions to medicine, to circumstance, a sort of micro-attitude that biased itself on only its efficacy, of results that couldn't ever be argued or denied, or solutions that couldn't be proposed, of lab-cells to lab-rats to lab-monkeys to lab-humans to veterinary-rats to veterinary-monkeys to veterinary-humans to bedside-humans, and the type of research that appealed to this case dismissed everything less explanatory. It was only about synapses, about salt and potassium, but, more importantly and sometimes it lost track of this, about the differences between these chemicals and humans, a sort of prejudice very common among the predominant humanism of the twenty-first century. We are not animals, or we are different animals (club rats and jazz cats), we are not a collection of synaptic reactions, vesicles, channels, transporters, receptors, axons and dendrites defined by amino acids or sequences of precoded compounds, but rather we're something different, something that defined itself by defining itself, something that escaped original definition by building upon itself before being able to be defined—we are a system resulting from a system, and, when we study the original system, we can only pile on research; nothing has changed in the way we go about studying the new cybernetic human, the sort of androids that couldn't even have been spawned in the most progressive science fiction. Aldridge is an online persona, limited only by some legitimate physical presence, and we must change the way we go about his studying. We are, scientifically, studying monkeys, and we're humans, as is evident by this club-monkey seeking a resolution to a complex cultural-physiological reaction that he faces, only wanting to overcome it because of some long-ago obscured desire to reproduce, but who really knows his intentions any more? Maybe he just wants dopamine or serotonin, but that seems to be a reductive answer to a problem more complicated than chemicals.

"...hello?"

"Yes, of course, my secretary will call with a confirmation for our next appointment."

This abrupt end didn't surprise Aldridge, as he knew he wasn't asking for straight-forward medical advice and further knew that this doctor's head was a mile away.

The zoo was in full swing today. The next door he walked into was another prized patient of his, a young-tragic professional football player, eight months out of a program at a large public university in Florida, America's favorite orifice, who had taken a sequence of hits to the head, an average of twenty worth noting every week, over the course of the last five years, resulting in a complicated regimen of cognitive-functioning medications that further resulted in heart problems, which were the reason for his visit today: Christopher "Big Goblin" Grant, dubbed so for his notoriety as a quiet type causing his teammates to create outlandish rumors about his 'secret' social life. Goblin was a fullback, a bowling ball with an armored head, originally projected to be second string and losing potential by the week, currently on the injury reserve list. He started his college career as a promising young star, composed on the field and in the classroom; he struggled to maintain this reputation, though, as he sustained more and more head trauma, he would take longer and longer on written exams, writing out long passages on the backs of the tests of trap lyrics from Tec 9 SMG Murder Killer, Fuegos, and Boat. When questioned why, he said it was an important part of his thinking process. Tec 9 SMG Murder Killer, having heard a rumor about Florida's Big Goblin, had written a song, "Gobbin' Goblin," that was credited as the source of the term 'gobbin,'' which came to mean something like 'tweaking,' or when one does too many uppers and starts to crash in spectacular fashion. Christopher Grant publicly denied any amphetamine use.

Tec Niiiine (x2)

Gobbin' like a Goblin (x2)

My nigga Big Goblin, he a armored truck (Big Goblin!)

Keepin' trap up on his teacher, man he don't give a fuck (don't care!)

Sly always flexing, sneaky widdat Tec Nine (Murder Killer!)

He a Gobbin' Goblin, tweakin' off dat pink line (addy!)

(he be) Gobbin' like a Goblin (x4)

Heard my nigga raw as fuck, heard my nigga famous (raw!)

Dat boy got some rumor, they just mad becuz they ain't us (dat boy famous!)

Listen boy, you want some good you come to ATL (Atlanta!)

We got white,we got pink, and we'll get you one them Kel (rifle!)

Gobbin' like a Goblin keep trap on the sheets (on that test!)

Street-raised, street-praised, I pump my glock to this beat (bow bow!)

My boy Big Goblin, he a ace nigga (gobbin'!)

You tell 'em every time you done and pull dat trigga (Chris Grant!)

(he be) Gobbin' like a Goblin (x4)

Big Goblin had, as it soon became evident, been raised in an upper-middle class suburban home outside of L.A., a comfortable existence that gave him ample room to perfect his athleticism. He did have an obsession with trap music, and was both scared and delighted that he had attracted the attention of some of Atlanta's more vocal killers. His background only took away some of his respect from these rappers, who quickly abandoned him as a thug but adopted him as a cultural icon for blacks who still had their roots despite coming from more well-to-do families, and of course they promoted his alleged abuse of addy, which was both unavailable and not interesting to a huge base of their fans, but they thought of it as 'on the come-up.'

The Goblin seemed to cramp the office. He was perched upright on the office bed, and squat legs thicker than the Doctor himself dangled stiff. He was wearing a giant's XL shirt, something that had to be tailored because no average-intelligence human could keep track of how many X's he required, a gray t-shirt with the logo of his team, the Portland Whiskers. Walking in, the Doctor twitched instinctively upon his eyes meeting the left half of the room, a black monolith with a gentle smile, head barely poking out between two shoulders that might or might not have been padded.

"Ah, Chris, how have you been feeling?"

Chris took some considerable time in formulating his responses these days, "I am—good—better (better!) honestly." He also had a small idiosyncrasy, somewhere between a tick and a speech impediment, that made him his own hype man, "I took the week off of cardio (you said!), and yesterday I hit the treadmill for a while."

"Of course, I saw the—"

"(wheelin'!)"

"Yes, I saw the data. I'm going to be up front with you," the Doctor assumed his eager-to-help posture, "there's a new program being researched, and it's showed quite a bit of promise. I'd like to talk to your coach, your trainer, your agent, anyone we need to, and potentially get you started on this."

Chris, after searching for his words, a furrowed brow and a face soft in its victimhood, "What is it?"

"It's a new therapy, basically, a chemical therapy paired with intensive rehab, an exercise routine, diet, monitored sleep--what you need to know is you'd be on campus for eight weeks."

"(Chillin'!)—I—uhh—" defeated by his own lack of control of words, "—I want to try another week—yeah another week—pl—please." Here was the Goblin, a high school hero, loud and proud, bigger than the rest of his classmates' lives put together, a man whose words only needed to carry a soft promise of physicality, never using hard-liners or dictating as much as suggesting with another, more present suggestion behind it. 'Just do it' had gotten him through so much, but not even anything as direct as that. It had always been the invisible hype man following his large person, *can you help me study for this pre-calc test (do it!)*, that had ensured his quality of life, and it was because of this that he had never had to leave his shell—everyone else fit inside. And, in college, he was a member of a cult of super-humans whose traditions reached across the state, unspoken rites and rules, presence defined by an unfathomable aura that moisturized girls who were previously invisible and brought the most elite frat stars out for pictures, often bartering cocaine and molly for gang signs to come out, which, of course, one blackout Goblin had taken advantage of—once—and had become the subject of a Murder Killer ballad and a minor fad on Black Twitter: an image of a preppy kid in sunglasses, boating shoes (without socks), khaki shorts above the knee, a button down shirt in blue tucked in, and a towering dark figure in similar attire with seizure eyes over him reaching a large sign towards the camera, comically distorting the perspective.

"when u tryna keep jamal off tha block but u gotta date with chads girl soon"

"when u goin law school to fk dem niggas up long run"

"when u bouta hit the sailboat but u gotta rep ya boys real quick"

The Doctor, displeased with the unexpected hesitation but ultimately sure that he would win Chris over soon, went through the rest of the check-up routinely, slightly skewing everything to the pessimistic. After the giant left the premises, stomping his way out until Pincock heard a delay, an engine start and struggle to back up from outside the opened third-story window. Pincock, a familiar excitement building in his gut, took to his computer, wondering where to start and what was up with popular music in this day and age.

Doctor Simon Rash, an old med school buddy, had recently been to L.A. and drunkenly shared more about his work than Pincock wanted. It had something to do with 'biological programming,' some sort of alternative to the dystopic ideas that have caused so many authors to drown themselves in alcohol and countless schizos in multi-phasic therapy with strong chemical presences—a treatment that could mush the brain in targeted areas so that a reformation of neural networks was inevitable. "Targeted dendrites to soma to axons, a reversal made possible by and resulting in a new constructed reality, quite exciting and I'm getting more involved next week," a rudimentary description that Pincock thought sounded awfully executive, a clear indicator that Rash was no longer within the university system, something he could only know indefinitely because of doctors' love to play off of false humility: to ask another doctor what they were doing was tactless surrender, instead both parties should flirt with each other until they've seduced the insecurities and securities out of each other, and only then would they kiss. Rash and Pincock had once kissed in med school in a small janitorial closet, Rash pinned against a Bauen eight-foot A-frame ladder, industrial burnt orange, and sitting on a matching stool, but these were different times. Both of them suspected their opposite had a wife. Neither of them liked the bristle of each others' lazy mustaches. Then, later, in L.A., established young-middle-aged professionals, they played inverted grab-ass, drinking craft beers because the first two gin-and-tonic's sat a little heavy and composure was their industry. They'd love to recreate their famous Rash-Pincock dynamic, but they needed a third party to bring the tension to light. Doctors are not overtly sexual creatures, having studied the body in a sort of top-down way, and, being young-middle-aged as they were, they were both unconvincing tops. You can't have two passive-aggressive tops.

Regardless, that was ages ago, and being passive in work got you nowhere:

"Dr. Rash,

It was a pleasure catching up with you last week. I was curious about the research you had brought up, so I looked up some of the studies that formed the basis of it. Today, Chris Grant, the Portland Whiskers fullback of Florida fame, came in without much progress on his cardiac problems that are resulting from his radical nerve treatment. I introduced him to your research. I understand that he's a little bit more high-profile than you'd care for, but I imagine we could work a low-publicity route.

If you could write me some literature to share with his coach, agent, etc. about the risks/rewards of this research, I'll share it with him.

Respectfully,

Dr. Thomas Pincock"

...

A tight shot of public transit train windows passing in front of camera.

Lewis, in voice-over narration, rugged and Zach Damon-esque, "I didn't know why they sent me here—the agency. I'm a secret agent. I'm a simple American man. I love women, beer, and spicy peppercorn."

A long shot of three young women tied to a railroad, revealing both urban surroundings and a breathtaking natural landscape, train in the distance but approaching fast.

Lewis, still in voice-over narration, "but I don't have time to think about that anymore."

Lewis' body double appears climbing up a massive cliff onto a giant plateau, cigarette in his mouth, Japanese helicopters shooting machine guns at him, rockets flare and destroy everything around him.

Lewis, now standing over the women, still being shot at by the helicopter, "HURRY, THERE'S NO TIME."

The beautiful women, struggling and nude underneath chains delicately that frame their genitals, "oh, we can't move. We're helpless."

"It's those Japanese!"

"Help us, Lewis!"

A close shot of the helicopter pilot, played by Bahman Baris, revealing a large scar under eye.

The imperialist pilot, Ichiro, "Ha ha ha! You will DIE, Lewis! You and a generation of beautiful child-rearing women! You'll never almost kill me again."

A close shot of Lewis' face, then pan down to the women.

Lewis, "Not my wives!" he rips the chains off his wives, who cover themselves just barely, and he begins to swing a lasso of chain above his head, cigarette visible, "bitten by the snake on one morning, still not afraid of the rope the next!

Lewis throws his lasso around the blades of the helicopter, the blades lock up and the helicopter begins falling to the side of the rail. Lewis quickly ties his end of the chain to a rail. The helicopter hangs suspended from the bottom of the railroad. The three women embrace Lewis.

A close shot of Ichiro, "You may have gotten me, but my son will be back for all of you!"

The women, naked but pressed into Lewis so that nothing is revealed, "You are so strong and clever! Our son will be stronger than his!"

"So will ours!"

"And ours!"

Very good stuff, and a very great set-up for a sequel. Zhang Li has outdone himself. All of the sex scenes took place in the first fifteen minutes, really just a montage of tasteful orgy coverage, followed up by an hour of Zach Damon fighting the Japanese imperialists to save groups of his recently-impregnated wives, all of them being placed in traps involving public transit (ninjas boarding a ferry, isolated in the water, but Lewis swims to the boat, fighting sharks, and kills all the eunuch-ninjas; kamikaze pilots attempting to crash into a jet loaded with women and children, Lewis expertly pilots to dodge until all the eunuch-kamikazes crash into each other; and, of course, the railroad climax) for some reason, perhaps it was a theme that the public had a common underlying anxiety about.

4: Dickin' Poor Man And Lickin' His Toes

Cierra had gotten through Stirner, which grew to be a dreadfully boring despite relatively short read, and was lost phantasmagorically. She saw phantoms in everyone's imagination, a movie in her head about imbuing his ideals, if you can call them that, into her reality. She was, naturally, quite cynical at this moment, thinking every bit of ideology she'd ever ingested to be some sort of 'spook.' An important part of every cynic's being is an undeniable desire to relate to other cynics, the comfort of other people around you when the bombs are falling. The one true hub of cynics, at this time, was the Board, the new park bench, where you could harass strangers and let strangers' aimless comments harass you. It was the only correct way for a cynic to socialize. It was the manifest of Diogenic forum, which could never have existed before the internet due to the sheer volume of malice that passed in whispers. Everyone wore great masks here.

It was now her ambiguous mission to win the approval (or not win the approval, because *fuck approval*) of the Board, or maybe to reason with them, or maybe to learn from them. The natural first mistake of someone on the Board is trying to apply Diogenic to the more Apollonian (or even Dionysian—Diogenes existed outside of the dichotomy) world of the personal, in Cierra's case, to try and relate Stirner to her life and take advice. Carefully wording the first post of her thread, she typed:

"To what degree do you think Stirner would've approved the seeking of vengeance? At an early phase, vengeance is an act of self-interest, but at a later phase it becomes an act of submission, as if someone had such influence over you that you were just bitter and admitting you were helpless.

For example, I'm a server at a restaurant, and I spit in shitty customers' food. Is this an egoist move because I'm taking some good feeling from the situation, or is this pathetic and pacifying me against actually fixing my situation?"

She attached a picture of a smug frog, have scoured the image section of a search engine for the perfect "uncommon Pepe" after seeing how popular these images were on the site, a little piece of culture that she might identify with, an inside joke with a rich history.

While waiting for a reply, she opened up her email and forwarded the email from Dave's account with the race-play BDSM porn to the "Contact Us" email address on the Stevens and Sons webpage with a succinct message describing the situation. It was very calloused, the way she typed, not even thinking about it. This was a formality, an afterthought; after all, one of the higher-ups should have already gotten an email about him salting people's food.

She tabbed out to see she had her reply on her thread:

"go back to ur containment board, frogfaggot."

And the second:

">posting a shitty meme

>pretending to be unaffected by spooks"

And the third, with an image of a popular fat man, FattyRants, with an orgasmic expression as he bites into a deep-fried candy bar with an overlay, four fingers up, a shaky hand, and eyes closed in anticipation of a heavy bout of diarrhea:

"Can we start banning Stirner topics? I swear some shitposter mucks up the board every fucking day trying to justify his shitty existence with this nobody's paranoid rants"

And then the thread shut down. The moderators must have responded favorably to a plethora of reports, which is not a common thing on the Board. It's its own democracy of sorts: there is an set of rules established by the autocratic owners of the site, but they are selectively and loosely applied based on the volume of people who actually have a problem with the post in question. There is still a bit of mass tyranny in play despite the Board's appearance as an ideal of anarchism. It was just beginning to dawn on Cierra, though she couldn't face the thought head-on, that anarchy results in nothing more than individuals deciding things, or she recognized that that was the case but didn't see the implications: she hated people, she wanted for some reason to empower the individual. She would soon become one of the unironic monarchists of the Board, a group lobbying for Inquisition-era methods of rule, a sort of post-Stirner pre-Stirner philosophy, or post-spook pre-Stirner ontology, or post-Stirner pre-spook methodology, resulting from long-lived cynicism. It was monarchism at least somewhat ironically but also authentically.

Regardless, this was all lost on Cierra, who was frustrated with her inability to reach the Board in any legitimate way. Both times now they hadn't even taken her seriously, and it wasn't because they suspected she was black or a female. She might have to really take the time to engage with others in their own threads before being savvy enough to sneak her own good thread in past the defenses of hundreds of cynical virgins defending the only true and pure thing in their life. The rest of their purity was tainted only by years of browsing vile and obscure pornography, hand-drawn images of horses from a children's show having brutal anal intercourse, genuine *whinnies* and *neighs* thrown in among voice acting, or computer-generated 3D models of young boys in sailor hats with rows of penises all ejaculating in spasm-like pulses, or even real videos of chicks with dicks railing fat neckbeards in blackface, an absurd oedipal projection. It was in this way that these men had become the eunuchs of the modern day, committing themselves to celibacy through the desensitizing of their pleasure centers until stimuli that could only be simulated were the only real thing in their life. This was of their own slow and undignified choosing, this life, and, for reasons unknown to anyone, Cierra wanted to commit herself to them—she just didn't yet know how.

She'd never done well sexually, a problem spawning from a rejection of her heritage and a further rejection of being treated differently because of her sex. She'd created a complex that was antiblack male because they were only going after her because she's black, antiwhite male because they were just fetishists, only talking to her because she's black. After so many years dominated by self-denial, Cierra started to question her own sexuality, just as the pegging pseudo-African neckbeards do. She became her own Übermensch in moving past the guilt of obscure fetish-chasing on the internet, moving past the conventions of healthy sexual experiences. The literature section of the Board banned porn, but other boards? She began a research journey into the depths of the Board's collective psyche. It all began and ended with a section for NSFW animated images and their sourcing. A Desi thread, one for messy facials, several for specific pornstars, squirting, huge black cock shemales, nothing out of the ordinary for the internet at large, nothing weirder than the stuff she had already found to make Dave send out (the very thought of which bringing a grin to her face and moisture to her cunt). And then, among all the hentai cordoned off in its own thread that she had the urge to click on, she found it. She had played a popular massively-multiplayer online role-playing game as a teen, her main escape from her social reality, and here was the natural extension of that—various characters from the game, their 3-dimensional models perfectly lifted from the game's engine, female elves, dwarves, orcs, humans, even one particular visually impressive animation of a female dragon, all getting their heads chopped off and brutally skull-fucked by giant orc men with hooked penises. Warmth spread across Cierra's body as her hand flirted its way down, a journey that had grown to be quite expedient as the habit is formed, and, as she reached her clit, lightning struck several times in the same place as she clicked on each of these images. She came immediately and violently.

There were only eight of these animated images in this thread, and she was not satisfied with the session though she was, for the first time, satisfied with the Board. Suddenly and unexpectedly, she had learned something about herself, something so far down that no other social interaction could have reached it. She hadn't found a name for this fetish in the thread, and she desperately looked around the internet with search terms like "orc skull fucking" or "dead elf porn" but nothing came up. What could she do? The answer was where she found the question. She replied to the thread with the most magical word, the word that came to be a quintessential icon for all she knew about the depravity of the Board, for this collectively self-deprecating society, the something-to-be-said for anything that catches your eye immediately in this age of massive access to information, the single word responsible for the complicated and deep-seated addiction that the Board inspired in its active members and even among its lurkers, the single word that acknowledged the fatal attraction:

"Source?"

...

Mein Gott, hilf mir, diese tödliche Liebe zu überleben

Heiko, after hours of shitposting and watching live-streamed games of *First-Strike*, a competitive first-person shooter, decided to watch just one more game. It was early AM, the time when such a decision could have massive repercussions for the next day. Heiko had class around noon, and, as such, had been reconsidering the risk-reward of wasting time watching people thousands of miles away play video games as the night passed into morning. This last game, from thirty minutes to another hour and change, could tip the scales, but it was strange addiction he had already confronted the consequences of many times before.

The professional players he watched were androids, born and raised to be an organic computer operating an inorganic keyboard per the restraints programmed into the game and the other organic competitors. A typical moment of dialogue during the stream, while in English, was really its own language, but Heiko still refined his ability to speak common English through listening to the streamers praise their viewers for donations and subscriptions.

"At least one top mid, just mollied me window."

"I'm hearing at least one apps, but this guy loves to throw his shit out by himself."

"Yeah, it's fake, smokes A, rotate."

"Smoked me ticket, bad smoke, I've got default, someone watching connector?"

"I was but now watching ramp, smoke came from palace?"

"Fuck, I'm dead, who the fuck just runs through smoke? One moving triple."

And then the streamer breaks in frustration, checking his stream chat and not broadcasting his voice to the in-game players, "Thanks for the sub, ex-tee-cee five-oh-three-two, welcome to the club, and, Quickshots, I think I played that right, he just did something nutty hoping no one was watching that angle. The edge of that smoke was one way."

It was like that forever. Each player logged more than fifty hours of matches a week, and many streamed just about every minute. There was a whole streaming world that existed in permanence, in a dissociative vacuum that traded watching your childhood friend playing a rented-for-the-weekend single-player game for watching your favorite celebrity get headshots and headshotted. At any moment of the day, Heiko could hop online and find a respirating colony of people donating money, spamming memes, and asking for advice on jiggling corners, gun patches, or smoke placements, and this was all for his relatively obscure game of choice, which was rarely on the front page of the most popular streams, unless, of course, there was a multi-million dollar prize at stake for a LAN tournament where all these streamers would be voiceless professionals narrated by undeserving commentators in stadiums of fanboys doing "the Goblin" dance every time the tally lights flare at the crowds, pale bodies of taut skin stretched precariously over protruding shoulders, elbows, and knees, in baggy jerseys supporting their favorite professional e-athletes.

Despite his inactivity in watching the streamers—no chatting, no donations, not even a login—Heiko often toyed with the idea of traveling to Cologne for the big world tournament, just for the absurdity of it all, just for the poetry of the event, the kind of temporal anomaly that would allow for such an event, the exact balance of societal time needing-to-be-wasted crossed with the distribution of entertainment resources and luckily stumbled onto by a group of programmers inheriting a game engine at the right place and the right time. These gamers were fighting lions in the Colosseum except the main event was often overshadowed by the streaming coverage of their collective training, which introduced the humanity back into the sport—despite the technical talk, there were jokes and laughs, people just playing their favorite game, people that weren't only the angles they were holding or the frags they had, though that was still a large part of their existence. The spirit he was watching had a hundred viewers at the moment, a part of the world-wide collective that collectively financed him.

Heiko enjoyed the sort of voyeurism he had in just watching silently, the silent majority of the viewers, a sharp contrast to his presence on the Board, where he posted freely and frequently. He had a subtle complex over the professional gamers he watched, knowing he was more social and worldly than they would ever be, sometimes even feeling pity that he contributed to their lifestyle, to their graves that they dug in sponsored gamer chairs in sponsored headsets playing on sponsored keyboards and sponsored mouses, listening to hour-long playlists of trap music and other burgernet trash music.

His phone vibrated—a text message from Effy. "I'm lonely, would you come sleep over?" This was probably the least desperate way that she had ever invited him over, other times hinting at other failed romances or manic breakdowns involving the deteriorating health of her mother, whom she was growing to resent. Heiko winced at every mention of her mother's cancer, of their more frequent bickering that he had heard one side of. She wasn't suited to handle the stress of a family member's mortality; it had her on a short leash and she almost never wore one. Regardless, Heiko jumped at the opportunity, closing his browser without hesitation despite having recently beaten off.

This confrontation of emotion from her didn't exactly imply any sort of sexuality in play, and he always caught himself wondering what her appeal was. It's possible that her only worth was in absentia, that every time they got together he longed only for the Effy of his mind but that his fantastic Effy and his real Effy could never meet lest she be compromised for the real.

He got up, redressed himself, almost four in the morning, and texted her blankly, "I'll be there soon." There are no convenient U-bahn lines running at this time during the week, so he'd have to unlock his bike if he even remembered the combination. The bike was rusty, the chain popped off frequently, and, even when it was working perfectly, there were a few links that would catch on the teeth of the lower gears, so he had to ride around peddling like a maniac, not that anyone would see him at this ungodly hour. It was for these occasions that he still owned the bike.

He wheeled the thing out of his building, through the courtyard by the many-colored dumpsters, the greatest commentary on the trash awareness of the contemporary Berlin resident, and out the tall front doors. It was damp outside, a sort of thickness of breath and refreshing feeling like a cold misty shower waking you up when you should be fast asleep.

Heiko lived on the northeast corner of Wedding and Effy east of Neukölln, where she belonged, close enough to Friedrichshain and far enough from Heiko for him to prove himself with every visit. He found himself on Müllerstraße after a brief and brisk ride down Barfusstraße, Müllerstraße turning into Chauseestraße at what could've been a park or just a lot that had been undeveloped since the Reich came down, cement slowly sinking into the earth and green life emerging triumphant, as had happened in much of Berlin until the next newest world came through with cranes and concrete. Chauseestraße took him all the way to Mitte and Friedrichstraße, where Berlin openly admitted its age, and it was about here that Heiko had only a vague idea of direction, knowing Friedrichstraße ran almost parallel to Wilhelmstraße, the first road he had internalized, and it ran right through Checkpoint Charlie, and around Checkpoint Charlie he should look for signs for the Jüdisches Museum because it's southeast of there, and, if he could keep that southeast line from Charlie to the Museum intact, he could show up straight at her door. And that was the case, some thirty minutes later, undelayed by traffic.

He buzzed her room, the door clicked, he walked in, grateful to be off the street. The Berlin around Görlitzer Park was a different world, a similarly impoverished and Turkish area to Wedding but much more militant in embracing and simultaneously rejecting its poverty. She was in the north, all the closer to the park and an area that housed artists and students alike because of its drug access and cheap rent.

"I can't sleep." She was wearing a t-shirt and panties, and Heiko was expected not to notice judging by her sleepy eyes. He'd made that mistake before when she had a fever once.

"Me neither." She had greeted him at the door and turned around before he replied, straight back into bed.

He followed diligently, a shadow breaking the solitude. She laid in bed, legs bent up and sort of balled up uncovered so that her ass was framed by her black panties and Heiko had a moment to look as he climbed in, taking his shirt and pants off. He knew by now that despite the asexuality of this encounter, it was the skin contact that she wanted, the gentle sweat that forms in the security of another body against yours. He cradled into her and pulled the blankets over them, his arm underneath and softly resting around her side and belly, which he felt compress by reflex. She pressed herself into him, two S's almost perfectly overlapping.

"Thanks for coming," she whispered amid a moan.

"I was already in the neighborhood."

She laughed and pressed her hips back into his, a slight hard rising through his boxers and finding its home between her soft cheeks, giving her the comfort of a history in an ahistorical time in her life, elevating the mood without forcing anything, and they fell asleep as comfy as that without saying much more.

Waking the next morning, however, Heiko realized quickly that he had missed his class., which he had already accepted as a possibility when he answered the late text. Effy had already gotten up, and she was nowhere to be found, hopefully getting a sweet treat for the both of him, but he wouldn't wager on it. The day had been thrown away before it started.

He texted her after a few minutes of quiet and wondering around her apartment, small talk with the two Italian students she shared an apartment with, both of whom Heiko were distant around, having been burned by at least one pretty Italian woman in his younger time in the capital. The city was an evolving source of etiquettes unknown to the rest of the world—a race relation protocol unique to Berlin, a Mecca of disconnected peoples. He had learned that Italian women were not worth the effort, and that was imprinted deep within him until he could someday unlearn it.

She replied, "I didn't want to wake you. I'm in class."

Regretting the decision to brave the night, he hopped back on his bike and prepared to make the same voyage in the quiet mayhem of Berlin around noon, dense, considerate traffic with bikers being worse than taxis and pedestrians the most dangerous of all. The warmth hit the street and brought up smells of city-defecation, a different breed of shit not quite as obnoxious but permeating the nostrils in an acquired scent, combined with bakeries pulling chocolate breads out of ovens, Turkish sweat and tea meeting savory döner, street pizzas and the appetites of the homeless about to be temporarily satiated, tourists' smell of fresh luggage, click-clacking in Mitte, a neighborhood of dense immigrant cologne covering the same döner smell that Heiko was addicted to.

He eventually made it home, a quieter area around noon occupied only by young families in parks and cigarette-smokers at the corners of buildings or smoking off lunch under the umbrellas of tables on the sidewalks. He parked his bike and wandered into his apartment, wondering what to make of the day. He could easily make it in time to his early afternoon class, but he had set a poor precedent already. Instead, he settled on shitposting on the Board, something that takes a bit of dedication up front, otherwise you'd browse without feeling the urge to correct the heinous crimes you see daily.

In this case, the Stirner-posting had continued, and at an ungodly hour for such things. He assumed all of the meme-philosophy he saw, like Stirner, alt-right faggots, or Žižek, was of American sources, those imperialists who mostly used the internet to spread their own culture and were loudly against common discourse, but it was odd for this kind of bait to be lingering this late.

In this case, Heiko saw that dreaded frog and the words next to him:

"To what degree do you think Stirner would've approved..." at which point he stopped reading, angry that either the American view was spreading or that they were just growing more dedicated to the cause, posting in their early morning as to not allow a moment of ethnocentric relief.

He typed reflexively:

"go back to ur containment board, frogfaggot."

He then waited for the his ability to post again, sixty seconds to prevent spam, but typed up a message immediately, elaborating a bit more as to not be recognized by his prose as the same poster.

"Can we start banning Stirner topics? I swear some shitposter mucks up the board every fucking day trying to justify his shitty existence with this nobody's paranoid rants"

Knowing deep down in his mind that this was an American behind this breach of his Board, he attached an image of a celebrity fatty, a still from a video that was often linked on the site to mock and identify burgers. He fought valiantly for this space.

...

Sometime around 7:13 AM, Simon Rash remembered that the office coffee pot was out of coffee as of yesterday afternoon, and he was on his way to work. He saw a sign for a popular franchise coffee shop that he used when he had to, and he had to. Parking his hybrid vehicle by backing in, he didn't bother to turn around, using instead the camera and the screen on his dashboard, a matter of principle. He prided himself on his efficiency and savvy. The spot he had chosen had a water drain that appeared to be exactly centered on the spot, as if the parking lot engineers had painted the whole lot in reference to this location. He was, of course, not perfectly aligned, but he easily could be with the technology he was sporting. His camera was centered on the back of his car, and his dashboard display had crosshairs of various sizes as guidelines for parking, green, yellow, and red to display distance. He scooted forward, reversed, scooted forward, and reversed, a perfect parking job. As soon as he tried to get out, however, he dinged a neighboring car, *not parked very well*, and cursed under his breath.

His problems could be solved with a dose of caffeine, he thought. There were several professionally-dressed women in line already, modest skirts or pleated pants and jackets, some with glasses, a look that he liked, and all with hair up. *Cappuccinos*, he called them, a better crowd than the *soy-milk-café-au-laits* or the dreaded *pumpkin-spice-lattes*, or, the worst of both worlds, the *almond-milk-lattés*. The *Cappuccinos* maintained a decent amount of self-respect and expediency in ordering, utilitarians like him seeking only to temper the reality of espresso, something he wasn't in the market for but respected all the same. He got closer and closer to the line, growing anxious over the impending interaction with an ex-cheery green-aproned teen girl, still bubbly in first impression but sarcastic in greeting.

"Hi, my name is Cindy, what can I get for you today?"

"A—uhh—medium coffee and a shot of espresso."

"Would you like an upgrade to a large for only fifteen cents?"

"Sure."

"Room for cream and sugar?"

"What?"

"Cream and sugar?"

"No! No, sorry, no."

"Okay, your total comes to three dollars twenty-two cents. Wouldyouliketorounduptofourdollars to donate to ShoesfortheStarving is that a debit card?"

"Uhh— yes, no, credit, please." It was a debit card.

"Okay, and what is your name?"

This was the moment he was fearing. They were probably watching him, and they would put it together that he was scared to mention that there was no coffee in the office. They'd know that he remembered, otherwise he wouldn't have come here in the first place. If he was prone to these kind of social anxieties, where would he fall short in his delicate research? They don't normally trust researchers with such fragile patient-facing interactions such as he was in daily. Luckily, he was a stallion, he just had to find his way out of this pickle with Cindy, who was probably being paid off. After all, she was working at his location during the time he'd be traveling, and specifically on today, the very day they gave him a test and he made a tiny mistake, but there was one way out of this, one simple way to fix this, "It's Simeon."

"Simon?" She wrote the name on the cup. "That will be four dollars."

"Yes! No—Simeon!" He was done for. Years of PhD research in such an obscure field, years that would never have gone anywhere if it weren't for them, years deluded then redeemed by a contract with a company that was known to gamble, that he knew to have jackals in several industries keeping tabs on their employees. All those years of not getting laid because of his dedication to research, and fucking Cindy, the double agent barista, had done him in, this little bitch prying into his life. She didn't need his name. He was the only male in the entire shop besides braces-glasses on the espresso machine, an unfortunate reminder of Simon's own undergrad experience, full of 'research.' He had done a lot of his own research, unmotivated by and irrelevant to school, into virtual reality porn and had learned some basic programming in an effort to contribute to the industry as VR emerged. He had some obscure tastes, so it only made sense to develop the VR landscape, though he was interrupted by a big contract from Cuquette, a pharmaceutical company known primarily for its popular compound alprazolam, or 'xans' in the hip-hop vernacular. He had studied biochem, the son of two doctors, and had done very well in school under the pressure of his parents despite his wayward focus. All of that was out the window now.

"Alright, Simeon, your drink will be ready very shortly!" A smile, possibly unforced. She was going to get a bonus for pulling this information out of him, and she couldn't even hide her smugness. He stood deliberately near the bar where the drinks come out, making the two pretty *Cappucinos* in front of him move away out of discomfort.

Was it worth the contract? Was it worth enjoying his job, worth the hassle of the executives and the thick-necked drones they sent out? He never used to worry about these things, only instead about Dr. Hatch's lazy undergrad work-study employee lab equipment manager. Things were so different then; things were so different last week. He had gone through extensive background testing recently, basic and more complicated psychological probing, the least comfortable of which being a film he had to watch about mother birds abandoning their young after humans touched them, which Simon knew to be a household rumor, but it was still quite convincing to see it, baldish little beaks with membranes for eyes desperately squeaking from the base of the tree, the strange way that its legs met its feathered body like a pubescent Simon observing himself in the mirror, blackface and all, pubic hair clashing with a complete lack thereof, and the little birds look moist or greasy. The contract also came with a prescription for xans, though it wasn't as much advised as contractually obligated within a regimen. Their reasoning was that studies had proven their employees were sharper over time when they weren't as ambitious in their free time. The combination of a recent dependency on downers and the threat of jackals made Rash especially anxious in the mornings when his system was still clean.

"Simon!" a braced mouth said, out loud. Simon dropped his head and avoided eye contact as he reached for the caffeinated drink, labeled 'Simon' for the world to see. If he wasn't already, the drink would put him right on his world's edge. He walked straight out the door, not sipping his drink down to a driveable quantity like he normally did, and he noticed that the car he dinged had left, replaced by a perfectly-parked car, surely another part of the conspiracy—they'd learned a bit about his obsessive-compulsive tendencies by questioning him when he asked for white-out to redo his name.

The drive to the lab was filled with tails and oddly-synchronized traffic lights, one helicopter and at least five pedestrians who could have been taking pictures judging by the angles with which they were browsing their phones. His building was located east of Raleigh, far enough out of the way to get a taste of the countryside he had no palate for. His parking spot, labeled neatly 'Dr. Rash' in white paint against the blacktop, was waiting for him, almost setting him over the top.

The noid walked into the office and scanned his card to get through the lobby without interacting with the secretary, Katie, the local Cindy, and continued eyes-to-the-floor to his desk in a room shared with a certain Dr. Ken "Kenny K" Klepp, a notorious amphetamine abuser and avid fan of oversized headphones. Turning on his desktop, which he shut off every night for security reasons, he proceeded through his routine:

-post-necessity checking of the weather forecast for the day.

-listening to a single Top 10 pop song and the viewing of its accompanying music video, in this case, "Saturday (The Morning of The Day After Friday)" by a nondescript white woman with a dark complexion and a lack of pictures taken from in front of her; the video featured a pool, a dangerously thick-jawed tall-dark-and-handsome getting out of the water in slow motion for a minute and a half, our esteemed popstar being approached by him for a kiss while she was sleeping, and bright lights, dancing, and images of a band and the back of the singing popstar.

-a quick sweeping of Katie's social media to ensure she was still married to the restaurant manager, which signified that she was still on their payroll, maintaining her image exactly as he should think it to be.

-checking his email, in this case seeing an email from his only ex-lover, Dr. Pincock, and the only man worthy of Simon's often-spilled-in-vain seed. He thought back on the moment in the janitorial closet, Simon sitting on a small stool, back against an eight-foot A-frame ladder, and the recollection alone required him to stand up while he still could and go to the restroom before he read the email, a bit of his routine that he normally saved for the afternoon.

Getting back after cooling himself off with damp paper towels, he read the email. Chris Grant. He looked him up. A stout fellow. Urban legend. Amphetamine abuse, standard today, but combined with excessive head trauma. This might be a good lead. The noid toyed with the idea of presenting the idea to his authorities, whom he knew to have the resources to keep it relatively quiet. After all, no one really knew much about his project at all. He had no one to talk to about any problems besides Kenny K and his boss, Stan something-Slavic, neither of which he particularly liked talking to. He would wait until he got home to send an email to Pincock through a VPN and a burner email address, just for safety. It went:

"Dr. Pincock,

The pleasure is all mine in talking to you. I see the subject as especially fit. I've got just the place for you and your friend. I shall talk to my peers and determine their opinions on the matter. I apologize for this vehicle of correspondence. I didn't want to send a personal email from my work address.

How are you? Have you talked to Dr. Hatch recently? Haha. I'm well, thanks, just busy and irritated at my snooping secretary.

I hope we can be professional in this.

DO NOT EMAIL ME AT WORK.

Thanks and with love,"

He hoped the line about Katie would put a halt to her work on him, maybe even her false-front marriage, if they were to find his email.

...

"Ay, chingadera, some greeting you've set up for me."

"You're no chilango, hombre, more like a chilito," the familiarly-dirtily-mustached grin broke in a cackle of forced laughter, joined in by his posse of bikini-clad women, South American and beautiful, bronze tits testing elasticity and asses not covered enough to worry.

"I look more Mexican than you do, David, other than that huevo-tickler."

"Aquí me tienes, yéndome," Mendez threatened, knowing that would straighten out the Turk's arrogance. The Mexican had a treat for him, the only reason for a visit.

"Lo siento, friend," he recovered and playfully added, "introduce me to your girls."

"Of course. Ladies, this devilish man before you is Bahman Baris, a famous actor for the Chales. Bahman, this is Lola in the yellow and Isabela in the black." The two women not directly adjacent to Mendez walked over to Bahman and posed themselves at his side, one hand each on his chest and dwarfed by his height. The way that his figure imposed on their little hands was almost comical, making him out to be some sort of god that might split them in half if he was endowed proportionately to his chest hair.

"Ohh, Movie Star! Much better than the last cabrón throwing his money," one of the girls said.

Mendez visibly took some offense. "Ayyy, shut up, petocha, that *cabrón* could have you boxed up and shipped back to whatever statue-praising favela you came from."

Bahman was cocaine-embittered that they didn't recognize him on their own. He was here in Del Valle, safe from the rolling worlds of slums but not from stoplight windshield rape, having come here from a publicity shoot in a remote area of the Gran Desierto de Altar, where his agent had arranged for a concert with him in full dress as Daniel Victory (by now, Bahman's agent had blended the fictional identities of Ichiro and Daniel Victory for convenience's sake), or, as the natives had guessed his identity to be, *el Naranjo, agente de bienes raíces ricos.* The stage was cheaply constructed, mostly budgeted for an extensive light show and a helicopter, in fact, the same helicopter that Bahman had ridden to get out there, having had to arrive several hours early so they could fasten a confetti-.50 cal machine gun with a directional microphone to the frame. The chopper was at the far end of a narrow stage in the shape of a funnel opening to the audience to make the whole set seem elaborate, walled with synchronized-LED-lit window screen and thin PVC designs in vertical stripes, blinking in contrast to the screen. It was to be a night show. For the budget, the show would have been amazing, but only thirty tickets were sold to two modest extended families who thought he was a New York real estate magnate and must not have been able to afford anything other than Chinese-American Hollywood gimmicks. Bahman had attributed his lack of popularity to his look, far from his natural appearance, and was frustrated with the staging in that he was shrunk from the audience's perspective. He still had some orange remnants under his chin that had made Isabela and Lola giggle, which he took to just be some sort of orgasmic predilection from finding out he was a star.

"David, I hate to break the suspense, but did you get any of her?" Bahman broke the multidimensional tension.

"Of course, I've got a sample here. Let's all get a little taste." He broke out a plastic-wrapped globe of what looked like raw crystallized sugar.

Lola broke her character, "ayy, roca? Let's do eeet," hoping only for a bigger bite of pleasure than her normal missions entailed.

The group dutifully tasted the bitter substance, pure as ensured by Mendez, who always had the purest, and a sort of plastic taste that could hardly be described, almost oily in a chemical sense. The session ended with Mendez re-dosing through his nose.

Who could tell anymore, but, moments later, Lola's unthonged and untamed ass bouncing up and down, a professional in what she does, and Molly's a professional in what she does, the combination of which, reverse-cowgirl and sensory overload, was about to lead Bahman to unfortunate ends, but he pulled it together long enough for Lola to start quasi-panting, soon taking a break and letting Isabella take over. The break was all he needed to avoid bursting at the seams; the drug has a subtle way of both decomposing and recomposing at the same time. He still felt on the edge, but he managed to maintain despite watching cunt and asshole appear at the beginning of every up-stroke and disappear behind seismic cheeks on every down-stroke. Molly is a decidedly feminine character, enhancing feelings to a sort of sensational level. Most men couldn't help striping their shirt off in the heat of her influence and feeling the weight of shame leaving their abandoning bodies. It was, in this and a few other ways, the ultimate drug for finding sex, a sort of moment-by-moment feeling being lent to even the most reserved of men during its wavering climaxes that, if properly timed, could end up in the perfect apparent confidence for getting laid. Bahman, in this case as well as many others, didn't need the Molly but used it appropriately as he busted across the faces of two eager South American Calzonsueltos.

While he'd love to glorify the night, it was terribly ordinary. And to summarize the night as just a few South American girls sucking-and-fucking would sell the night short; he made it back out to proper Del Valle, a skyline dominated by fifteen-story buildings with radical lights trying to catch your attention, full of clubs that would last a few months until their sponsors faded away in their own presence or fell victim to more legitimate externalities. What he learned from the neighborhood of appearances was that no ladies in this district were *beyond all that fuck shit*, which would have been perfect for him except that he couldn't derive influence from his *Chalean* fame. The problem, as it quickly became apparent, was a Mexican-American Dream, a city founded on tax returns and alfalfa trade, the most Yankee of commodities. The freeways had given way to the Free Way, and, in support of his first impression and against his favor, the area thrived off of visibly extravagant wealth; he was, a natural result, a marginally small figure here, much like the countless Top 100 DJ's that were hired on a weekly basis.

He was only overshadowed by the Art Deco, a force to compete with the most sadistic of wealth's desires, a combination of we-can't-do-that with you-can-pay-us-enough-to-try, a sort of preemptive bailout for architecture firms that were willing to sink themselves to whoring out for elite Mex-pats or, better said, migrant owners, a brand of egoists seeking only a place where their resources exceed expectations, which somehow became this asymmetrical mass of unworkable one-way streets. Molly was the ride that never quite made it down the road to Bahman's hotel, too far down the strip to be relevant, which was his worst fear: that he would, anywhere on this great planet, be irrelevant, as he was the very moment he busted a nut across eyes lost in greater fame, disappointed by his exhausted, slightly limp dick.

He thought to himself, grinding on the next slut of the night, a Maria, no more different than any Isabella he'd met, that he should return with his bounty to Berlin, the home of his shenanigans and the only place he had ever been that mostly ignored his status in a tolerable way. In Berlin, he was only an attractive Turk with family and friends. Here, in greater Mexico City, he was colored something more abstract than Turkish with a single (albeit well-connected) acquaintance, leaving him at the disposal of income, which he could barely compare with given the extreme wealth of certain oil and chemical investors that had struck riches and avoided taxes in this metropolis. Berlin, however, offered nothing to these mega-rich and instead offered much to the socially-influential or fun-depraved, those Berliners of course sucking any dark dick for the promise of any rainbow of influence or fun (which often coincided), the subtly-overt theme of that generation, any and all genders willing to submit, and it was exactly the ambiguity of offering potential that really drew blood to Bahman's dick; in fact, the mere thought of returning to the great Mecca made him hard enough to go for round three on his new friend, her first session of the the night (with him, at least), Maria, or so he would call her, under the stairwell, wizard-style.

The night would have to be cut short, however, for he had a flight in the morning, some hours from this moment.

...

Fowlst, heart beating out of his chest, was listening to a little diddy about a mythical hybrid of some sort of imp and a bowling ball which may or may not have been an analogy to his addiction to a breed of stimulus. The routine was to rip enough bong for him to believe that his heart wouldn't react to synthetic-bass-heavy music and then to have a manic breakdown as his heart broke out of his ribs with incessant surging, at which point he would switch tabs to a video with a hundred million views, Petey, the child, sawing on the fiddle while his dad recorded, and his dad's later-recorded voiceover obscuring the virtuoso's work in post-production with lyrics of his own. The source of the popularity of the video could not be isolated to either technical talent or the shock value of watching a little boy being exploited so.

A black screen, introduction, white text appears fading in and shrinking until it all fits, centered on the screen:

"So, as a context for this, I know a gay guy who was expelled from my undergrad for his second rape accusation from different people, the more recent one being a baseball player, and this is to be sung to the tune of *Devil went down to Georgia*"

And then the boy begins feverishly and mechanically destroying the riffs, falling and rising to set the stage and then relieving the violin's pressure against his neck.

Randy went down to Portland, he was looking for a hole to steal.

He was on a find for a good behind, and he was willing to force a squeal.

Came across this young man, looking for a diddle and feeling him hot,

Randy jumped the first good chump, said, "Boy, I'd get his man slot."

Said "Bet you didn't know it, but I'm a baseball player too,

And if you care to make it fair, I'll take a nut from you.

You pitch pretty good ball, boy, but try my pitching too,

I'll let my diddle unfold inside your hole, because I bet it'll pleasure you.

Guy said, "Now, my man's Jesus, and he said it's a sin,

I won't take your nut inside my butt,

No chance I'll let you in."

Randy do a bit of blow and prepare to diddle hard,

'Cause hell's broke loose inside your head and the young man's shown his guard.

And if you win you'll put your happy diddle in his hole,

But if you lose, you'll be disenrolled!

Brief instrument break with a parallel but also slightly tangential riff of falling then rising

The young man opened up a case and said "let's get drunk bro,"

Pong balls flew from his fingertips as Randy was aglow,

And Randy put a hand upon his ding and tried to lay a kiss,

And his gland of semen started up and it went something like this.

Slow build-up, sinister sound, violin screeching, Petey's entire body shaking at the energy, violent sawing and falling climbing falling rising and off

When Randy started, the man said, "now why's your zipper so undone?"

"Lay down on that bed right there and I'll show you some good fun."

Mire on his mountain, run, boy, run!

Randy's gonna dowse and have his fun,

Dickin' poor man and lickin' his toes,

"Randy it's too tight," He smiled, "No."

Violin solo calling out and answering only to itself

Randy hid his head because he'd knew that he'd been seen,

And he knew he had to hold his diddle if he's to get out clean,

The court said, "Randy, you ain't coming back, and do no more cocaine,

We done told you once, then another snitched, we find you in disdain."

Mire on his mountain, run, boy, run!

Randy's gonna dowse and have his fun,

Dickin' poor man and lickin' his toes,

"Randy it's too tight," He smiled, "No."

The most tragic part of the entire video was the satisfaction on young Petey's face as the violin again left his chin and rested on his leg upright, knowing smugly he'd hit a perfect rendition, a smile growing across his face, and he looks above the camera, beaming at the cameraman, his father, almost giggling and completely ignorant to the degeneracy that he would be exploited for. The child made it at least a year and a half before the video-sharing site had grown enough for his peers to find such a video. It was about eighth grade when it all hit, and his social life suffered greatly at his insistence that he was innocent of the plot and loathing of his father, who his friends began to idolize, much to the detriment of the Aldridge family image among the community. A divorce, moving in with his mom in the city next-over, wanting only to get away from everything. He found refuge in his Spanish class, where the students were forced to go through a program to find a pen pal from a Spanish-speaking country. Peter, in all his depression, found more than just a Spanish speaker. In his free time, he found a Chinese, an Australian, a German, and a boy from a few states away who had also bore the brunt of the early internet, someone who had clicked the wrong link to torrent a punk-rock song titled "Virginia is for Lovers" and subsequently had federal agents bust in the front door of his house, seizing his computer and eventually letting him off as innocent of Possession of Child Pornography after months of scandal, though not everyone ended up really believing his story.

From these distant friends, he'd learned a lot about life and became a bit more cultured as a result. His German friend, Heiko, an artistic type who'd write long tracts of poetry or play scripts about cat empires in his backyard, introduced him to house music. His Chinese friend introduced him to terribly-scripted cinema. His romantic friend, funny enough, later reintroduced him to the internet in a positive light.

He was now an EDM producer with a large following, and he did music reviews and meme coverage on top of it all. The latest Lil Tec 9 SMG Murder Killer song was a bit trite, as the Atlanta music scene had the capacity to be, so it was especially fatiguing to force himself to listen to while his heart tried to kill him. Nonetheless, it was his profession. Instead of waiting for treatment, he was forcing the issue. And the music reviews took much less out of him than it did to make his own music, which he produced incrementally based on his own inverse reaction to the sounds: the more unpleasant the better. He took it to be the flooding of pleasure centers, tragically the dykes of his brain had succumb to a sort of traditionalism, rejecting his own authoritarian approach to the music he wanted to listen to. He enjoyed, or he thought he did and thought they would as well, the peninsula he had created, more beach access to dopamine from all angles with these heavy rhythms and foreseen drops, but some base of traditionalism among his synapses created a soft spot along the water, a lapse in the consistent structural integrity that was, no doubt, the result of new-meeting-old, that became a problem when the water levels rose. His only solution being his most recent manifest that *opioids are the opiate of the masses*, or, in a pinch, just a pinch of some good weed. Regardless of the civil engineering of it all, he had been personally advised against attending or participating in concerts by his cardiologist.

He gave the song a three out of five because of its excessively low RPL (rhymes per line) score of 1.5, where many trap artists and, more popular, hip-hop artists could maintain a healthy 2.25-2.66 RPL throughout entire albums. He felt generous in giving the song this high of a score, but he *was* a bit of a sucker for trap music, a guilty pleasure of his, and he also appreciated the base of meme culture that arose from the song, a bowling ball in a nice shirt, empty eyes, and the smug white kid, almost knowing this picture was golden before it was taken:

"when danny boy hit u up for some lean"

"when u find out who buyin ur ho ass nigga mixtapes"

5: Krampin' My Style

BRUUUUUUP. Click, unclick. "Uhhhgh." *Sluuuurp.* "Ahhh."

"Just you today?" She seemed especially smug-dark today.

"Yeah, I'm the only one actually necessary 'round here."

"Uh-*huh*." Skeptical, as always.

"They's at a conference in Point-and-Shoot, South Carolina."

"Are you ready for the check?" Never to let him relish in her presence.

"As much as I'd stay and enjoy the view, yeah." He watched her turn around towards the register, walking, less-than-prominent ass cheeks bouncing in sync with steps, kind of staccato, not his kind of girl in some ways but preference falls behind convenience, just like he'd get caught up listening to Bryan Luke and his hit single "#BlessTrucks" just short of looping at the office of JF Trucks. She wasn't a Bryan Luke girl; in fact, he fantasized once or twice, she was probably a girl with tastes far better than her position allowed for, just like him. He'd seen her give the evil eye, far worse than she gave him and his friends, of the cynic to her boss on a few separate occasions, and it was this glance that made his cock wish her ass moved in smooth, drawn-out motions, attuned to something like Philip Glass's first violin concerto, winding to find and expecting what's real, growing to slow and easing the blow, an ass that words struggle to keep up with, instead relying on an indefinite gliding through an aural plane and maybe even finding itself in his oral reign or oral rain shining to twine. A motive: uncapturable, an impossible narrative, airy and daring (derrièring), ruthless yet caring, schöner Götterfunken striking him in the dick as the immediate come-on leaves him breathless and struggling to keep up, soft, throbbing chords. Elegant melody. The fairy's dance, light on her toes, joined by all creatures of the forests, all nymphs, elves, rabbits and birds, a heaven-sent cacophony of sound dying back to a quiet focus on the fairy, the black waitress's ass, dancing lightly on its way to the register.

The cynicism sets in then. She becomes self-aware that she's a body, a fairy in his imagination, being misused by the very gods to his benefit, an infinite cabal of masculine gaze, a hallway of mirrors and she's smoking a cigarette, impossible to avoid and even more impossible to struggle against. A fairy to a toy, a little wind-up nut-buster configured only to dance. Dark circles under her eyes. The dance slows, becomes heavier, the embittered language in her movements now seeks to pleasure you in a spite of your fraternity. The cynic's pleasure is the smell of a shitty world. Her slow and deliberate dance pleasures her, because she brings you down below her level as you hopefully grow aware yet unchanging. If it's unavoidable for her to be the subject of the gaze, it's impossible for you to not be the voyeur of this delicate fairy dance. She's enjoying this part more than you are. In fact, you're quite uncomfortable seeing the malice in her eyes.

In a moment, she even realizes that she's enjoying this, and that her infinite cabal of femininity (her own hallway of mirrors) has blessed her with such an image. She is beautiful. Whatever gods she affected have crafted her perfectly. The dance returns to a childlike innocence, more experienced, however, than any cynic or idealist. It is the image of innocence that comforts Ted, the fat JF Trucks logistics analyst with a greasier erection in a greasy diner, as Cierra walks back towards him with the check, her eyes ready to receive, his to give, a vibrant dance between them, a powerful cadence building up as she takes each step. Closer and closer, pressure building up, nearing climax, his forehead sweating and a deep warmth building inside her—

The phone rings. "Here's your check." She was distracted.

Groveling, he tipped her for the experience and finished his coffee so he didn't have to stand with a hard-on.

"Typical" Teddy Wozniak wanted nothing more than to be the Genghis Khan of STDs. He had, some time ago, gone on a drive-along with a JF driver as a part of a new industry-education course program, and he stopped to lick and be licked by a couple lot lizards, later being tested positive for gonorrhea and accepting antibiotic treatment but only taking about a quarter of his prescription. A year later, the original hue of his discharge had evolved from a creamy white, yellowing eventually, and had recently matured past the first traces of a light green into splotches of sewer green. He was harboring a signature and hoping it would be resistant to the advancing marks of the generations of scientists who had created families of drugs to deal with his own biological concoction. He was also purer in that he was his own laboratory. He took it as a sign from his own gods that he experienced no pain when urinating, a non-falsification or even a permission to carry on his life's quest.

He'd been saving up his cash for sunnier days, hoping to one day travel the world after a sufficient harboring period, hoping that he could spread his seed across the faces of members of all nations, eliciting the reaction of a global epidemic of a brand new strain of disease derived from his very genitals, the penultimate mark to leave on the world, biological, undeniable, a cold, hard truth. Napoleon—he was held up by tens of thousands of devoted soldiers—but Teddy Wozniak conquered by himself. *Wozniak's Disease*, maybe they'd call it on the newsreels. There might be a hashtag campaign about him. The probable infertility that results from long-term untreated gonorrhea would be replaced by his seed carrying a different life. He could create an entire species, generations of a species.

The logistics analyst could ask for nothing more out of life but much less. The rest of his day would be spent haggling lanes with a produce distributor after a shipment of peaches got into a fender bender and were subsequently soiled from a commercial perspective.

...

Dougie Wallace, a smooth-ass cat, thought back on his first tour in Berlin, a different Berlin, newly reunited with its estranged twin brother, West Berlin, and absorbing so much of his culture. Dougie was a hit for these people, many of whom had never seen a black man, let alone *two*, who were 'brothers' (the brand cleverly designed to impress that they were both actually *brothers* and also brothers in the African-American sense, though, in reality, they were neither, often bickering and biologically more distant than your average German and Swiss citizens). The group was formed in the mid-80s by a German producer, an enigmatic closet-recorder who went by "Aggie," who saw the imminent downfall of the Berlin Wall as a potential gold mine. Incidentally, a French artist, after being paid off by the German producer, made a series of similar cartoon heads with varying colors and expressions meant to represent the many faces of Western influence at the East Side Gallery, in two cases, *The Wallace Brothers*, two dark blue cartoons with big lips.

Needless to say, the German producer was right. A burgeoning Eurojazz scene's floodgates opened. Wallace became a star in two cities in the course of one night, then in only one metropolis by the next afternoon. City bright lights and sometimes sometimes-beautiful German women, oppressed culturally (metaphysically), were thrown onto him as the producer hashed out album after album of auditory gold, *Lordy Lordy Great Heaven Above*, a chart topper, followed immediately by an ambiguously dark Christmas album, *Krampin' My Style*, which tried to manufacture a hip, new image for the aging half-goat half-demon. Unfortunately for Dougie, the projection of himself, a tall black man, as a horned devil who kidnapped and ate children, as was smoothly sung in the intro track—*Hooray! Hooray! I'll Eat Today!*—was a little bit too much, and he had trouble finding a bed to share for a few days after the album dropped other than with the more dogged types.

He and his partner lived a little under a decade in the limelight, falling off as all sorts of new industrial and electronic sounds were on the come-up. They had also been written out of almost all income, growing a heavy dependency on continued popularity. The producer signed them out of obscurity and kept them at a distance, so they lived hand-to-smooth-ass-mouth. After his short-lived fame, Dougie's favorite album, *Jazzpussy*, was sold to an American Chinese film director to be used in movies about Americans.

Dougie hadn't seen his producer in years. The last time he had, the producer's daughter, a spoiled little brat of a thing but cute at that, had asked him if he recently laid out in the sun for too long, for which the producer laughed heartily and pulled her back, offering her candy to *be quiet now, Mäuschen*.

The little blond girl reminded him of his own niece and the last time he visited his family in the States, the acid taste left in his mouth from the look on little Cierra's disappointed face when he gave her a parting gift: a cassette of one of the more obscure *Wallace Brothers* albums, the pun of which was lost on the anglophonic little girl who consequently took offense, *The Los!er*. The entire album was a sort of stream-of-consciousness exploration of an unnamed (autistic) savant who felt displaced as a child and grew up to lead a nation out of some Freudian drive. The album would, unknown to Cierra, have massive parallels within her own life as it developed, but she never listened to most of it, having pried the cassette open in an early *(utterly Jungian)* existential fit and lit its contents on fire. The album, however, like all of Dougie's lyrics, was written entirely by the producer who was really living out his own fantasy through every jiving song. You could only get such a fatalism-in-libretto from a post-postideology German.

...

The bottom line is that cat's milk, if gone unchecked, goes sour.

"Well, Miss Cindy," he said, eyeing the gummy alligators coated in a malic acid solution, "I have a habit of destroying myself whenever I can. Just this night I drank too much."

Miss Cindy was a Deep-South Chinese-American belle in full church dress, wandering around the convenience store looking for some kind of dressing to go with her pretzels because it had recently been made illegal to purchase pretzels without dressing, and, apparently, pretzels couldn't be branded either.

"Get some ranch—that's quite tasteful, isn't it?"

At this point, other people were in the store, and Miss Cindy herself was behind the cash register paying for her pretzels and Thousand Island dressing, $1.59 for the entire purchase, and Heiko gave her a glance to make sure she was counting the right change. A slender olive-skinned woman was browsing for sunflower seeds, olive oil-flavored, and a black man was right next to the check-out getting his week's chewing gum. A Nordic looking fellow wandered in and headed straight for the back of the store.

After a little while, a part of the floor near the black man started getting staticky and then more so until there were great currents blue arcing out of the floor, some even spilling underneath Miss Cindy, who hadn't felt so revitalized in years. The black man was confused, and Heiko was studying the floor for any cause—a stray insect with a metaphysical dilemma, perhaps.

The olive-oil-skinned woman, noticing the voltage, got suddenly flustered and stormed out the door. The Nordic man followed. Heiko followed to make sure he hadn't just been robbed blind by a new sleight-of-hand. He saw a distant woman and an angry man mid-confrontation.

"Yes, of course that was me! Why'd you even ask? Or did you think *maybe* someone else did that?" He tried to reason with her.

She kept turning away from him, "You're making a scene. I don't know why we do this to ourselves."

"Babe, don't do this to me."

...

Friday morning, to Heiko and Berlin alike, was early afternoon for the rest of Germany. He emerged from a wine slumber, the kind you don't really sleep through but rather endure strange dreams about growing static in life or harboring a fetish for olive oil, and cracked open those tall doors out onto the street, looking for döner. The Turks teased him a bit for his bedhead and puffy face, but he got out favorably with a chicken dürüm and checked his phone to see if Ihsan would be working yet. He was.

"Bahman got into Berlin around midnight," Ihsan said, which Heiko assumed meant his molly was almost at his door. "He's around here somewhere."

"That's awesome. Prince Charlie's is going to be lit."

Ihsan, in his manner, took the smug look of a choosy beggar, "Are Effy's friends coming too?"

"For some paprika crisps, I'll get anybody," Heiko said, remembering that he was carrying a bag with a warm meal in it. He unwrapped it and took a satisfactory bite, sauce splitting out the back of the wrap and savory meat-juice making a run for his chin.

"You're going to like Bahman. He's a *los!*er, a real go-getter."

"What the hell is a *los!*er?" A tomato popped plump between his molars, coating his mouth with a fresh flavor.

"So Bahman is a star in China, and one of his directors listens to this American jazz album on repeat all day. I'd love to get over there someday. Seems like a hilarious place."

"How did you get to know this Bahman?" Heiko had full cheeks and took a hand off the wrap to stuff his free hand down the tube of chips, getting it stuck and flailing it about carefully until it came out.

"His dad owns the sport-betting place my uncle goes to, met him there a few months ago but he's barely ever in Berlin. I'm going to call him right now, actually."

The entirety of the dürüm and one half-liter of beer later, Bahman walked in the door of the shop. Affirming his suspicions that the shop wasn't a real business, there had been no other visitors to the shop since Heiko had arrived, and Ihsan had given him several free parcels by now. Heiko wondered if he was meandering in an underworld parliament of gambling.

"Ihsan, valedor! It was a long flight, how glad I am to see a friendly face." He was as physically big as he probably appeared on screen, Heiko thought.

"Ichiro! Danny Victory! Welcome back to this depraved place; I'm sure you'll add to it."

"Of course, of course. Who's your friend?"

Heiko, choking a mistimed handful of chips down, straightened up as he was involved. "This is our friend and source of women for the night, Heiko, the poet!"

Heiko reached a hand out, the other hand blocking his potato-paprika cough, "nice to—CHEHMM—nice to meet you, Bahman, I was told you're an... famous!"

Bahman faked blushing, his most convincing skill, false-modesty, but also genuine in his lack of effect in the bright city, "but that doesn't stand up to a poet around here."

Heiko, reflecting on his night of watching Americans play video games, posting pictures of frogs, subsequently berating others for posting pictures of frogs, and drinking copious amounts of wine, blushed genuinely. "Ihsan told me you just came from Mexico."

"Big sack of molly golf balls," Bahman beamed, quoting a Lil Tec 9 SMG Murder Killer lyric.

...

Alyssa was watching Fatty again. She had seen his entire collection of uploads, having put herself under the radar for some time now, silently watching the infection of social justice grow. Any minute now, Uncle Dave would be reported to his superiors, found out by her democratic corner of the internet; any minute now, Fatty would die of any number of health complications, hopefully something entirely minor cascading into catastrophe because of his peripheral problems.

The effort to find Dave's identity and rescue Alyssa was spearheaded by one of her followers, a certain icon of a sexually-ambiguous pink-haired Hispanic holding a sign, *me tiro al perro*, with the name Davida Mendoza, self-identified as a feminine-of-center, masculine-presenting genderflux (feeling aporagenderous recently) social justice activist, focused on bringing down the oppressive cisnormativity with xir pink hair and blatant sexual frustration. Davida had been on a man-hunt for Dave and pulling out impressive resources to do so. It took xer minutes to find his identity after being alerted to the cause when it was shared to xir blog, though xe had not released the information yet, waiting for a civilized plan to action. Xe amassed a lot of support, having a blog with over a hundred thousand followers xerself. Xe had made a video promoting the cause and started a hashtag campaign, #DaveThePoopWatcher, which went viral on its own after the original activists' push, its cause being lost on a heavy majority of people using it who tagged a 'Dave' they know. Incidentally, Dave Stevenson, the poop watcher himself, had been tagged by a joking friend and thought nothing of it. The flooding of tagged 'Dave's led to many unwarranted persecutions by zealous internet small claims courts, which, in turn, put pressure on Davida to release the real Dave's information to save thousands of regular 'Dave's from trouble, though, admittedly, xe liked to watch the mayhem.

Alyssa was watching all of this unfold at a distance. It had been two days since she released the video, and she had amassed more than a hundred thousand new followers on her blog and the video itself had half a million views. She was on track to overthrow Fatty, only if she could catch up before he died else his posthumous rise in popularity would eclipse her own postheinous one. Calculating that it might be an appropriate time to harvest, she sent xer an approval to release Dave's information, and she also called Katie to tell her the truth about her soon-to-be ex-husband. First, she had to look up statistics about differentials in police brutality between races to make her tear ducts well up.

Riiiiing. Riiiiing. "Hello?"

Sniffle, "Aunt Katie? This is Alyssa."

"What's the matter, dear? Are you crying?"

"It's just that—I can't—I can't..."

"Alyssa! What's wrong, sweetie? Why'd you call me? What can I do?"

"Uncle Dave—he—he sent me a weird email the other day and I have to talk to you."

"Oh, no."

The Tacoritodilla, the latest in taco innovation, manages to trump its predecessor, the Quesodilla Crunch, insofar as its crunch is unaffected by the sheer volume of cheese, a critical layer of soft tortilla separating the two. This disgrace of a human had not noticed a glob of cheese on his chin, then must have decided it wasn't worth it to drive back out to pick up another Tacoritodilla to reshoot the video after seeing it in the post-production. What a treat for Alyssa's viewing pleasure. *Furthermore,* he said, tongue occasionally exploring the trail of cheese under his lip but never quite reaching the bulk, *it's structural integrity allows for a consistency in eating where the cheese doesn't run and hide, pooling elsewhere in the wrap, but instead pinches off wherever you bite into it, allowing for a perfect complement of nacho cheese with every delicious bite.* She kind of wanted the cheese to pool up in hopes that a mouthful of it would find its way directly to his arteries; he might otherwise survive a gradual intake. A light sweat was forming above his brow as he looked down at the taco concoction and back up at the camera. *While it still isn't as cost-effective as the Cheesy Gorjita, I would rate the Tacoritodilla an eight out of ten*, five greasy fingers raised, his other hand wiping his chin and sucking goopy cheese off his palm, then three more fingers raised, *a pleasant treat to mix up your routine.*

...

"It looks like you have *a glob of cheese* in your artery, Jacob. This has got to stop."

"I don't know how it got there, honest. It really hurts though."

"We'll schedule an appointment for this afternoon, but I'm warning you, you won't be able to keep this up for the rest of the year."

"I appreciate the unsolicited advice," he took a pause to breathe, "but, other than this bit of inconvenient cheddar, I'm in perfect shape."

"Can you just make it here this afternoon, say, three?"

Fatty sighed, sounding like an avalanche crashing through the phone speakers in Pincock's ear. "...I don't think I can get out of my house at the moment."

Dr. Pincock sighed in return. "I'll be by this evening, okay?"

"That works. I never get guests any more."

Dressed in his normal way, a bright Hawaiian shirt with a lab coat on over it, the Doctor went through the rest of his day routinely, checking emails with charts about cats' blood types and a boxer's cat blood, wishing for a magical transfusion between the two difficult clients, thinking about the musician's strange circulatory system and wondering what he could do to selectively stop a heart from beating. Then he saw the reply from Dr. Rash. There was a paranoia present that Rash had never had. Rash was always self-absorbed, which is the first step of paranoia, but never open enough to consider others' effect on him. The general effect of the email was similar to the old Rash, frantic and generally incapable, a sort of hiding-in-plain-sight-because-he's-bad-at-hiding in social interaction, just the same as when they emerged from that steamy closet years ago, passing a janitor on his way to get a ladder, and Rash blurting out uneasily, "of course I've never kissed a man," as if deep into interrogation.

Pincock could never work directly with him again, and considered cutting off correspondence and losing the opportunity to be the pioneering face of a new generation of treatment, not that he knew exactly what it entailed at this point. Or, he could play his cards close to his chest without folding. He replied, against Rash's direct orders, asking what the research treatment was like.

He also got an email from Peter Aldridge, asking how safe it would be to play one more show before treatment, the importance of which was precipitated by a rumor that an Iranian Chinese movie star would be there. The Doctor understood this younger generation less and less by each bit of information he learned about them. He replied and advised against it, but not absolutely, with a sentence that could have been interpreted as a reference to *Que Sera, Sera (Whatever Will Be, Will Be)*, which is not a reassuring message from one's cardiologist.

It was nearing the time for Pincock to go on the house call. He was aware that Jacob made his income on the internet in some way but never had the curiosity to find out how. Pincock was fairly health-conscious himself, having studied the collections of plaque in arteries and EDM hearts for some time. He didn't eat fast food because it occasionally irritated his pyloric valve, and after a long day he would much prefer to read a book in peace than place himself in another variety of zoo.

Papers shuffled before his face, he signed off on all sorts of lines signifying his approval of procedures, medications, guest requests for larger benches in the lobby, and so on. Eventually, he was mentally prepared to go home after a trying time with a new patient who was convinced of the benefits of bloodletting, seeking to get a prescription for blood thinners.

"I can feel all the toxins flowing out of my body."

Don't make fun of him. His brain hasn't had a steady supply of blood for months; in fact, he may be suffering from a state of perpetual ischemic stroke.

Burbank to Eagle Rock, a short drive but further away from the Doctor's home. Eagle Rock; what a place for a fat man to make a living off the internet. There's certainly some inherent angst out there, some bitter state of being from the second-rate films combined with a steady birth rate of creatives who got the hell out before they struck gold. In Jacob's case, no doubt, he physically could not move away.

Getting to the house, all looked normal, a little bungalow of sorts with a front yard and yet-living grass of a dead variety. As he approached the door, however, the scent of a million salted oils invaded his nostrils. Shedding a few tears, he knocked on the door.

He heard an exasperated yell from inside, "I'm—come in!"

He waited patiently, thinking Jacob was in on his way. He eventually knocked again.

"COME IN!" A voice answered, some sort of cry-scream with a single crack in the voice.

He walked in to a dimly-lit living room with a sort of shrine to cheap cuisine, take-out boxes stacked delicately in leaning towers supporting platforms of pizza boxes, open and closed, littered with empty paper cups strewn about on their sides, long cemented by grease into a stable structure with rings that could be used to date the scene. It was the hearth of the home, the Doctor gathered immediately, stepping on an empty bag with a crunch.

"Welcome to my home, and thanks for coming," the neckless mass of miasma uttered from up on his dais, a custom-ordered XXXL armchair that quadrupled as his bed, dining room table, and recording studio. Tucked into the sides, between his massive legs and the chair, were several empty bags of Tacoritodillas, leftover cheese oozing from the bags and becoming a part of him, porous skin absorbing goop through the very folds in his body. He was an evolved creature, and, when he talked, his chin- and neckfat bounced up and down and back and forth with magnificent communicative ability, a new Total Physical Response.

The empty bag, now greasily attached to his foot, offered some resistance to being lifted, a gluey stretch as Pincock nearly stumbled over himself. He pried his foot off, finding the source of the problem to be an orange-brown puddle of nacho cheese that had fused the bag to the carpet. A professional, this fatty, he thought as he noticed a rather expensive set of lights and a camera in front of the throne attached to the blob by a wired (jerry-rigged) remote. "I did not imagine all *this*."

"Yes, it's become something of my masterpiece," Jacob replied, splitting open a bag of spicy and numbing fish-flavored chips, one of his favorite imported snacks due to the dulling of others flavors after one indulges in a numbing flavor (a fatalism-in-snacking). "I don't know how familiar you are with whad I do, but I'm a thothal eadder and reviewer of local rethdaurantth and delivery appth." *CRUNCH.*

"I wasn't fully aware, no. A social *what?*"

"A thothal eadder," he answered smugly while his numbed tongue was sluggishly bouncing around, "it ih a thing on the intehnet. People watth me ead."

Losing more faith in humanity by the second, Pincock holstered his reaction and calmly took out a myriad of charts to do his consulting.

"I underthtand where you coming from, buh I awtho think you don' know mush 'bout thith movemen caww' Thize Ath a Wotuth of Twanqwuiwity."

"Thighs As a Lotus of Tranquility?" The Doctor, somewhat incredulous, was unsure if he wanted to appease his fattening curiosity.

"THIZE. Like THALT. Like big." The creature before him was jiggling about and getting flustered.

The Doctor, thinking he might tease a new milestone of heart-rate acceleration and calorie-burning out of Jacob, journeyed a bit further. "Ohhh, SALT, of course. Yes, yes, I've seen a video or two of Davida Mendoza giving xer presentation on SALT."

"Yeth, yeth, brave perthon. And thothe invethtors at Thtevens and Thons believein what xe thays; they aw thponthoring xer."

His succinct and matter-of-fact answer hushed the optimism for the fat man being riled up. The Doctor resigned. "Good for her, good for her. Let's talk about you, though. You're dying."

...

Skullfucking aside, the rite of passage and the numbing of attention to be able to browse the Board in a mindset that might allow for some genuine interaction, Cierra was diving right in. She had, like every other member presently there, just masturbated, and was only now considering that she should have included some sort of bizarre 3D animated porn in the destruction of her manager. Or maybe not. Maybe that would be lost on the world at large, the unknowing majority maybe even thinking it was a red flag, that it wasn't his own because he couldn't know this depth.

Present today was an abundance of social anxiety on the literature board, some mention of the hypocrisy of feminist ideals termed 'Ideological Stockholm Syndrome' with an attached drawing of a naked woman with hairy armpits and a woman in very conservative dress, subtitled, *DIFFERENT THINGS EMPOWER DIFFERENT WOMEN AND ITS NOT YOUR PLACE TO TELL HER WHICH ONE IT IS*. The arguments therein devolve to strawmen references to some obscure Chinese film with an orange antagonist singing from a helicopter, arguments pro-West or satirically anti-West. Somewhere deep down in the thread, buried and not replied to, the image of a sad frog is found, overlayed on a map of the Europe, with the text:

"Liberalism, like any great ideology, is inherently contradictory. Rugged individualism involves non-intervention on others' lack of individualism, which is a natural trait in humans. Good luck finding a community who prides itself on a lack of shared traits. As it stands, the only alternative to this example of feminist logic is ubiquitous ideology that doesn't espouse contradiction but instead is fatalistic within its ideal, such as consumer capitalism, religious fundamentalism, or technofuturism."

And then there was a link to an hour and a half long lecture by Slavoj Žižek about the sorts of ideological strife that distract people from the real, about how environmentalists create evil characters in their minds instead of engaging a greater phenomena, that we as humans are surprisingly weak, that we've supported a exponentially-rising population through little gimmicks and we're running out of them, that there's a thin veil of technofuturism keeping everyone high on life, that the behind-the-scenes work is rushing around recklessly trying to keep the average Joe or Moe's stomach filled and his heartbeat slow as it can be. There's a cult of privatism about this secretive work, resulting in the only ideology being presented to these Joe's and Moe's (or Dave's) in the form of cotton candy parading up and down the aisles at the baseball stadium, a non-nutritious fabric of brightly-colored and artificially-flavored substance-without-substance, that fills you up for the moment but dissolves in a moment in your stomach. More importantly, that this cotton candy is being delivered to your stomach in new ways; there's already several apps out there for it.

But mostly, in the thread, the replies were as follows:

"why is there so much shitposting today?"

"Islam is right. Fucking Western women fucking chads moaning and simultaneously complaining about his hard cock."

"its bc the jOOs"

Or, Cierra's own post:

"why do you virgins always spam my board with your sexual frustration?"

Which got a quick reply:

"virgin detected."

Which prompted Cierra to close the thread, report the thread as 'not literature-related' and move on. The thread promptly shut down due to a complete lack of literary reference other than the video of the lecture, which was really based on film theory, and everyone moved onto the next one, a thread about the last time you masturbated to a scene in a book, which was never reported and taken down but instead harbored much legitimate discussion of vivid sex scenes or descriptions of nature and aesthetic that sent blood to untouched cocks and endorphins to obscure corners of obscure brains. She replied to the thread, somewhat jokingly but with a kernel of truth:

"The last lit scene I flicked the bean to was the orc massacre scene in *Dimensions of Aerozoth: Looting of the Nordgar Keep*."

She got a few quick replies:

"is there a grill on my board? inb4 'sharpie in pooper'"

"sharpie in pooper so we know it's real"

"you know what the drill is. we need proof of you getting off."

"OMG same the orc scene was so fucking hot. New Queen of the Board?"

Cierra, disgusted and flattered at the direct sexual attention caused by the first euphemism for masturbating that she had thought of, didn't reply further, causing a hive of opinions stinging each other for falling for her 'bait' reply or other optimists believing she just disappeared after garnering more attention than she wanted. Regardless, the legend was born that there was a worthy female on the Board. It was certainly not the first time, but there was a certain fatalism-in-posting to openly admitting to having a certain set of genitals, like sports journalists asking women's volleyball players about their relationships with men or female politicians being asked about the decision to not have children.

Here she was, a dark girl, admitting a part of her identity to an audience of depraved anons, the first time in years that she differentiated herself on favorable terms, and, for some deep-seated reason, she enjoyed the attention.

She soon found herself dropping hints to various threads about her identity, creating an abstraction of presence, an invisible eye watching over all of the activity of the Board, separating and conquering opinion via dejected individuals resenting her newfound attention or rejoicing collectivists finding something new to rally behind, the Board's own paradox of their standard of anonymity. There were soon other posters trying to drop subtle hints of femininity, most of which were taken to be Cierra's own, or others claiming to be "not the other girl on here," and occasionally Cierra would even call out other feminine posts as not being "Our Queen" and shaming those individuals who had almost gotten away with their bluff.

She wouldn't have guessed and still couldn't define what her newfound breed of 'positive' interactions with the Board were, but she was certainly enjoying herself and had forgotten all about Dave, her now-absent boss, a new John having stepped in and filled the exact same shoes with a slightly less-convincing gait and the same pace of voice, like a suicide-hotline telemarketer selling smiles.

"If they ask about the special, what do you say?" He managed to imply a 'ha-ha' with his smile.

Cierra, blacker than ever in her new dissociative state, dryly replied, "it's Linole-yummy."

"Perfect! Wow, this is going to be an easy transition for me. The whole crew here is fantastic!"

And hours later, at Señor Flanker's lecture, "Die Rübe, an obvious metaphor for a certain hegemony in nature, for convenience's sake we'll compare the story with humans, though it could parallel ant colonies or bacteria or even some plants, requires two oxen to pull it, which mirrors the sort of codependence that humans have created among all their domesticated products and the sort of imbalances in ecological systems that result. In the same way that domestication is a product of chance and selection, the king questions the farmer if he had the best seed or if he just got lucky. The king, sort of a metaphysical god figure to our story, endows the farmer, or the one lucky ant who finds a piece of food on the ground, with a large reward. However, if there's one thing we know about ecology, what is it? Anybody? Cierra?"

Cierra, slumping in her desk, did not perk up, "uhhhh—"

"What usually happens when everything is going *too* well for an organism in their environment?"

"Uhhh... something comes along and kills it?"

"EXACTLY! My goodness, Cierra, I wish the rest of the class were like you. Yes, folks, every species that is doing *too* well will surely have some new stroke of selective chance take advantage of it, like the Bubonic Plague taking advantage of the dense populations and low sanitary conditions of Medieval Europe or a surplus of carrots leading to a surplus of rabbits leading to a surplus of foxes. So, within our metaphor, the brother to the farmer, his direct competitor, first appeals to a rather human condition, shiny things, to appease the King and secure better standing, almost paralleling a mating ritual among birds (we're all familiar with the recently-popularized concept of peacocking), but then he seeks to eliminate his brother, the competition, which is the most direct of ecological forces in nature: two ant colonies at war over resources, a constant state of battle. The rest of the story, as with most of our dear Petrov's examples, hasn't been explored quite enough in an *ecological* sense, and, as such, is up to much controversy in biological interpretation. However, I'm sure most of you understand the obvious parallels of the first part of the story."

6: The Societal Gap That Is Filled With Nacho Cheese

Dave, contrary to what used to be his normal demeanor, cried silently into the too-firm hotel pillow that had craned his neck into soreness throughout the course of the night. The tears mixed with drool and snot into a pool that Dave was too low to care about, so he tasted a sort of stale saltiness that might have at least put part of his mind into the present. The flavor blended well with the false cheeses of the Tacoritodillas he had gorged on, evidenced by crumbs of ground beef and sour cream staining his white sheets and whiter thighs under his pit-stained white shirt and light blue boxers. The man was a wreck.

Some sort of vicious beast had swallowed him whole. His family had completely outcasted him in a single moment and he had quickly turned off his phone's notifications for social media, though, in his void of support, he was still perusing the muted insults being hurled at him by leagues of quasi-anonymous soldiers of social righteousness, names and faces he'd never met but who thought they knew him through and through. Katie had kicked him out of the house despite his plea of ignorance to all of it, despite his reasoning that they had a healthy sex life and that she might have known him better after years of marriage, that she should be the only one still believing him, that she was the only defense he might have against the tsunami of injustice crashing down on him. In a telling moment, she turned away from him in tears, thinking that he had been the very source of the tidal waves, that he had shaken the base of their marriage and brought upon their house some epic disaster that she hadn't deserved.

"I don't understand how you could do this."

"Babe, don't you see? There's nothing to understand! I have no idea what happened either. I don't understand!"

"Years of my life," she sobbed, "years of my life and I feel like I don't know anything about you."

"You do know me," he pleaded, hoping that he was telling the truth, hoping that he knew himself as well as he thought he did, hoping that everything that framed his own self-image might be structurally sound enough to maintain the pressures falling onto him, "you know me more than I know myself."

"How can you say that after what you did to Alyssa? How can you—"

"What did I do to—"

"How can you stand there and tell me that I knew about your perversions—"

"What did I do to Alyssa?"

"Don't you fucking deny it. She told me everything, she called me in tears, about the hidden cameras, about the comments, about the email you sent her—"

"What?! What did she say?"

"You fucking tell me what she said. Go ahead. I'm waiting. Tell me what she fucking said."

"Babe, I don't know, I don't know anything about this. I need you to believe me. I need you. Please."

"Get out of this house, Dave. Get out of this fucking house and call me in a few days with your pathetic little story."

Depressed into the darkest little corner of his being, he turned the key in the ignition and fled the neighborhood for a hotel, stocking up on beer and cheesy taco-concoctions in hopes of outlasting his own apocalypse, hiding in his own pathetic nonunderstanding loathing.

The email from Stevens and Sons was cordial and depressing at that, referring to him as some sort of wayward asset that had to be pushed to the side due to questionable behavior.

"Mr. Dave Stevenson,

Due to some recent displays of unprofessional conduct, namely, the alleged communication with a Steven and Sons employee containing links to profane and racially-charged content, you are hereby laid off indefinitely without pay until the issue is resolved. We do not wish you to take this as a dismissal but rather a period for us to decipher the situation.

Please do not reply to this email but instead seek legal assistance as a channel to communicate with us."

His own mother wouldn't return his calls. He didn't have many personal friends outside of associates or frequent customers at work, and he wasn't sure that they wouldn't have heard about it. Regardless, before the first night of his misery, before the darkest hours of his life, after a six pack was emptied and greasy wrappers surrounded him, he called a regular from Linole-Yum, Teddy Wozniak, one of the logistics boys that Dave had chatted up so many times and had often made loose plans with.

"Teddy, it's Dave, from the restaurant."

Teddy, hearing a voice that he associated with his coworkers' presence, turned on his charm, "Dave Stevenson, howthehellareya?"

"I'm well," Dave said, "hey, I was wondering if you'd like to get a couple brews with me tonight, my wife's having a girls' night at the house and I need to get out."

"Dave, I thought you'd never ask. It just so happens that the rest of the gang is in South Carolina on business. Let's hit the town."

Dave, unsure whether to be uplifted or to feel worse about himself for arranging a situation where he would either be in denial or spilling far too much, sluggishly got up and dressed himself. The place to go around here was luckily across town from the restaurant, a certain bar known to the locals as "No Hope's."

Hope's was a dark room, lit only by low-hanging soft bulbs above pool tables and the indirect amber lighting behind the wooden shelves that housed the liquors. It was frequented by all levels of the trucking industry as well as contractors and a bank of electricians that all worked for a local electrical conglomerate. Among the transporters were inspectors, liquid haulers, oversized loaders, car movers, dump truckers, pairs of team drivers who mirrored each others' every move and only talked to twin sets of haggard-looking prostitutes (the team connivers), recruiters, instructors, logistics analysts, like Typical Teddy here, and just about everyone else that could get you and your problems or solutions from anywhere to everywhere.

As for the women, there was an assumed dress code of cleavage and a perfume of cheap cigarettes, outdated and overdone hair and obnoxious lipstick. They moved in shadow-circles talking to men they'd known for months or years, elbowing each other or eyeing their clients to see who was willing to really spend that night, ordering mid-range lagers from the weaker of their prospects and then cozying up to the stronger ones in public display, satisfying themselves only on the shame they could cause, shame being the primary measure of their success. *Jerry's always talking about his lane* or *Larry's a little too excited tonight, wouldn'tyasay?*

"Two Moore's Lights, Skip."

"And a couple doubles of Tommy Davis."

"It's nice to finally get to see you out of that shithole, Ted."

"And now we're in *this* shithole," Teddy said, looking somewhat uneasy.

"Aren't you a regular here?"

"The girls know me too well."

"A-ha, you always struck me as someone who did well for himself," Dave said with the honesty of a fading six pack in his belly, grabbing his new beer and pulling it closer to him.

"You work in logistics for long enough and you know how to get any cargo into the right lanes, if you catch my drift," Teddy said, picking up his shot and matching it against Dave's own shot, "cheers, buddy, to the girls' night at the house!"

They took the shots, and Dave immediately felt the taste of a dangerous drunk on top of the burn of the cheap whiskey. He washed the feeling down with a swig of beer, hoping to trick his mouth into only feeling a buzz, something less self-deprecating, but the damage was done.

"So what's in South Carolina?"

"One yearly company-wide orgy at a lodge in Point-and-Shoot."

"Andyou weren't invited?" The primary effects of the whiskey were setting in, the arrhythmic and unpunctuated meter of speech. "Another couple, huh?"

"I—uhh, another couple, skip! The girls—they know me *too* well."

"I wish—I don't havethat problem." Dave said, sinking into himself.

Teddy replied absently with drunken joviality, leaning in but looking over his shoulder, feeling it set in further. "Hey, Dave, maybe *youknow THEM* too well!"

"No, man, nah." Dave, sinking through his stool; the only part of him visibly above the bar was a hand on a bottle of Moore's Light, light blue and silver label on brown bottle.

"Hey man," man's floodgates opening, "man maybe they're... not even worthit." Teddy continued, slapping a hand onto Dave's shoulder, not knowing a trace about what he's talking about and mind admittedly wondering to a certain dancing fairy sprite sucking the green right out of his swamp-bulb.

"D-do you think they're noteven worthit?" Dave's face emerged and noticed the hand on his shoulder, firm and distant, the superposition of concrete and dream as Dave's eyes matched Ted's own, empty as they were in fantasy of jungle sex.

Teddy, not even snapping out but rather being affirmed by Dave's voice, which took him back to the only place he ever saw her. "They're only good for one thing... and *HICC...* SOMETIMES... noteventhat." The hiccup brought him back into the present, which was an image of Dave leaning towards him, awkwardly craning his neck and pouting his lips, eyes closed enough but still reflecting light enough for Teddy to know he could see. "Hey! Woah." Teddy pushed Dave back with drunken force that took him right off the bar stool.

"Woaaah!" *CRASH.*

"Woah. Woah, woah, woahwoah." Teddy repeated to himself, unsure of where he was suddenly.

Dave got up on his feet, still bent over, hand on the floor, started leaning, tried to make his feet catch up, ending up connecting a few brisk steps with his weight in front of him, leading with his head, until he crashed into the back of a pair of knees with a leather skirt, causing an immediate collapse. Dave turned his face trying to avoid a face plant, and the prostitute rode him down to the ground, landing with his face splitting her legs, a lack of underwear strictly apparent and a pressing matter.

"Oh my God!"

"What the fuck!"

"Who is this guy?"

The bar briefly went into spasm, a loose circle being formed around a dazed whore performing her services openly and apparently pro bono publico. Was it a marketing ploy? Tax-deductible charity? Passionate romance? Her hips were too deeply bent for her to just stand back up; she had to commit one swing forward, a grind across his face, to get her weight off him. The greatest damage of the incident was that she had broken his nose on impact and then smeared his blood across his face with this movement, but that wasn't the immediate impression that the bar got when his face emerged from the skirt, a brilliant, broad red brushstroke from his upper lip up to his receded hair line and even painting the peak of his hair; vibrant, the color of love. *Sex is violence*, the prostitute may have deflected towards the situation, if she had such an eloquent vocabulary.

Instead, before she turned her face to meet his completely but having felt his nose in her cunt and having heard the sounds of the accident as they happened, tried to play it off with a joke after a squeal, *"oww*, buy a girl dinner first, baby—" and she noticed his bloody face, "OH MY GOD!"

At that very moment, she decided that she would never refer to anyone who approached her vagina as baby; the imagery was too powerful, seeing a bloody balding face emerge from the leather hood she wore. Teddy pulled Dave up before any more realizations could be made and made for the door.

Dave was in a numbed whirlwind, last clear analysis being that he was leaning in for a languid and thoughtless kiss, then on the floor, then a sanguine flavor and the smell of piss. Now he was on the steps of the bar, empty-handed and by himself, holding his nose without knowing why. Teddy rushed back out with paper towels and fresh brews.

"I never thought I'd see *that*, and I come here pretty regular."

Dave, now intoxicated by the pure stimulus of it all and closing off his nose, "wh-whuh 'appen?"

"I, uhh, I don't really know," Teddy said, sobering up and wagering that the attempted kiss would be forgotten. "You're a lot more fun when you aren't at Linole-Yum." He cracked a beer on the edge of the steps they were sitting in, taking out a healthy chunk of wood.

"Mahdose, mahdose." Dave pleaded.

"You got snatched."

"I 'unno."

"I don't know either."

"I'unno nomo," Dave continued, on the verge of tears.

"What?"

"I'ust 'unno anymo."

"We all get too drunk and fuck around with the pros, man."

Dave sterned up, "no! No! You 'on't know. I din't raper."

“Woah, woah, woah, no one accused you—“

“No ban, I din't raper. I 'on't even lye poop.” On pronouncing the plosive, he spit a bit of blood that had been making its way into the crevice of his lips.

“Poop? Wh—?”

“I 'ON'T EVEN LYE POOH!”

“Dave, man, let's get you a water.”

Dave struggled on hearing this, anticipating a great resistance against him putting the Moore's Light against his lips, which was met without. “I 'old you, I 'ON'T EVEN LYE IT!”

“No one said you did, man. Hey, I'll be right back, you stay right here.” Teddy got up to plead for ice for his postpartum friend.

Dave was left mumbling to himself, piecing it all together or failing to do so, “I 'on't een lye pooh, I 'unno.”

Teddy reemerged, sitting down and pressing ice against the bridge of Dave's nose. “You're going to look a lot different at the restaurant with a broken and bruised face.”

Dave mumbled unintelligibly, “it'on' ma'er.”

“What?”

“It 'on't ma'er! Nuhng ma'ers!”

Teddy, somewhat turned off by the pathetic person being define in front of his eyes, someone far removed from the grease-director he had previously known, replied, “Dave, let's get you home.”

“I can't go 'ome.”

“Why not?”

“Mah wife in't at girl's night. She leavin' me 'cuz she tink I like mah niece's shit.”

Teddy, doing a one-eighty of judgment with this new depravity, replied dumbfounded, “uhh, what?”

And Dave explained the rest of his situation, slowly and without most consonants, that one day he woke up to a number of concerned calls from family and family-friends about what he had sent a number of people close to him, to an email from his work, to allegations of pedo-coprophilia and socio-sexual racism and interracial cuckoldry, to the actual rape that his own dear niece was accusing him of, to that video she made that went viral, to the threats he was receiving from sexually-contrived Mexicans, to his having no one to talk to, to this crazy night that he still hadn't pieced together. At the end of it all, Teddy explained the night as it happened, truths told.

Unfortunately, underneath a veil of empathy was a sinister sympathy that Typical Teddy was harboring, just as malicious as the obscure strains of gonorrhea that had made their way into his heart, causing a swelling in his aortic valve that he didn't know about. This sympathy was paired with an envy of infamy, of a slight embitterment caused by Dave's resentment of Teddy's secret dream-come-true. Behind the commiserative patting on the back, *"I'll help you get through this,"* was a congratulatory patting on the back, *"can you help me go through this as well?"*

...

Feeling his lungs warm up to the intake of a bit of harsh hashish and some mild cannabis, Fowlst was attempting a listen at his set list for this evening at Prince Charlie's. His heart may or may not have been in the right place, but he'd been assured that there was some molly for him tonight that would put it there. Heavy drops, something routine to his psyche by now, still made his heartbeat skip double now and then, eighth notes in 3/4 timing filling in the filled measures. Gentle melodies of wind instruments breaking the cacophonies of post-synth sounds clashing with themselves, bridges to choruses offering him the only respite of his own work or the occasional tab-switching to his indulgent fatalism-in-music to take a rest. The hash helped, having numbed and dumbed and superimposed, honing and toning him up. Depending on his mood, it blurred the lines, sharpened the lines, or did both at the same time, and it was in this way that its effect mirrored his own music.

He'd sent an email to his cardiologist from his phone while the plane was beginning its landing procedure despite the pilot telling him not to operate any electrical device at that time, a second rebellion. The decision to fly across the world to Berlin was based on a safe indecision: he could always be compensated for the flight despite ducking out of the concert, one of the many protected rights of the veiled artist.

Since the condition appeared, he hadn't noticed a special sensitivity to the lights and general rapture of live performances; it was only the volume that got to him. He could tell from the transitions, some of which having been masked by excessive light build-ups, flashing strobing and seizing lights and vapor machines blasting the opioid masses jumping in their own preferred fever.

His own experience with molly and this volume problem had left him at a loss of solution. The drug by itself aggravated his heart problem, but combining it with the stimulus of the show resulted in more ecstasy than anything. His heart could have been taking a beating, but he didn't know it, and where did that leave him?

He was supposed to meet up with the dealer shortly in a corner store of all places, the sort of place where more illegitimate than legitimate business is done. The venue had promised high grade MDMA, a very courteous gesture, the kind of stuff that could be spoon-fed to post-traumatic worriers such as himself, though his teaspoon was likely to be a tablespoon and he'd be in more of a mid-traumatic stress situation than those lucky souls drinking mollywater at the doctor's of yesteryear, cold white floors and walls and labcoats creating their own sanitary stresses. The good news was that he only had to press play; his show presence was that exactly: he pressed play, wearing an oversized owl mask that had layers of neon-lit circles for eyes and an outline of sound-reactive multicolored LEDs, the stuff of transrealist biopunk dreams, embodied further by the artificially overstimulated body underneath, either jumping maniacally and flailing about or completely idle in a distant concentration at the astounding light show going on around him, all of which stimulated the crowd.

Of course, a part of the courtesy was their delivering to him, but he requested to try some a few hours in advance as to get accommodated with it all before going live. They were going to be busy all afternoon, so they gave him one of the connects, a certain Ihsan, no doubt one of a handful of distributors handling the massive and targeted demand for the drug, for, in the city so bright that it blinds the souls and eyes of generations, one must look out for only their own audience-family on any given night.

If the molly was good and feeling good, he was going to go. His mind was set on meeting Bahman Baris, one of his favorite celeb crushes who would surely match his large on-screen presence in person, and so he set off for the address he was given.

Walking in the little store, a cash register on a quasi-desk with several refrigerators directly across, and two walls of various crisps, crackers, candies, and condoms behind that, he asked the clerk, who was conversing with a soft-looking German, for Ihsan.

"Who's asking?" Ihsan had been directed to ensure that every customer was planning on trying to get into Prince Charlie's this very night.

"Hagen told me to come—I'm the DJ at Prince Charlie's tonight."

"And Aggie wouldn't deliver them to you, that lazy son of a bitch."

At this, the German seemed to perk up as if something crossed his mind, but let it go.

"I wanted to gum a little bit now so I could test it out before dosing fully." Peter seemed knowledgeable at this, and Ihsan looked as if he would comply.

"Ach *so*. Of course. Are you excited for tonight?"

"Very. Just got off the plane and I'm trying to track down Bahman Baris, heard he was going to be there. Have you heard of him?"

"Well fuck me, that tall son of a bitch does have some influence around here." Ihsan reached under the counter, ignoring Peter's inquiry, and brought out two bags, "is point two enough?"

On sight of the crystals, Peter's attention snapped away from Chinese cinema. "That's plenty. What will it run me?"

"Aggie told me it was *on the house* for you."

And just like that, Peter was gumming a quarter of the contents of one of the bags, bitter bitter and chemical bitter bitter makes your jaw clench and your face squeeze up like sour. A short walk away and into the basement where trains were brought to you by dings and timers, and here was his train after a longshort nine-minute countdown just having missed the train before. He got on, stayed for several stops, got off, waited, and got back on in a whirlwind of comeuppance. He again got off the U-bahn, displays flashing and sound confirming *einsteigen bitte, bitte bitte bitte, einsteigen bitte, zurückbleiben bitte, bitte bitte bitte,* taking steps to the beat of the hearts of the crowd around him, *boom, boom, boom, boom,* putting his shoulders into each step, *boom, boom, boom, boom, like a Goblin,* wrists flicking and jaw tensing by the step, *boom, boom, boom, boom,* looking into the beautiful shiny eyes of passersby, *boom, boom, boom, boom, tsssssssschhhh,* the train's doors closed, all at once, *boom, boom, boom, boom,* a pretty girl rushing down the steps every part of her bouncing, blonde hair, the sun in strands the sun am Strand, falling out of a black knitted cap, *boom, boom, boom, boom,* realizing she wasn't going to make it in time to her train opposite his, departing, *boom, boom, boom, boom,* flustered sigh dropping shoulders in a heavy resignation and her neck looks soft and sweet-smelling and if only he had the faculties to tell her sugary things, *boom, boom, boom, boom,* gloomy gloomy given the sunlight she deserves but no, *boom, boom, boom,* boom, he should keep walking and up the steps but he'll never see her again and suddenly there's another one, *boom, boom, boom, boom,* walking down the steps, slower, brunette, deliberate, skinny pants on skinny legs that he wanted to run his hand over, the texture alone surely overwhelming him, *boom, boom, boom, boom,* walking past her and starting up the stairs, feeling like leaning but not actually, stepping in rhythmic motion, *boom, boom, boom, boom,* emerging to the early setting sun shining light on his back, warm starting at his shoulder blades and moving through his ribs and out the front of his chest, *boom, boom, boom, boom,* Torstraße, Rosenthaler Straße, no, Weinbergsweg, the tongues of these people, *boom, boom, boom, boom,* cars parting like some heavenly sea for red and green stick figure things, *boom, boom, boom, boom,* beautiful people on comfy wooden benches at the patio, beautiful planters with blooming colors, *boom, boom, boom, boom,* the metal door handle will be cold, cold and a press of the wrist, *boom, boom, boom, boom,* they don't know, not the couple walking down the steps two-wide, oh my, what a fabulous pair of breasts surely under that shirt, soft cotton over soft mounds of pale-cream strawberry, *boom, boom, boom, boom,* don't look, wait for them to pass, sweat probably apparent on the forehead, *boom, boom, boom, boom, bin nockh mew da yah ickh owckh voss fear, boom, boom, boom, boom,* suddenly door and sweaty fingers grasping at slippery slick card in moist and warm gushy feeling pocket, peripherals closing in but pleasantly, *boom, boom, boom, boom,* open door and freshest of fresh breaths, the kind that a Buddhist would wait a thousand years for, *boom, boom, boom, boom,* green plant sitting on a table in front of window, stalky green and its enjoyment would cut your soft fingers and wouldn't that be unpleasant in such a mood, *boom, boom, boom,*

boom, still might go to it, peripherals distracted by shifting lights, a mirror! *boom, boom, boom, boom*, looking rough, were his eyes always black? *boom, boom, boom, boom*, towel soaked in cold water, now, *boom, boom, boom, boom*, now music, music, einsteigen bitte, *boom, boom, boom, boom*, fibers of being flexing to the beat across the universe, some forecast we have here, folks, sunny all day in the heart of man, *boom, boom, boom, boom*, it all worked so that he could be here, a storm chaser of his own breed, *boom, boom, boom, boom*, chasing the stormy stars, thirteen hours by plane away, *boom, boom, boom, boom*, deafening bass and beat, something post-industrial, a sawmill discotheque, *boom, boom, boom, boom*, something he created for this place, something that was projected onto him just for this and the upcoming moments, *boom, boom, boom, boom*, the stars have aligned and he is intimate with humanity right now! *boom, boom, boom, boom*, hearing the echoes of himself like some ear for mirrors! *boom, boom, boom, boom*.

...

"Who's Aggie? I thought we got this stuff from Bahman," Heiko, between chomps of chips, said to Ihsan just as the American left the store.

"Aggie's the guy above me buying all this."

"Oh, I thought—" Heiko's brow drew confused.

"No, he just gives it to me to sell, but he also has me give away a lot of it."

"Sounds expensive."

"He's a *promoter*."

"How is it?"

Ihsan straightened up from his leaning posture at the register, proud, "our entertainer should be feeling himself by about now."

Blühe wieder, bunte Welt. It was a beautiful world, especially with a tense jaw. "So let's dose before midnight and then little redoses until the lights die down and the sun comes out."

The plan was set, punctuated by a succinct *crunch* as Heiko peered down into an empty tube. "She should be about to get to the station. I'm going to go meet her there so she can find this place."

He set off for down and across the street, but who should he find next to a homeless man divvying up a bounty of cigarette butts and splitting them for unburnt tobacco but Brock the Gray on the streets of Berlin. The eyes told all, or maybe only most. Maybe it was Brock's blood, a son or grandson or cousin, but it was definitely him in there. Gold eyes opened like twin crowns upon his rugged cat face. The feline, unaligned with any provincial faction or alliance, sat close to the beggar, having no doubt gone through some turbulence in life since his last reunion with Heiko. It was clear that the cat had abandoned the society that he had built around himself at some point, instead seeking less and more wholesome, relying on handouts but not unattracted to the notion, somehow even crossing the Elbe at some point on his journey to Mecca. And what for a Mecca, the city of undying beggars, a fatalism-in-politics, what had brought him here? Love? The prospect thereof? Had love dragged him across fields and forests through winters and rains and dumped him here? Had love been the wind or the railroad? A balloon? Had he arrived here unceremoniously and lived out a new life of streethood? The streets here were far different from the stream and creek of Wilhelmshaven. The cats here banded together but without common fur and only based on the genre of trash that they dragged in. The ins and outs were nuanced, dangerous lines never to cross or crossed daily for survival. He had surely once belonged to a clique, trading effectively and providing levels of material wealth impossible back in the northwest. He would have been a prudent risk-taker, managing effectively a portfolio of resources, of trash-can-schedules and restaurant-regulars willing to share bites of chicken, of streets and courtyards. What had changed? Could he have thought back on Barney and the Senate being torn apart by the fiercer of them, only to be routed themselves? Could it be open battle's obscure reflection, street society, that he had finally gazed directly into and surrendered himself to the rest of the spirit? And how long could he survive as an apolitical actor? How long could he live in peace? There was no fish for dinner on these streets but only the occasional crust of sweet bread that his companion beggar would give to him as he surrendered himself to a street-rolled cigarette. Those eyes, gold-crowned beggar, staring deep into Heiko, who now wished he had some sock cake to share.

Kleine Brötchen für kleine Jungen,

Keine Brötchen für keine Jungen.

The moment was over quicker than it had happened as Heiko continued past, pretending to be unaffected by the heavy souls he was walking past and glad he didn't have a cigarette to give to the man. As he looked past, he saw a familiar princess appearing from the underworld, her own gold crown falling around her neck as her black cap failed to restrain it or just petals emerging from the leaves, a button nose like the eye of a sunflower and her eyes like its escaping aroma, creamy-enchanting only after you've walked away. She was turning and turning, looking for him.

Blumen hab' ich mir bestellt.

"Effy!"

"Achso! There you are." She turned into the sun and began walking his way, peering down the street for an opportunity to cross. She was in dark, knee-high boots and a black skirt, only a strip of leg at the bottom of the thigh exposed, with a floral blouse tucked in at the top of her waist, petite shoulders framing her body, cream color sneaking out through dark mesh sleeves, with sunlit hair tastefully concealing the subtleties of her figure.

The way that she hesitated before the cars, not that she could have passed or that he would have tried, but her gentle passivity and appearance of apathy towards the swarm of cars charmed him. It was just another silent note in the bank of Effy's incantations, evidence for some feeling she would maybe later express in words.

And then, briskly, she walked across the street with a familiar grace, skirt appearing to be the only limited factor to her infinite stride cut finite by black on either side, and it was the same certainty in Brock's eyes that now met him in the form of a stripe of flesh, a teaser-trailer for what might be to come and think of the flower! Sweet nectar of Tochter Europa herself being slurped right up, the taste of vitality, the fountain of youth, the very fertile crescent in its pleasantly warm and moist climate. He would taste her by the end of the night. It was upon his shoulders a great boulder, a *los!*er to be, something he could force in the less poetic moments of life.

"Are you ready for tonight?" She smiled, concealing her magic from the sounds she made.

"I'm going to peak."

She laughed and grabbed his elbow, both of them standing on the sidewalk before the crosswalk. "Optimistic, I see. Did you try some of the fun already?"

"I was waiting for you and your friends," Heiko suggested.

"Oh, *yeah*, they had dinner plans so they'll catch us in a while."

"Sorry, you know how Ihsan is," Heiko played as if to be on her side. They began walking, Heiko simultaneously following and leading like he often did. "We actually just met tonight's DJ. He took a little sample."

"I'll have to ask him about it when we get there before it hits us." She was in the middle of a conjuration, appealing to the spirits of foreign beasts in an effort to inspire some covetousness among her own wild dogs, some sort of conservatism or territoriality. Her own wild dog, half walking behind her despite her not knowing where to go, seemed terribly a cat person in the heavy majority of things playing out, and it wasn't past her to see texts from him and think of the positives, of the time he outdrank her in a direct competition and then carried her sick self home and took her so or the boyish charm he could exhibit in the summer sun; she would then see his texts reaching out, supporting her, as less the evidence of a chronically lonely person and more of some sort of ascetic savior, but he routinely and often rapidly invaded this image like the abnormal cell growth forcing itself into her image of her own mother. And just like that, two steps further towards the shop and she started crying. "I don't know—"

"Effy!" Heiko tried to console her, one of his stronger suits and a card he'd be happy to play, "what happened?"

"Claudia called. I don't know."

"What happened?" Heiko had his arm around her and she nestled her face into his shoulder and neck, the infertile crescent.

"Well we started talking about class, and she made a comment about my dad—"

Heiko mhm'd and deliberately stopped her from walking further, guiding her to a halt facing him and half an arm-length's away, hands on her shoulders.

"And she—she started getting mad at him—and I tried to tell her it wasn't his—fault," tears flowed freely and sobbed predicting words.

"Well she's—"

"And she started yelling—and I started yelling—and we're both yelling and neither of us knows why—"

Heiko, knowing why, didn't say a thing, instead pulling her back in. "Hey, it's very complicated, but I know something simple."

Effy, sensing salvation, sniffled up towards him with opening eyes.

"That you're a sweet girl and we're going to have a lot of fun tonight."

And just like that, her arm around his hip and his around her shoulder, they took to continuing the short walk to the store, pausing briefly out front for her to wipe her eyes.

Ihsan's dark eyes appeared over a colorful candy bar display. "Na?" He said dryly.

"The rest of the party will be through here soon." Heiko preempted the question to avoid its proposal. "When's Bahman getting here?" Of course, wanted the answer to be *much later*.

"He's been in and out all day, so probably soon." A lull appeared, and Ihsan turned it towards Effy, commentary on how he felt on her or so she thought, "Hey Effy."

As normal, she gave him the least interaction she could, "Hey Ihsan, how're things around here?"

Ihsan, taking that as confirmation that Effy still liked him as a person, began to talk about himself as he opened up a beer and the store gradually became less and less open to foreigners and Effy's friends arrived and the sun set and Bahman arrived and chatted about Mexico this and China that and somehow sat in the middle of every arrangement and wore a brilliant purple v-neck that made his dark skin burst as some sort of exotic import-entertainer dominating the conversation and in between laughing belly ha ha ha ha to bring eyes back on his goofy but adorable smile and his dark locks of hair falling to the side of his eyes bouncing with each ha and Heiko watching Effy not watch him and Ihsan watching Effy's friends forget the name Ihsan and replace it with Bahman's friend.

Night fell upon them, the balance of light slowly favoring the light bulb's matte sheen to the sun's pervasive light. Now the bulb and its street-legions were the only source. Shadows filled the crevices of faces differently, bodies acquired uncertainties and spirits acquired unknown intentions, attentions, and retentions while intentions, attentions, and retentions acquired new spirits. The molly was mixed into several on-the-house shots of equal parts digestif and energy drink, the latest bomb to hit Berlin.

Night should have helped him, Ihsan thought, less distinction and more desperation, and certainly less denial. It was proving to be the opposite, however; it was serving as a cover with which the girls could be less shameful about keeping Ihsan at a distance. It was a genuinely low-light interaction. Heiko and Effy were lost among themselves talking a small circle around her pressing personal issues, though Ihsan only saw the connection being made, the occasional hint of enthusiasm breaking the speaker playing house music above their heads, *boom, boom, boom, boom*, the coming-up of the drug reflecting in the moving and distorting shadow-proportions reacting the changes in expression and movements of the head, *boom, boom, boom, boom*, and the moisture he could now sense, probably smell, accumulating around the very thought of tall-dark-and-handsome over there, and his own excitement being aroused from the impending rush he was going through.

Effy thought the night would help her too, but she was battling a deep anxiety that she had since avoided for some time, accelerated by the rate of her heart. She was normally one to play it cool, but now she was sweating. Among the group, Heiko was the only link to this problem of hers, so she was in the middle of an extended breaking down and telling him the depth of it all, of her absent father buying her mother occasionally and loose knowledge of his shadier dealings, even of a time that he stayed with them for a week in hiding once. Quietly this time, that she didn't trust Turks, she really didn't, because she associated them with the side of her father that she didn't know, and that she really feels guilty taking molly because she's falling in the same traps her father set, *boom, boom, boom, boom*, and that she's taking out her anger on her sick mother, swear-screaming at her on the phone, couldn't bring herself to go see her, *boom, boom, boom, boom*, her fucking friends don't even give a shit about her and they don't even know and why does she even keep them around? *boom, boom, boom, boom*, but who else would she keep around?

My size should have helped me, Bahman thought as his heart started racing, knowing that he took the same dose as the others, *boom, boom, boom, boom*, I'm too big, they can't not see me, I can't avoid their looks, *boom, boom, boom, boom*, what have I gotten myself into? I'm losing control, the light bulb is radially distorting until it splits into two radii traveling circles around each other and four light bulbs now, *boom, boom, boom, boom*, looking down to three sets of wide eyes on what-were-their-names' faces staring right deep into his own and let's go let's hit the club! *boom, boom, boom, boom*, let's get out of here.

The group united briefly, all interrupted except Ihsan who wasn't in a conversation and was unluckily noticed as such as Bahman's voice crossed the boundaries. "Let's go find some music and get ready for the club, I heard this DJ is awesome."

And so the group began, all appreciative of Bahman's talent for such leadership, with Heiko and Effy immediately falling to the rear to continue their conversation, leaving Ihsan oscillating between forcing himself between the horny girls and the presumably horny Bahman or just walking behind them, shamefully trying to chip comments in here and there. It was a good night for a walk, so the group took a liberal approach to finding a destination. It was early yet for the city.

Heiko, feeling the onset of fatigue from pulling the weight of Effy combined with the artificial energy from being pulled by Molly, felt he could alleviate the situation by trying to change the subject, *boom, boom, boom, boom*, thinking it was only the result of a drug-addled mind not quite strong enough to be drug-addled, not listening to the complexities of her emerging story but shouldering it off as anxiety, *boom, boom, boom, boom*, and his own anxiety mounting as a direct result of her, would she do this all night? *boom, boom, boom, boom*, she doesn't smell good right now, and he couldn't even hold his fantasy of her in his mind, *boom, boom, boom, boom*, should he send her home? *boom, boom, boom, boom*, did he even want her anymore?

Lena, one of the three what-were-their-names, was losing interest in Bahman by the second. His initial allure was the ethnic-ambiguity-but-some-kind-of-exotic curious feeling she got from him, matched with his height and deep voice. He had just commanded her attention, but he really hadn't shown any distinct personality, *boom, boom, boom, boom*, just a generic big person of sorts, not a cultural icon or a leader but just an empty sort of face, nothing more than the body he'd been born into, *boom, boom, boom, boom*, and what little he revealed about himself was something about him liking Chinese movies or something and he might have been the drug dealer for the night, *boom, boom, boom, boom*, or maybe it was the Turkish guy that's kind of wandering around with us, he wasn't cute, was he? *boom, boom, boom, boom*, she wasn't normally one to be caught up in the pretty lights, having her head on somewhat straight as is said, but sometimes she went off the deep end in an occasional night-like-tonight, *boom, boom, boom, boom*, but it's early, she had plenty of time.

The group arrived at a coolly lit biergarten with gentle house playing and a slight light show behind a waterfall which caught the eye of the group immediately, Bahman being the first to succumb to the pretty scene and walking straight to the closest table. The seven pulled chairs in to sit together, Heiko and Effy again seeming distant and Ihsan deliberately placing himself next to Bahman with a girl to his left and two on the other side of Bahman on his right.

Bahman, with a wave of relief crashing over him as Ihsan injected himself in, Ihsan being some semblance of empathy and similarity and distance from the studious eyes of the wet females, *boom, boom, boom, boom*, maybe Ihsan could even break the ice with a few of them and draw some attention so he could get lost in the waterfall imagery, *boom, boom, boom, boom*, red and yellow lights barreling through, moving fisheyes through water flashing to the music, looking sweet and cool, *boom, boom, boom, boom*, wait, why is no one talking or was he talking?

Ihsan, initially satisfied by having a cute girl sit on his left, proximity and a tinge of warmth coming from her or perhaps being inspired into him, *boom, boom, boom, boom*, it's been a while, and I've finally cornered one off from him and I think her name is Lena, *boom, boom, boom, boom*, but what do I say and what is this silence next to Bahman? *boom, boom, boom, boom*, he should be talking right now, why isn't anyone talking? *boom, boom, boom, boom*, is he trying to get rid of me? *boom, boom, boom, boom*, are they trying to get rid of me?

Effy, conscious about her wet eyes ruining her makeup and the general risk of being caught being a person in such circumstances, pretended to check her phone and stood as Heiko dragged a chair to her and pulled another one for himself, *boom, boom, boom, boom*, she sat abruptly, cold metal teasing and tingling exposed skin, and looked down, slowly harboring resentment that Heiko did not seem as available as normal, *boom, boom, boom, boom*, he doesn't understand because his mother used to hug him the same with or without sock cake, *boom, boom, boom, boom*, and the only person she had to talk to didn't understand, *boom, boom, boom, boom*, and it was going to be a long night.

The biergarten was an underwhelming experience, filled with nervous false-belly-laughs and Ihsan delivering his commentary too quickly in an effort to get it in at all, resulting in chopped and screwed conversation, and Heiko and Effy off to their own, some tension spreading around and between them, and, just like before, Bahman announced that it was time to go have some fun at the club. This second act of leadership did not carry the same weight as the first, however, due to his dying conversational suave and living-breathing-growing anxiety.

The club was just as it should have been expected. The moment was marked by Bahman turning the corner into the large alley-like entrance to the venue, which sat off the road and between buildings, and immediately a bouncer called him over with an emphatic gesture over his head and a loud voice. The group scurried over with him, but the bouncer stopped Bahman's procession to chat with him while waving the rest right through, past the long line that had formed.

Bahman, happy to see a familiar face and abandon the now four titillated nipples that seemed to still be chasing his gaze, enthusiastically greeted his friend, *boom, boom, boom, boom*, he was even able to suspend a bit of anxiety after convincing himself that all he needed was new people, *boom, boom, boom, boom*, but the feeling crept right back up as the sweat streamed down his temple and he was losing certainty that he was speaking normally, *boom, boom, boom, boom*, and the lights from inside were starting to pour out and they looked sublime, even reminding him of a Sonoran performance he once gave, *boom, boom, boom, boom*, simpler times.

Ihsan, ecstatic at the loss of Bahman, began to get the attention of all the girls, grabbing Lena's arm and leading her to the dance floor and the rest of them followed, *boom, boom, boom, boom*, employing only the most aware of dance moves at this early hour, the slow building-up of the best climax he'll ever have, *boom, boom, boom, boom*, he noticed the DJ in a large, electric owl mask, looking like he drank too much molly water with eyes like those, *boom,*

boom, boom, boom, the world was in no place to find out if it was the same guy he'd talked to earlier, *boom, boom, boom, boom*, but no distractions here on this dance stage, not in this deafening bass and flashing dark room.

Heiko, knowing that he couldn't yet abandon Effy without some kind of excuse, told her we would join her outside after getting them drinks from the bar, *boom, boom, boom, boom*, but drinking at the time seemed like a lot to take in and he was sweating like a maniac, so he asked for waters, *boom, boom, boom, boom*, and Effy might not have been happy with it but she needed it and if that wasn't a metaphor for everything she—*boom, boom, boom, boom*, he gave her the water, she shouted in his ear, something along the same lines as earlier, no progress out here where she can hear herself, *boom, boom, boom, boom*, time for her to have lost herself, told her just a few minutes on the dance floor because he was starting to feel really good and look how beautiful it was in there, *boom, boom, boom, boom*, Effy, this was our night, this was going to be amazing, I wanted you to feel amazing, *boom, boom, boom, boom*, oh, and you should drink this water.

Peter, feeling good, was finally accepting it all. His father didn't mean for the video to take off, and it had really paved his own way in the music industry as it was, *boom, boom, boom, boom*, in some ways the creativity of it was quite charming and even admittedly funny, and what a time and place to be thinking about this, at a club in this lovely city, *boom, boom, boom, boom*, this must have been good stuff, it had made him forget about his heart condition, and he was even beginning to lose himself in his own music, *boom, boom, boom, boom*, he felt like all was well in his universe, a fleeting feeling that he been previously only associated with the reliving of his traumatic incident, *boom, boom, boom, boom*, but that was a different house, and this was the new house!

Heiko and Effy joined the rest of the group on the dance floor, Bahman still absent. Effy first joined their little circle but leaned further and further out until her only connection with it was Heiko, who was now standing between her and everyone else.

Effy, the anxiety still mounting and the realization slowly unfolding that she couldn't be here with all them anymore, tried to force Heiko to go through the same confrontation she was going through, *boom, boom, boom, boom*, that she didn't actually love her mother and she hated herself as well for it, that the guilt was crushing her while elevating everyone else, *boom, boom, boom, boom*, he wasn't even listening, that asshole, why does he even get to stick around her? *boom, boom, boom, boom*, she's miles out of his league and failing at his only purpose.

Peter, getting into the music, was feeling the stars line up for him, *boom, boom, boom, boom*, feeling the benefit in what he had produced, his spiritual outpouring, for the first time, *boom, boom, boom, boom*, his very blood channeling the sounds, reverberating and resounding, *boom, boom, boom, boom*, bouncing to the music.

Bahman, emerging from the crowd coated in sweat, starting to look desperate, forcefully grabbed onto Ihsan, *boom, boom, boom, boom*, help him, Ihsan, he needs to get out of here, *boom, boom, boom, boom*, Ihsan pushed back, telling him to fuck off, his last connection being cut off and he can't have it, trying again to grab Ihsan, *boom, boom, boom, boom*, and Ihsan puts some muscle into the second push and knocks Bahman off-balance.

Heiko, trying to make a loud gesture by deliberately walking away from her, began making his way directly through the crowd to get away from Effy in the most direct way, *boom, boom, boom, boom*, cutting through his friends and was going to whisper that he'd come back to Ihsan but Ihsan and Bahman looked like they were having a chat, *boom, boom, boom, boom*, he passed by them and *boom*.

Bahman, stumbling and bumbling, crashed into Heiko, who had two cups of water preventing his hands from adequately catching himself. Bahman's height caused him to fall down onto Heiko, whose unawareness led to him crumbling from the top down and landing on the side of his head. Bahman scrambled up, saw blood and an empty expression, yelled, the crowd began breaking up and forming a circle at the time time, and Bahman ran towards the DJ, the closest authority.

Peter, feeling a new sense of pride, threw some new loops into the current measure, making dramatic gestures to hype people up. Molly had made him a new man, *boom, boom, boom, boom*, and he was going to be here all night, *boom, boom, boom, boom*, and everyone was going to be with him in his house all night.

Bahman, sweating, wide-eyed, and frantic, yelled at the DJ and twisted his hand as if to turn a dial down, in German, "TURN THE MUSIC OFF AND GET HELP."

Peter, not even able to remove his over-ear headphone from his ear inside his mask if he tried, hearing only something about a 'hole' and thinking this sweaty wreck of a person was recanting the line that followed him everywhere, 'if you win you'll put your happy diddle in his hole,' shouted back, mute to himself and proud of his new voice for the first time, in English, "MY NAME IS PETER FUCKING ALDRIDGE, AND YOU CAN NOT STOP THIS HOUSE!"

Part Two

Harmony and Understanding

It wasn't a short sequence of events that led Cierra to sticking a marker in her asshole, taking a picture, and posting it on the internet, but it happened. She was the Queen of the Board, complete with a title and a consort of eunuchs who gave her constant praise, manipulating the few confirmed images of her to please their fetishes and even starting a crowdfunding campaign to prevent her from having to work and leave them periodically, though she might not have had to anyway after being so brutally sexually harassed by her old manager.

As she got more and more involved with the Board, she became increasingly open to using her femininity, utilizing particles such as "grill here" or signing off "t. femanon." The reaction of the other members was dominated by negative attention, sometimes in total skepticism that it was an actual female posting on their beloved and later in personal and perverted attacks, name-calling "roastwhore" and also "virgin sperglord princess," but the lasting result of this attention was a following of interactions guaranteed with every post; she led a posse of cellar-virgins by the virtual scent of her genitals. As she kept posting, her tone and syntax began to be familiar with others and eventually there were always allegations of the Queen in their midst when she interacted, hinting or not, and this resulted in blatant requests for her to further expose herself, "tits or gtfo" and the like.

The now famous picture of her tits, matte black body resulting from unnatural light behind her and computer screen reflecting dull off of the curve of her breasts and shoulders, a piece of paper with the time and date hanging from her mouth and the picture cut off at her nose, had incited a riot of false testosterone where only collective self-loathing was before. Before the tits, there were only sad frogs who talked about spilling pasta all over the place in social situations, but now there was a plethora of smug frogs calling her out as if they understood the female psyche and could bring about a collective benefit: further degradation furthering mutual dependence, a virtual opening up to another human being in the form of specified anal penetration, a call of desire confirming she was needed and an action confirming they were just as important. The sheer volume of requests for this picture made her feel pressured; she could never retreat to her previous innocence. She was to be the Queen or just another witch, and to be a witch here was quite dangerous. There had been horror stories about angry frogs acquiring personal information and prosecuting accordingly. The pressure accumulated in a thread dedicated to her on the most desolate section of the Board—the board of miscellany. By now, a majority of posters had saved the picture of her tits and many had found lookalike pornstars, many of which flattered Cierra, and most threads would contain some form of the original picture with any number of adjustments made, photoshopped dicks or cum or even Pepe looking onto the scene with a grin on his face.

So, despite maintained complete anonymity, she gave into the pressure and prepared her anus, reaching back, ass towards a mirror to stage the picture appropriately, struggling to the timestamp in frame without including too much of her face. The picture was to be from a low angle so that they got a satisfying look at her pussy too, which seemed to be even more consecrated to the Board as if it weren't to be abused but for the most righteous act. As she looked between her legs at her phone's screen reflecting the full image before it, it dawned on her that the head of the silver marker sticking out of her asshole between her upward-pointed round butt cheeks made the shape of a crown with a silver marker and a piece of notebook paper as a globus cruciger, the symbolic ass-accessory of the coronation of an internet empress. The Board was incredibly impressed and celebrated with much talk of coming buckets, and the new Queen herself then commissioned several original skullfucking images that were made pro bono by some of her more talented followers, some of which even attempting to interpret her own images into the 3D graphics.

All of this excitement had numbed her enthusiasm for the Thursday lunch, but there the bus was and its doors slid to the side as a liftgate rose out from underneath. There was the beautiful male nurse, the 'real' social actor. He was charming in his naivete about the real going-ons of the upcoming generation; he lived in a bubble. He didn't know of the sorts of despair that could be present in as mundane a job as his because he didn't have that touch of doubt from a young age. His family probably went to church every Sunday and had barbecue or takeout afterwards. He stepped on the platform on its way up after exiting the passenger seat, and once he got up he smiled warmly at a spacey Hal and a trapped Carol, bracing as if Hal might lose grip of the bar and fall on her. From inside the diner, Cierra could even see Jade a few seats away looking on her favorite tall, black helper with lust, and he didn't even take offense to her. His smile didn't waiver.

She began to resent him in the same light as her uncle. He was one of society's clowns, costumed and with a painted face, performing his best trick to secure his share in the circus. The worst problem was that his smile was painted on so cute and his costuming was so clean. He looked almost holy, wheeling Carol to the front door, and an entire bus and Cierra were watching him. He was a strong, beautiful figure, broad-shouldered with a sheen highlighting every bit of curvature on his muscled body, and he always had a smile that matched the brilliance of his shirt.

That smile would never greet Cierra like it did the others, however, after she gave herself up to the Board. There was in her a new inspiration, a base depravity and an asocial distance, that kept him and the rest in otherhood, something she had felt sparks of before but was now being singed by. She felt the creeping conscience of the virtual blood oath she had taken: the damnation of Dave Stevenson. The furthest other was the man who used to avoid this lunch for fear of his mother-in-law dragging him into gossip entwined with outdated cultural references, a fatalism-in-linguistics, about Clyde going postal or the Spice Girls' inability to get over it. Dave wouldn't be around, however, and his mother-in-law had taken the news about him very poorly, and she couldn't be bothered to return to "that ghetto restaurant."

What did she think of Dave anymore? Nothing. He had been stripped of his name tag just as she was granted her crown. His reign was long over and he was banished from her world by agents of her will. The silent and resentful tolerance was over, and she had overtaken him, though the crown wore heavy on her, a queen at the forced servitude of her hidden subjects.

The social contract of an internet empress is admittedly convoluted, much unlike the honest moral dynamic of this angel in front of her, wheeling in senile mouths constantly emptying themselves complaining that they needed to be filled. She admired the peaceful gait of his work, the warmth of his smile, and the ease with which he moved people. Her power was derived from far away, a desperate and deceitful plea to the beaten-down wills of others; he just pushed and pulled.

He and Carol walked in the door, mid-conversation, "—and don't let Hal have coffee. You know how he gets when he has his coffee."

"Well, Mrs. Keanes, Mr. Wozniak is a grown man, he can do as he pleases."

"He's an airhead and Kay would have joined us if she didn't feel threatened by his very presence."

He pulled her chair up to the table and began helping her get seated, "Mr. Wozniak has a lot of trouble getting around, ma'am, I'm certain that everyone is safe around him." His voice was deeper and warmer than his smile.

"Well he certainly won't get past *you*," she said, eyeing him up and down, "thanks, darling."

Looking back outside, Cierra noticed Hal hobbling towards the front door and herself, holding his lower back with one hand and waddling with the other and wearing a lot of mustard green. He smiled, sparsely-toothed, "Hello, sweet-cheeks," he struggled up the first step, "is the coffee warm?"

Mind in the distance, she replied, "for you, Hal, always."

...

"I don't know, we just wanted to have some fun," Effy slurred between sobs, "all of our friends were doing it and we thought it was a safe environment."

"Do you think this wouldn't have happened if he had not taken the drugs?"

"Of course not!" The sharpness of her reply cut through her sobs, "we wouldn't have even been there!"

"So do you think everyone else there was on drugs?"

"I don't know what everyone else was doing! We were hardly there for five minutes when he fell!" She was defensive and defenseless.

"So, if it's okay with you, I'd like you to talk me through the night leading up to that."

"Well we had planned to all go out and have a very fun night, the kind you only have once in a while, not that we were celebrating anything but not that we weren't."

The reporter nodded, lightly taking notes and barely breaking eye contact.

"We were with some of my friends, some of his friends, the normal kind of thing."

The reporter nodded, not taking any notes but breaking eye contact to glance at her journalist's pad.

"And I had gotten into a bit of a fight with my mother, who's very sick—"

"*Mhmm.*"

"And Heiko knew everything—really, he knew everything about me and the situation, maybe more than I did—and he was trying to get my mind off of it, not that he was distracting me from it but not not distracting me."

"So Heiko was very kind to you? Was he a nice boy?"

"Oh, Heiko's always been amazing to me, the most caring you could ever meet."

"Did he often go out clubbing? And with drugs?"

"He had done molly a few times, with me once or twice, and he went out but usually only when I dragged him out. He liked to read and write, mostly, and spend lots of time on the internet."

"So he had done drugs before, but he wasn't addicted by any means?"

"He was not a fucking drug addict."

"—and he spent time on the internet—what did he do on the internet?"

"I don't know his internet habits! What do *you* do on the internet?"

"I browse social media, watch stupid videos, laugh at silly things, and read the news."

"That sounds like what he did."

"Okay, continue with how the night went, please." The reporter's brow showed disappointment but she scrawled nonetheless.

"I don't know, I really only remember talking to him mostly. We started at a little shop that Heiko's friend works at."

"What's his friend's name?"

"Ihsan."

The reporter noted.

"Then we went to a biergarten, where the effects started to hit us. I remember a beautiful waterfall and, oh, of course! The other guy there was Ihsan's friend."

"And what was his name?"

"I can't remember his name. I must have been really feeling it at that point. And at this point Heiko is starting to feel it a little bit, not that he lost control or anything at any point through the whole night."

The reporter noted.

"He was big, and wearing a purple shirt, and dark. And loud."

Noted.

"And what about the others you were with?"

"I only really knew one of them."

"Yes, Lena Wallace. What happened at the Biergarten?"

"I got a little sadder, Heiko got a little happier, we left in about the same state."

"How long were you there?"

"Maybe two hours"

"And nothing else happened?"

She thought about her situation, something that had taken a strange background presence to that night's trauma. "It was getting dark and we were starting to roll, you know how it is."

"Mhmm."

"We talked, but honestly I was in my own world. Heiko was actually kind of between me and the rest of them, them and us, and I don't even know what was happening a meter away somehow."

Noted, somewhat at length.

"So we left the biergarten, or the big guy suggested we leave, and it all felt off."

"What do you mean *off*?"

"I don't know, I don't know if everyone was feeling like I was feeling or if maybe one other person might have been so the others were kind of doing the same with that person."

"Okay, what happened when you got there?"

"The guy kind of left us right at the door, but he got us in right past the line, which was nice considering our state."

"Do you think he works with the club? Or knows the management?"

"I saw him very friendly with the doorman, but then I didn't see him until it happened."

The journalist snapped back to the neglected notebook, started scribbling, and Effy naturally waited a moment for her to catch back up. Effy was in a black jacket with a white t-shirt, standard fare, and her eyes looked as if they were just beginning to recover from being swollen. The stream of tears down the valley of nose and cheek was a dried estuary, a trace of brine visible.

"Okay, and you guys went in?"

"We went straight to the dance floor, and then Heiko went to get drinks."

...

The helicopter rotors cut through the sound of orgasms and hot and spicy chips crunching in Guo Qu's mouth, but Zach Damon reassures all fourteen whores, "Grunt harder, tofu sellers!" They were in a garden with a decoration of monolithic stones propped up in an eroded circle with camera angles censoring them, clever angles and top-down perspectives. The women were on their backs, all pointed into the middle where Zach stood, presumably erect.

On the very arrival of his words, electricity connects them all in simultaneous ejaculation, the very touch of the gods; the whores' eyes droop low as he enters each of them just off-screen, Zach himself proceeding down a line of them and anointing each one faithfully and inspiring between them a sense of unity. His gentle touch brings them together in pleasure, all fourteen of them, this being the sequel to *The Thirteen Hairbands and The Beautiful American*, titled *The Thirteen Hairbands and The Beautiful American: The Second Mistress*.

These blessed of concubines to be partners in bliss, these women who've been purchased by a beautiful doppelganger, produced a choral arrangements of gasps and moans in contrapuntal rhythm and tone to his gentle voice's conjuring, this man who calls a mere six hundred Chinese women to his throbbing unit. Daniel Victory, or Ichiro (who could tell anymore), however, still circled above the scene in a helicopter, hoping only to get himself off at the spectacle of it all.

After all, there is no loser with Zach Damon, and pleasure can be enjoyed by all from the image of the creamy breasts below. Despite his evil disposition, Daniel Victory missed the sweet embrace of flesh on his flesh, kisses and their connecting, and his evil might even have been caused by his very passion being deprived of this godly trace.

And it would be for our orange-faced antihero to decide what to do with his passion, circling through the clouds above, to intervene in the festivities or let Zach continue to conquer, appreciative thereof?

Daniel Victory came, stringy helicopter rocket snot, bounding and stretching down into the open-air scene below, landing on the new mistress and splattering across her face, and she looked up, vision obscured by the discharge but still seeing the machine disappear into the clouds, and she considered herself blessed by a holy divinity.

Zach Damon, knowing that the semen was not his own and further knowing that Daniel Victory had probably been its source, kept it favorable, "did you see that, my stinking whores? Above the sky, we've been anointed with the sparks of the gods! A kiss for the whole world!"

The film's music, as usual, had come from a German musician, a real *los!*er, featuring several tracks out of his dedicated album, *Jazzpussy*. The main soundtrack was a cheery little ditty titled *The Rapture Bop*. The movie had a strange resolution, which wasn't that common in Zhang Li films, but it served its purpose of distracting Guo Qu from his shortcomings, such as his not being a member of the Communist Party, an exclusive club of bus drivers.

...

It was simple, almost comic, just a pulse of bass over mostly symbols. Then, suddenly, high above it, a saxophone, a single note hanging there, unwavering, until a piano took it over and softly realized the irregularity of the tempo. This was no composition by a performing monkey, this was the breath of humanity escaping this piece of brass, filled with such pep, a zest for life. The first six beats set a course for 8/8 timing, but the last two notes brought an asymmetrical friend with them, the ninth, the first three of every nine for the rest of the song, and it's easy to see how jarring this was to the conventional mind: a song out of balance.

The intro of "Gotta New Gnome," a playful expedition into a growing jazz-folk scene, a sort of previously impossible bridge between brass and strings, was smooth electric. Dougie believed that not enough people knew about the history of the gnome, feeling himself to be some product thereof, a late and abstract symbol of good spirits and bountiful harvests—that's the one thing about both garden gnomes and jazz: they don't appeal to desperate Germans. They do, however, appeal to the Deutscher who has adequately prepared his plot and knows that only a poor twist of luck could best him. The good Deutscher knows exactly when to sow his seed and when his seed is sewn properly, and he can nourish the sewn seed until the seed splits the ground and seed becomes stem. These poor twists of luck come in many forms, however, so a well-placed gnome, perhaps in the rafters of a garden shed or in a bush overlooking the garden, will stealthily guard the home. Also, in typical Deutscher fashion, the gnome adds a bit of Wilhelm das Erste in der Erde, a sort of fatalism-in-idealism, for that the Folk is known. The gnome itself, like Wilhelm the First, looks like the schnapps-drunken, negligent woodsmen that allows the Jew to be cut down in the night, and, as such, escapes much blame out of ideological alignment, much like many other famous German traditions. There's a little known fact which Dougie knew that Wilhelm the First's own court, by the Grace of God, was populated solely by gnomes. Contemporary jazz, like gnomes, seems friendly-negligent in its woodsmanship, letting worries and sorrow pass freely without the proper permissions, which, again, in previous times, led to the cutting of the Jew.

So, the Wallace Brothers, jamming with some of their favorite cats, spread the ideals of the new gnome, a sort of post-plastic, hand-made, ambiguously-American little thing. Ironically, the group's German producer contractually abused the musicians, though it was clear that he had some greater influence from the south eastern part of a divided Germany, particularly exemplified by the shady rise to prominence he enjoyed in the nightclub scene. Aggie Mann had his hands in every corner of the zone. Dougie Wallace just enjoyed the lifestyle.

But as they moved on with their set, Dougie, dressed in violet and sex, began the steadily-complicating verse of the intro to *The Los!er* and thought on his family, specifically on his estranged American niece and the lack of symmetry between her and his own similarly-estranged daughter who he knew to have recently gone through some trauma at that black cat's own venue, no doubt some new chokehold for things yet undepraved. He hadn't confronted the issue, having only heard about it on the news, seeing his own daughter talk about some loser hitting his head and being on too many drugs.

His relationship with his daughter was complicated—he had worked late nights in smoke-filled rooms when she was most impressionable, often fighting with her mother when they were ever both home and fucking at the peak of their arguments, climaxing in troughs and nadiring in apices.

Maybe it was finally time to talk to her, he thought to himself as he murmured verse after verse of misunderstood and asocial genius:

"art house, smoother, darker, smokey, starker,

sounds flying by, telling why, long black sigh,

thinkin' back on ol' sweet Jack's glassy, glossy eye,"

He would call her in the morning, his morning, early afternoon and scattering the prostitutes from his flat. His strongest ability as a father was his ability to be battered emotionally despite only supporting his loved ones, though his support (while consistent) was largely distant. He was always there when he was there, but he was never there, his presence being removed by several clauses in a drunkenly-endorsed contract with a glorified drug dealer.

The call went as follows:

"Lena! How are you?"

"Who is this?"

"This is your father."

"Ha ha, funny, are we still meeting up later?"

"No, this is Dougie,"

"Dougie? Sorry I thought you were—"

"your favorite *Los!*er."

"Oh my God! Hey Dad."

"Hi, sweet Lena, I'm sorry I haven't caught up in a while."

"Oh, Dad, you know I know how it is between us!"

"Exactly, dear, but you know I wish it wasn't like that."

"Don't worry about it!"

"I do."

"... So what's up?"

"Well I saw you on the news late last night."

"I didn't know they would actually use that!"

"I'm sorry that I didn't see it until it was on the reruns— work, you know—are you okay?"

"Oh, Dad, you know me, I'm always okay."

"Yes, dear, I know how strong you are."

"It was a freak accident."

"Yes but I know how those clubs can be."

"*Dad*. I didn't really know him that well."

"Who was he?"

"He was a friend of a friend mostly. We were there with this movie star."

"A movie star! My own daughter with a movie star—"

"A Turkish-Chinese movie star."

"Was he from Hollywood?"

"Chengdu, actually."

"Oh, I've heard cool things about California."

"No, it's not—"

"So was the guy American?"

"No, Dad, he was just some German guy who liked Effy—"

"Effy?"

"Yes, Dad."

"You know how—"

"Are you just going to lecture me?"

"…No, I'm sorry. I just want you to be happy, you know that."

"…"

"Well how is university?"

"It's fine."

"…Listen, I love you. If you ever need anything at all, you know I'm here for you."

"Thanks, Dad."

…

He did miss the kisses on his skin, but it was what's behind the kisses that he missed, something he hadn't felt in some time and could certainly use now. Despite the cold, Mexico City was settling his stomach, and the dry heat made his skin feel clean. A park was visible, lush green, that perked him up a bit, and he was completely dependent on the little things at this point.

The Chalean actor had been scrambling mentally for some time now, on a personal tour. He had been to Mexico City after the incident to find himself, then he went back home to find himself, a place he hadn't been in at least two years, then he came back to Mexico City to find himself and Latin women. He had been here for six weeks in this stint.

He was in a weird place; his retreat into himself had left his charm outside, and he couldn't be bothered to flirt with Spanish in conversation. The inside of a moderate penthouse is a barren place when the women again dress and leave. It could be said to have been inspired by a studio apartment, but it had expanded horizontally in the later concepts. It was a blend of dark-stained wood and white, what looked like floating lights above white counters with dark-stained wood cabinets, white curtains pulled open to display a painfully bright day, something that was in the process already, and he considered descending his floating staircase.

He didn't. At least, not for a while—a short nap. The natural light crept up the stairs and into the hall but could not reach the depths of his lair. He had a concise dream that he contacted the owl-masked DJ and commissioned a work. Then he got up at last.

He wandered down the stairs, fondling himself to feel something, something he hadn't felt in some time and could certainly use now. He pulled it out, but it also just sort of fell out. He made it to the base of the steps with his dick out, wishful-thinking that one of the girls had passed out of exhaustion or mutual benefit on her way out. You never could know these days.

However, there were no prostitutes on his theater-style couches, but there was a small leather wallet with a bag of cocaine in it, or at least wishful-thinking there was.

There was cocaine in the wallet, and there was a small metal spoon in the wallet, and he did some cocaine. It was strange how he grew to miss the rather unpleasant physical sensation of doing excellent blow. It was batch by batch. The fourth line of the bag tasted better than the second, but the first of the next, even on the same night, was rough.

This line brought him to an equilibrium. Where he had been far off the ledge on both sides, he now balanced on the edge and felt the rush of adrenaline from the challenge. In this sense, he had been elevated in several ways. The complexity of the approach of the drug on your perception is doubled by its fade. Where he had been tumbling before, baseless, he was free-falling now, a new base of operations, and then he did some more cocaine.

It was almost time to go drink on the beach, but he could again hardly be bothered. He knew what would happen out there; the nearby pros would seduce him again, they would do cocaine all throughout the evening and perform imaginative sex acts with some amount of social engineering involved, then the night would come and a malice would fills their loins, and they would fuck like animals until the night began to soften again.

Then he would be right back where he was, which, admittedly, was where he wanted to be, but it seemed strange to him that he should have to go out and engage with all that again just to end up right back where he started. Did he have anything new to do? *Oh, that's right, the reason he came back here.*

He texted Mendez.

...

The principle problem with the night was the harassment he got from journalists the next day, asking him about 'clubbing culture' and its dangers, and how he felt as a part of a tumor on the younger generations that manifested in a young university student being put into a coma and a touching interview with his watery-eyed girlfriend.

He began to write a short manifesto that he would never send off.

"This shallow conservatism has no place in my generation, we who call forth the very gods of the human spirit in rejoice, and those of us who might be more apt to receive this spark of divinity should be allowed and encouraged to do so. I'm certain a set of royal ears famously complained about the volume of notes in a certain arrangement of sounds that would later be celebrated as the voice of the Catholic God, and here I sit, molly-hungover on a couch in a hotel in the city of God, and am chastised by some base organisms who thought these questions might legitimate their existences.

I tell you, I was celebrating life like you cynics never knew how, and I know this because I too was one of you until it the fire touched me, until I saw the very essence of humanity being celebrated and I was its shaman. I directed holy eyes. They saw all of us, and I'm certain poor Heiko was having the very deepest moments of his life leading up to and possibly causing the accident.

You just don't get the experience until you're in too deep, and only once you've drowned can you appreciate the air again.

You all might soon or already have made the connection that I was the unknowing subject of a viral video when I was a younger child. I lived without oxygen for thirteen years as a result, and only through this divine intervention have I again learned to breathe. I was baptized in the water of molly, prayed for the drop of the bass, and devoted myself to the show of lights and sound, and I will continue to perform these sacraments on pilgrimages across the world, spreading love and joy."

He did, however, write and send an email to his cardiologist, explaining delicately that his services would not be further needed.

"Just keep swimming.

The mixtape begins with a short sample from an animated film on the theme of swimming, an introductory play on the contents of the rest of our favorite vessel's latest release. After the sample, Darnell introduces himself, apparently in some sort of investigation involving his two nephews. The first verse is in the style of Boat, a rugged banger with a wad in his pocket and humble beginnings behind him. Now he flaunts his wealth and people raise their hands when they see him. The verse ends with that familiar aphorism in his circle of cultural icons, "Fuck 12."

The next break goes back to Uncle Darnell as he's about to call his second nephew, Yacht, who is notably a cheerier figure full of charitable spirits. Yacht, however, has some asocial characteristics that seem to hinder him. Namely, his introductions are strange: atonal, arrhythmic, and long. After a long greeting, he introduces himself and immediately propositions any women that can hear him to give fellatio to his friends. He follows this with another set of atonal, arrhythmic, and long greetings, concluded with a close variation of his first greeting and finally a return to it.

A quick transition, the next song features another artist, Jerry Seinfeld, formerly known as Blueberry, another artist out of Atlanta, and is a sort of promenade of the sheer power and fame of the duo. The hook enforces that everyone knows them, that everyone wants to be them, and that they have a very distinct look. All in all, the intro lays great foundation for the rest of the mixtape: the two faces of the red generation.

The first verse opens up with the duality of Boat, that he's loyal to his friends in beginning his verse with a shout out, but also that he wears bright jewelry like a crown in a fierce act of individualism. He then goes on to describe how women look (frisky) when they see him and his friend Jerry Seinfeld, especially when they are counting their money. Lucky for his lady friends, however, in a stark contrast with the normal rugged nature of Boat, he does practice safe sex, keeping contraceptives in his socks just in case a women falls onto his erect penis.

The hook reiterates the dominant theme and then Jerry Seinfeld offers his own input, opening with a further confirmation that everyone knows them. The artist then opens up a clever metaphor for how easily he has carnal relations with women, that most women become aroused (*like the* Ganges – the imagery is a bit disgusting, admittedly) and he can maneuver around them just like Jesus could have walked across the river. Jerry then pitches his music production service, quoting a basic package for $500 and pointing out that the jewelry he wears is an adequate reference of his abilities. He works efficiently, and, because of that, he and Boat are way up. After a couplet about his dominant sexual performance, he closes with a segue into the hook, that he and Boat are very popular on tour, a line that bigDawg9012 adequately annotated with the following comment on RapIngenue.com: "yacht a good rapper not a dead ass."

The song closes with the hook, and then the fire alarm goes off; the next song's come in hot, the littest of the entire work, featuring Lil Tec 9 Murder SMG Killer and Young Jeff, one of *Simple* magazine's *275 Closet Autotuners* [#ClosetTuners] *To Watch Out For*, though the hashtag campaign didn't find as much success as was projected. Furthermore, the campaign backfired a bit among the more political followers of the scene who caught onto the fact that one audio engineer, a Turkish-Armenian out of Canada, did work for 274 of them.

Peter was continuing his tour against the direct advice of his doctor, and he was enjoying his concerts in a way that he hadn't in a long time. He found moments of lucidity as he broke down his body with biweekly shows stimulating him far past his limits, a cyberpunk meditation, and he was the voice of something higher, the masses waiting to delight in him, lit up with a multicolored flashing owl mask and, most importantly, mirrors for eyes, a recent addition he had made to reflect his developing belief system. The glasses flashed unpredictably the tens of thousands of lights they would see in a day, dependent on his errant motions and the preprogrammed light show and the glowsticks and backlights of the crowds.

...

"*El Naranjo*, how have you been?"

"*So lala*, hombre."

"My friend, I saw what they said happened, but you must remember where you are now," and Bahman opened his eyes to the hundreds of beautiful people surrounding a massive free form deep blue with smiles, drinks, and assets.

The volume of cheeks alone stunned him, and he was some veteran of this kind of scene: the sun-touched skin smooth and softer in perpetual motion, giggles, bouts of flirting horseplay, or simply a consistent stride along the sides of the pool, the semi-crescents of the outlines of every teal, salmon, and white bikini there, leading past the flat stomach until it met the succulent, the complementary or matching top piece. Magnificence, the embodiment of the spirit as it applies to the appearance of health. The image could be summed up in a single word: ripe.

The music was Mexican light house, a nice electronic melody, cheery, with highlights of vihuela reinforced by the drum and bass, a Mexican Ragga Bossa Nova, and it all seemed like a music video (and it might have been). Regardless, the palace of pleasure is no match for the early afternoon craving for cocaine, so Bahman followed Mendez through the crowds, into a postmodern building with mostly glass walls. They went up the glass stairs and did blow on a glass table, looking down through the table and the glass floor below to see several pairs of breasts preparing tequila shots. Mendez yelled down, they came up, and the meeting continued, though they couldn't see through their new table.

The women were bouncy, giggly, and all sorts of fun, but it wasn't yet the time to get distracted. There's a delicate, unspoken balance to blowing your load. Ideally, you keep loading up on blow which somehow prevents the early load-blowing, and you maintain from there for as long as you can. When and only when the world is dying, as the remaining survivors fall, do you give in for the first fuck of the day.

This happened around five, Bahman with two girls, bouncy girls, fantasy manifest, as was normal for him, eagerly awaiting his cock, which slouched to attention under the blood pressure of the cocaine. Still, the girls weren't in it for the physical act as much as the spirit of it, and all parties had fun. Bahman emerged, sweating, from the glass building again, the fourth time he had left the building in the four hours he had been there, and sat by the pool, where he looked around and listened to the music, now some dancehall techstep, something harder for the hardened that remained, and he again enjoyed bouncy women dancing almost naked, bouncing booty for pictures and smiling and laughing white teeth clashing tanned skin, and for a moment he forgot the trail that he had left to get here.

Mendez popped down on the seat next to him abruptly and checked in on the movie star.

"No complaints, hombre, un chorro de chiches," Bahman gestured a panorama and the both of them again lost themselves in the orgy around them, still an uncountable mass of fleshes.

"Now you understand."

"I could live like this."

"Ah, but you must work, hombre—" Mendez sat up and turned to Bahman, "when will you be back over there?"

"Luego."

"*Luego*? Or *luego luego*?"

"In a few weeks."

At this, Mendez sat fully upright, "Tell me when."

...

The social contract weighed heavy on her shoulders, which wasn't where it started. The fervor for the Queen had turned into a bizarre wasteland of paranoia, betrayal, obsession, and threat. It had happened quickly. The original images she had posted had run through the process of the meme. Anytime they were referenced or posted, the threads deteriorated into Pepe drowning in his own come with a grin on his face, which would in turn be replied to with cynical personal attacks and deconstruction of her possible motives. Worst of all—she was mute in all of it. Her presence had been flooded by impostors, and the only way that she could enforce her will was to post more original content, something she had done only once since her original usurpation.

She missed Señor's lecture, titled *Interspecies Polyandry in Schneewittchen: Marxism in a False History*, which was, as he had warned the previous week, rather theoretical. She imagined him jumping around passionately as he referenced his favorite academic, a name she would surely never forget, for less than five students, at least four of which on something behavior-altering. In a strange way, she felt warm thinking about his desperation without her there; he really never called on a single other person, and he openly ranted in class about how much better she was than the other students. This came across, unfortunately, in her shallowest and most dominant sense, as pathetic, and she wasn't in a place to subject herself to pathetic display.

She was scanning the Board, but not the literature section. She hadn't been to the literature section for a few days, instead spending her time on the random board. It was six fifteen in the morning, and she had to get to work in forty-five minutes. She had set an alarm but disabled it after waking up curious about the state of affairs around four am. It was pervasive, this relationship she had. She had literally opened herself up to countless faceless people, and a cult had developed. As is the process of any cult, the late stages tended to favor blood orgy, and time moved quickly on the internet.

The state of affairs was as follows:

-five dedicated porn threads: midget, futanari, disturbing, originating in 'foreign' films, and gifs from a Super Mario flash porn game

-one thread on the deconstruction of women which inevitably saw a few references to Her Majesty

-three threads that could all be TL;DR'd as '>nigger thread'

-a roulette thread where your post number assigns you how often you can shower

-two feminist bashing threads; notably, one had turned into a light cuckold porn thread

-a thread about the Antagonizing Orange which inevitably led to posts and pictures comparing the King and Queen of the Board

-a thread dedicated to controversial frames from the portrayal of Sand Man in a Chinese blockbuster

-a thread dedicated to the Queen. It had just hit its bump limit, so it was about to die and be reborn after a full 278 replies. This thread was the most chaotic of the front page, ironically with more disturbing porn than the disturbing porn thread on top of many variants of the original two pictures she posted, the latter of which taken from the forced perspective of her sitting on your face, which, essentially, was a close-up of her asshole. The original post, as normal, claimed to be the Queen herself with some clever trick up her sleeve, a reason for her visit, seeking only to degrade Her followers. The third reply was a Pepe, and that was the end of it all. The thread went down a malicious path. It was a sexual revolution of sorts, that many of her followers now spoke of her as a 'race-cucking niggress.'

She had to stop and get ready to serve salty grease.

...

Smoke House, not a grill but a bar, not a house but a hole in the wall in an alley. Cool purple, wooden bass guitars, the juicy sax, tall, dark, and good with those hands, deceptively nimble with their size, precise and fast, slapping strings sensually. Smoke House was his home base, the laboratory for his musical experiments where ratty people gathered, where the cats chattered, and where the rhythm pitter-pattered. He was safe here, deep in the Wedding district, surrounded by ethnic non-Germans or the iconic ironic Germans, delicious foods at better prices, artsy but uneducated, edged.

He was delving further into folk-jazz, past lawn ornaments, and into something far more German with a new sound he had labeled *Der Schimmel Writer*, a saga about a German songwriter who ultimately brought about the beginning and end of cozy music venues like Smoke House. The first song, a long, slow progression, minimalist with accents of accordion played by a friend of his filling the small room past its capacity, was about the humble beginnings of the writer, Heiko, a student of language and music whose father was a German folk musician, fending off the death of German traditions after the *Loslers* took it all too far.

The album went on to tell the story of the boy's life, how he became the assistant of a local Streichgraf after impressing the entire string section with his technical knowledge of the instruments despite never having played any of them, and how Heiko slowly finagled his way into being the next Streichgraf through the marriage of the daughter of the previous Streichgraf, which appeased those patrimonialists who wondered about the future of the craft. It was around this time that a black man appeared in the story in the island of West Berlin and jarred everyone with his new music, and then Heiko played the black musician to his advantage, harnessed the progressive music and manufactured it into his own albums, reacting to the new waves of sound entering the young city-state.

However, the new wave that the black musician had been a member of broke free, and Heiko couldn't monopolize all of it, and soon it was revealed that he had been a bit heavy-handed in his dealings with musicians, and the revelations turned public opinion of him until his own family abandoned him. The New Wave claimed his daughter, who basically excommunicated him, and his wife fell ill under all the social pressures. As all was crashing down on him, Heiko embraced the new music by investing heavily in commercial venues that still stood to his day and became a ghost in the industry. Some say they still see him wandering around clubs, keeping watch over his properties, or so the song went.

Most of this was just background to the jazz-folk sound, however, and couldn't have been extrapolated by the seventy-two words in the entire work.

After the second hour of consecutive and concurrent accordion, slap bass, keys, and drums, Dougie was tuckered out, and he sought the comforts of a prostitute to ease him into sleep. He called his daily driver up and walked next door to a quieter bar that would play the audio from television news without any visible screens.

It was there that he heard a voice that he didn't want to see.

...

"Heiko did seem like a sweet boy, but I still think he partied too much."

"That's not what some of his other friends have said."

"Of course, but they also like to go out."

"When you say *go out*, you mean going to clubs—partying?"

"...I think the whole thing is rotten, if we're being honest."

"What do you mean, *the whole thing*?"

"The lights, the sounds, the drugs, it's all too much."

This is where the latest soundbite of the interview cut off, and where Dougie stopped listening.

"Do you think the drugs are the cause of the problem?"

"I think drugs are a symptom of the problem."

"Do you think the problem is especially big here?"

"Ha! What do you want me to say to that?"

"Well, this city is known for it's clubbing scene."

"And this is the first incident of its relative infamy, is it not?"

"So you're saying it's better here than other places?"

"You want me to either betray my city or put myself in extreme denial."

"Well it's not *that* black and white."

"But you want it to be so that it can be a headline."

"Are you offended by my questions?"

"I just think you came in here with a goal and it has nothing to do with my story, or the story of the things that happened—"

"Now that's not—"

"—and that's why you didn't use almost any of Effy's story, because she wouldn't and couldn't budge from her perspective when you tried to push—"

"—we used a lot of—"

"—you tried to push either your boss's—"

"Alright, now—"

"—or your own *viral* interpretation of the world on her, the poor girl."

A pause. "Okay, I—"

"Fuck you." When she said this, cold, her eyes were on fire, and the reporter cowered into her notebook with nothing to write and scribbled feverishly even though the interview was being recorded; maybe she forgot in this powerful moment, maybe her journalistic instincts had been undermined and uprooted, and all she was left with was her own void of person broadcasted for anyone who would watch this part of the interview that would be cut. A long silence followed, which Lena broke. "Do you want to hear about me?"

The reporter, surprised, said "sure."

"I think this entire image is manufactured. I think the problem and the cause are the same fucking thing, and it's this image we drill into people, this deformity we produce en masse, this *thing* that we put into ourselves and feed it until it spreads and infects every fucking thing in us."

Notably, the interview was in English, and Lena spoke very fluently, owing to her father being American-born-and-raised.

The reporter seemed to be recovering from sobs, but these thoughts brought her back into personhood. "That's—that's not bad."

"No, it IS bad—" the reporter tried to interrupt to say that's not what she meant, and Lena was going to oblige, but the reporter withheld and Lena continued, somewhat sympathetic but still strong, "it's actually the worst thing in the entire world, and there's your headline," she smiled, and she smiled, their smiles met.

"Lena, who *are* you?"

"I don't want to say, otherwise that'll be in the headlines instead of what I just said."

"I understand," said no reporter ever.

"Who are *you*?"

"Well, I told you, my name is Meriam," at this point, the cameras cut off, the crew grumbled, maybe even a gurgle was released with the indigestion, frustrated by what they saw as a good lead turned into dogshit, "I've been a reporter for six years, three of which I specialized in social media and viral stories."

"What have you learned from the whole thing?"

Meriam looked for words, "maybe that it's all bad."

...

He had had to abandon the XXXL armchair and trade it in for IVs and a XXXXL sanitary green hospital bed. "CAN I GET THOMETHING THALTY?"

What had started innocently as a splintered numb-and-spicy potato chip had turned into a nasty infection in the roof of his mouth, but that was hardly the cause for his current tenure in the hospital. The real problem was the glob of cheese in his artery.

He was beginning to write the next post for his newest campaign, THALT, THose Arteries Look Terrific, a subdivision of the now-wandering intentions of SALT, an umbrella movement which had developed into several different sects, noteworthy of which was a post-new wave feminist group that praised phallic monuments. THALT was admittedly not as popular as its rival mother. The guiltier or more empowered of the followers might have been thrown by the tubes in his nose and the general mint environment, and he was also not wearing a FattyRants shirt for the first time in several years. Instead, it was a harsh color combination of the normal sweat stain green and cotton candy blue text t-shirts that he sold enough of to suspend his existence.

The tests were a disorienting process that Jacob had gone into with some skepticism. Lots of needles, as it always was, and things plugged into him. There were bluemen all around him, nameless sometimes or with a nametag but without a face, rooms with closed doors and the sanitary air. The whole experience had done a number on his psyche.

This afternoon, the stress left him in no mood for soft lines. The nurse had been ignoring his buzzing all day, at least seven calls without a single serving of snack peanuts. Where had he gone wrong? What had brought him to this point? How could he have put himself out of reach of the changing world of fast food at such a revolutionary moment?

The Chocoritodilla was debuting this very Friday, and it would be somewhere between professional and personal suicide to miss out on this opportunity, and suicide was not the answer at this moment. Fatty had been feeling fear for the first time in his life, and it had him burning hot. At this rate, you might have been able to see his cheekbones in less than half a year.

His cardiologist was out of state for the weekend, somewhere far east for some new age medicine, not too far out of line for the cat blood expert. The waiting room was full of weekend-wounded has-beens, slowly growing impatient. Whatever Pincock was doing, it better have been important.

...

The routine fifteen-mile detours he took to work had put him in a perpetual state of chronostress, avoiding the same restaurants, which was a shame this morning because he really could have gone for the new Breakfast Tacoritodillo again this morning. Today's route on the clockwise-rotating azimuth of approach was the first of many trips where two points on his journey would be eclipsed by a bit of his destination. He reasoned to himself that he liked to see new places (he didn't) and that he preferred to not eat at the same restaurant for reasons of agency (he did).

Today, he coordinated his car with his dining app and his GPS to find the suitable destinations for breakfast on his way to work. At the most convenient exit, there were several good choices: the chicken-and-biscuits joint, Uncle Charlie's, known for its steep flavor-to-sanitary-standards ratio; and Uncle Jeff's, which was a biscuits-and-chicken place known for its reactionary approach to the changing times of the early internet age, its lemonade, and its owner, who was fabled as a stern, conservative, completely-absent father to our own beloved Young Jeff; and the normal SubStandard, a sandwich shop with a consistent standard across all franchise locations worldwide. His choice for today and tomorrow was Uncle Jeff's after a routinely-disappointing series of sandwiches from SubStandard.

Uncle Jeff's was fairly clean, especially compared with his shoddy brother-company across the street, Uncle Charlie's. The biscuits-and-chicken company had a consummate scheme of colors, a brilliant red and a clean white, a theme reminding you of your grandfather's favorite slice of an extinct America, a paradise where you could sip a milkshake while smoking a cigarette in the middle of a high-school day in a keen diner down the street. The food was good, and, more importantly, he had never been to this location. As he was pulling in, however, he noticed a certain "Linole-Yum!" restaurant that shared the same parking lot, and he deemed it to be a safer location due to the fact that even he hadn't heard of it.

Rash parked his car after a seven-point turn that ended four inches from where it began, turned the engine off, and noticed someone eyeing him from the driver seat of a car parked across the lot, a suspect man with darkness under his eyes and a bandage on his nose, but to acknowledge this acknowledgment would undermine the entire facade. He must remain naive. He exited his car and entered the restaurant.

There was a nondescript hostess, and Rash didn't meet her eyes. "Two, actually, I'm going to meet someone here, but I'll go ahead and put in an order—"

"—sir if you could give me just a—"

"A blueberry waffle with two eggs, sunny-side-up, hash browns and a coffee, would you recommend black or with cream?"

"Your server will be with you in just a moment. Her name's Cierra and she'll be happy to take your order."

"Thank you, my name's Sam Booth."

He scooted into the booth, checked the grip of his boot against the linoleum by pressing his heel into the floor, and opened the second menu across the table and upside-down from him as if his friend was in the restroom. In the booth in front of him he saw the shape of a large man in a sweat-stained short-sleeved collared shirt, a real man's man, no doubt, sitting across from a similar body, their guts pinching the table and probably providing it with the structural integrity it needed to hold the behemoth sandwiches on their plates.

He looked up reviews for this quaint place while he waited and was impressed by a good score and something in a review about cheese. He was interrupted by a beautiful black server skeptically looking at him.

"Welcome to Linole-Yum!, my name's Cierra, what will you have to drink?"

"—my name's Sam!" he burst.

"Hello, Sam, can I get you something to drink?"

"I'm ready to order, Cierra."

"What would you like?"

"Would you recommend black coffee or with cream?"

"I'll bring out some pack of creamer and you can try it out yourself."

"But what would you recommend?"

"I don't drink coffee."

"But if you did—?"

"I think I would take it black if I did."

A raucous bout of laughter arose from the booth in front of Simon, "I bet you would, sheeit."

Neither Simon or Cierra were the least bit distracted by this comment. "I would like one of those sandwiches that they have, hashbrowns, and a coffee, black, and a coffee with cream and sugar for my friend here."

"Okay, I'll have that out for y'all in no time."

The boiled peanut gallery with the sweaty bellies again chimed in, "but when are you going to have *that* out for me, honey?"

This one caught the server's ear, "Teddy, if you don't shut the fuck up, I swear I'm going to shove that straw in your dick and give you a new infection to talk about."

"Jesus Christ, do you talk to your other customers like this?"

"None of my other customers brag about their Mongolian STDs."

"The hell you just say? I want to talk to your manager."

"Yeah, go ahead, I fucking dare you, we'll check the tapes for all the harassment y'all throw at me, you pervert lard-o's."

Simon, seeing this as some elaborate performance, too specific and personal for a normal interaction with the world-at-large, chimed in, "Hey, hate to interrupt, could I get two waters too?"

"Well, Bill, I guess we'll be taking our business some place else tomorrow morning along with our tips."

"Oh, I'll miss your tips? I couldn't even feel them anyways." The server seemed to be getting aroused, Simon thought, possibly a break from character, while the men seemed to have already entered the post-coital shame, a reflection of the state of things, that they had been born and bred only to be cast by a corporate-intelligence construct as greasy idiot extras in an effort to normalize an otherwise surreal hole in the wall. He thought it strange that his company placed these ridiculous figures before him in one of their own establishments known for a world-class ham-and-cheese sandwich. It was quite circular, a cat chasing its own tail, as his life often was.

The server had returned to the kitchen and reemerged with a steaming plate of coronary problems, placing it abruptly before the scientist and offering somewhat of a sneer, "r'yago."

Simon expertly cut her off, mid-*yago*, "could I get a carry-out box? My friend is having a family emergency," he gestured outside to the strange man in the car that he had noticed earlier, a bold gamble. In his mind the greatest likelihood was that there were two agencies' operatives present, and him linking their gazes together may cause hell back in their respective HQ's; alternatively, if the server and the observer were in bed together, he was alerting them to his own awareness. He was, in a way, done hiding, and this morning's addy withdrawal had really put him in a weird place.

The waitress, visibly stunned after noticing the man outside, now starting his car, ran for the front door, yelling at him. "DAVEYOUFUCKINGDICKHEAD GETTHEFUCKOUTOFHERE I'MCALLINGTHEPOLICE YOUFUCKINGSICKPEDORACISTFUCK," the greaseballs turning, laughing, and applauding, the beaten man's car peeling off, and the server collapsing in the parking lot, crying, and Simon getting up and walking to the server's station to grab a box for himself. Despite his fatalism-in-assocation, he was quite ready to leave this place.

As he was moving farm-to-table to box, he heard the vulgarer of the two comment in awe, "that Dave's really got his own thing going."

Simon walked out the front of the restaurant, handed the sobbing waitress a ten dollar bill and said, "sorry about Dave, he's really got his own thing going. Keep the change—Sam's treat," though the bill would've amounted to $12.94. In his own way, Simon was an elite member of his own agency, far hidden from the visible actors of the world. He got in his car, started her up, and left for the back corner of the parking lot, where he ate his sandwich in solitude.

When he got to the office, he noticed that the receptionist was finally back, but the pictures of her and her family had been taken down. She was, all in all, just another pawn of the greater machinations in the world, another crying spy-waitress for a board of rich white men, and Simon took pity on her with what he thought was a warm glance that made her pretend to check her phone immediately. "Is Kat good today," he asked, pretending to not know her name.

She took it as a STEM-ish way of asking if everything was ready for the simulation. "Yes, everything is ready."

He took her strange and distant response to be a bad sign, so he went ahead and decided to dose the patient with the uppers instead of the downers, just another instance of his ability to act as an unpredictable saboteur.

...

Mein Vater, mein Vater, jetzt faßt er mich an!

By an honest mistake or a precise maneuver of anticipation, Simon Rash administered the first and only positive session of modern therapy. It probably would have been inconsequential to any of the subjects other than Das Wunderkind, as he was beginning to be known to himself as, but, as it was, the brain-dead Kraut was a cat-characterizer and the calico kitty calls to each cortex differently. The addy was stimulating nightmarish storms at first. The picture projected inside his head was a kitten meowing, showing its little fangs and scrunching its little face at a red ball on a string, but the picture projected inside his brain was quite sinister.

The kitten chased the red ball that was bouncing in suspension, dangled above his little soft self, and it bounced delicately against his little soft head and images of a rock splitting Carl's head wide as the sky filled the subject whose heart was now pounding to the arrhythmic blend of music his damaged auditory channels would channel to him, some sort of fatalism-in-sound, something like this coming right out of Carl's exposed gushy brain:

"IT COULD GET: some wind for the sailboat, the railroad for these workers.

It's always around me: all this noise.

Er reitet so spät durch Nacht und Wind: der Vater mit seinem Kind.

Ich habe auf der Welt: du.

I should have: stayed on the farm and listened to my old man."

Carl, the model for cognitive, sensory, and affective domains in learning, seemed to have become a pure outlet of cultural data, red red red flowing out of him like the lifeblood of Heiko's brother that he might have sought revenge on the poor cat for stealing his fishy fishy and Heiko couldn't give him sock cake anymore because the cat's head was split open and rot ach rot alles ist rot and Mutti fattened the boy up until he couldn't stand on his own and now he can't stand on his own:

"What could it be?

Why are we running around?

Mein Sohn, was birgst du so bang dein Gesicht?

Bist du alles, was ich will?

Did I sign up with you?"

Effy, the broken hymen appearing in the head of the cat, the questions of his and hers and what for a future they might have in common and what in common they might have for a future. The drying blood crusted years ago with something lodging itself right between them like recognitions resulting from questions posed:

"All these are the days my friends!

Let it happen!

Vater, der Erlkönig!

Du!

Goodbye yellow brick road!"

And recognitions realizing that results are far more complicated than previously planned, the need for molly bright lights or the desires thereof and eating Turkish food everyday in Berlin from the streets through the big doors to the safety of watching people playing video games in a Jargonsprache he had only mastered through his diligent consumption:

"1, 2, 3, 4, 1, 2, 3, 4, 5, 6,

Try to get through it, try to bounce to it,

Sei ruhig, bleib ruhig, mein Kind,

Bist du, bist du, bist du,

Oh, I've finally decided,"

Had he been quiet all his life? Had he been bled like a split-head cat, like Carl the master of musical nonsense? Had he ever been heard, or was everyone hearing and nodding and never comprehending? He sounded normal, had heard various recordings of himself, a normal pace and the words seemed like they were where they should have been, but there was some void of semantic purpose:

"Two lovers sat on a park bench with their bodies touching each other, holding hands in the moonlight; there was a silence between them; so profound was their love for each other; they needed no words to express it;

I will not vanish; you will not scare me; I might as well do it; I'm not that stupid;

Ich liebe dich; mich reizt deine schöne Gestalt; bist du nicht willig, so brauch ich Gewalt;

Du, du allein kannst mich versteh'n; du, du darfst nie mehr von mir geh'n;

You can't plant me in your penthouse; I'm going back to my plough;"

If he was so, if he was bleeding and aphasic and flowing fluent, then so it was and so it would be, Heiko, the ultimate victim refusing to feel a victim in all this, silence silent like not saying no but not saying yes like a boy in a big world, fattened up by Mutti and thrown to the dogs but maybe some sock cakes would settle him down, maybe bomb's down on catwalk and flashing apps now, go! go! go! was all he needed out of this great big world and without Effy he would still be Heiko just like without her father she was without her father, maybe her being the most of victims, stuck in the realms of rote rote rote not even seeing the rot rot rot only repeat repeat repeat and maybe that's why people understood her is because she could read read read but never could she ever in her little life write write write:

"And so they sat in silence on a park bench with their bodies touching, holding hands in the moonlight. Finally, she spoke, "do you love me, John?" she asked. "You know I love you, darling," he replied, "I love you more than tongue can tell; you are the light of my life: my sun, moon, and stars. You are my everything. Without you, I have no reason for being!

Take the next ticket to take the next train; why would I do it? Maybe I was ready all along.

Dem Vater grausets, er reitet geschwind, er hält in Armen das ächzende Kind, erreich den Hof mit Mühe und Not; in seinen Armen das Kind war tot.

Du.

Maybe you'll get a replacement; there's plenty like me to be found: mongrels who ain't got a penny, sniffing for tidbits like you on the ground."

Silence. A kitten batted at a dangling red ball on the screen.

What even the coolest of cats fail to realize in this dark age of neon light is that it's all illusory, Heiko might have thought to himself had he not eluded himself on one brightly-colored night. He might have realized that the superimposed stimuli of the post-cyberpunk-as-aesthetic age may even be dangerous, a brand of fatalism-in-light-emitting-diodes. What he would have realized if he ever spent a second in Chengdu, outside of his bubble of streaming video games in English, a foreign-not-foreign language, is that there are greater strokes of humanity in a single city street or village road than all of the vastness of the internet put together, that no amount of markers in anuses or collages of baby pictures that ultimately form portraits of Adolf Hitler could ever be a sum to compare with the fruit vendor smoking cow-dung cigarettes until enough Mandarins are sold to pay for the street-barbecue intestines at the local street-intestine vendor (smoking cow-dung cigarettes and saving up for a batch of hot-potty intestines in the air-conditioned restaurant). But he never went to China, so he never experienced the spices of life outside of the Turkish street food he had every day on his way home. His affinity for a proper digestif didn't extend to the culturally-enriching flavor of baijiu, the rural warmth of plums snaking their way down your system and revitalizing the numbed peppercorn receptors in and around the very intestines he would have eaten earlier, the porky-poopy taste not completely removed. God and Chairman Mao bless, and the collages of Adolf Hitler might even be appreciated on these streets. If only these bridges could have been gapped long before this incident, but now Heiko was in a comatose state with an IV pumping drugs in his system to condition him to react to virtual stimuli, and some might even say that it was the worst possibility realized, a sort of Glassian listening-to-music-in-headphones-on-public-transportation-and-watching-the-world-pass-by manifest. These were the days but not for Heiko. The crucial link that was exactly that: a link without a link; another member of the anonymous; an asocial social being, a routine creature in a rotten rut. What does Heiko think about in his more conscious moments given that he had spent collective years of his life imposing himself on an oblivion? What is the moment of lucidity? It is the mastication and spitting of these very years. To spit his life is to deny his oblivion, that he doesn't need a digestif (and so was maybe not even missing out on baijiu) because he hadn't yet consumed. He had tasted every combination he fancied and rejected it, forming, in his own way, a collage of flavors that ultimately left him craving a cigarette and some intestines, with the exception of possibly the most popcorn entertainment that he would ever admit to, an oxymoron to compare with his greatness. 'Flashing upper' and it could be very fresh and clean, which is not to say that the Genghis Khan of Gonorrhea wasn't involved but also not that he was, for Heiko may not have known at the time, but Teddy was more involved than he could ever imagine. There was no easy way for him to reason it out given the drug cocktail he had been given. What could be said for certain was that no one else had felt these things in this order and intensity.

Of the things he had certainly never learned was an elephant in his cranium dwarfed by a mouse that the cat was chasing. Unfortunately, he was always given sock-cake and never took it. Your average sock-cake-eater falls into one of the two sock-cake-eater categories: those eaters that like the sock and those eaters that like the cake. Like in many aspects of his life, Heiko existed in a theoretically-impossible superposition outside of his own dichotomy. The cake was sweet but would be covered in lint and cat fur if it was without a sock to protect it from the pocket it was carried in. The sock performed its function diligently (other than the hole in the big-toe), but a sock with no cake was a dull image that didn't reference any wispy sweet memories in his mind, oh sweet sweet mist of morning touching on the lake and the smell of catfish and sweet bread. Fish and bread: another distinction that failed to distinguish him—he could have been a baker, but, more importantly, he could get the railroad for these workers. The smell of fish to him was fresh and clean, though he had once heard that the city folk thought it to be rather rude, that smell of home; some distance for him from them and them from him was their lack of faith in the home, for he always believed in the home unlike that little bitch Effy with her rich daddy and his music and band of musicians and all the cool concerts she was afforded and abused with copious amounts of and now she's where she is. Where is she? These are the days. She was out on the town, her. Her and her changing band of musicians exposing her to new and exciting and him being home watching video games but home for her when she needed home which was more often than she wanted to admit. He thought he might have picked up the hobby out of practicality, the more socky of his characteristics, that he might spend a lot of time sort of waiting around in the earlier and middle hours of the night on texts of passive-aggressive aggression on his warmth, that she wanted to like the smell of catfish but she only liked the cake and that the holes in his socks were an absolute embarrassment to everything she stood for, that she had thick thick wool socks that seemed like they were made out of the cat fur in his pockets to him, that she was so warm in the winter but so cold in the summer, that she knew everyone but no one knew her except for him and he only knew her and she didn't know him as well as the social media hashtag campaigns and 'flashing upper!' and old-internet culture, a boy genius mocked by his father, das Wunderkind und der Erlvater, new-internet culture, basement nihilism anonymously and the skepticism of gender. What of a life, and these are the days, my friends, and these are the days. Be quick, else you'll miss the sweet clouds of morning time and the voice that added the myth and mist to the mystique so sweet cream as if to fatten the vapor into bubbly bits of heaven or melt-in-your-mouth sock-cake. What those city kids didn't realize was that the baker had nothing on the mother, the fisher on the brother, the bullet on the rock to the head. Blood clogs the pipes of the city, so we drain the blood accordingly, reactionarily revolutionarily . Society was the schedule of blood-letting. Molly was like a burst of blood, a rebirth of nerve for a moment and then lost gone gone. Movies were like a dream of blood, a pleasant out-of-body experience to remind you what it felt like. Money was like an IV of someone else's blood, something didn't belong but it still felt alright. Cats knew blood, or did they? Was that really Brock that he had seen then and there? What had happened to him? Was Brock the city incarnate? Would he bleed if a rock were to beat him on the head? What if a sock were to treat him to some bread? The streets are dry of blood. Different days he lived in.

It was that very first swig of baijiu, this new feeling in and around him, the kindest of awakenings to all. There was some derivative of a kitten on the screen, some sort of furry creature with cartoonish eyes and perky little ears. It couldn't have been Satan, though, or a demon or hell-spawn. This, no, this was too unassuming, assumption being the most base characteristic of a proper and upright no-good evil-doer, the prescription of description, some sort of political spectrum with red people on one end and people on the other. Effy with a red streak. Mother with a red outburst. Cat with red spilling out of his hell-spawn head. Blood-letting. Dies Irae. Bloodthirsty demigods were we, choosing who and who not like we should have any say in the matter, life being a race of knife carving in order to stab your competitors in time and at some point our thumbs flipped around and we got a better grip and the grip led to the ship, the ship being a device of effect, something to reach further than arms allow, and what would the ship be without the whip? Whip into chip, naturally, some sort of sociological phenomena that couldn't be studied for hundreds of years. It went from public beatings to anonymous public contributions to a thread about three-dimensional CGI orc skullfucking. It will take hundreds of years to study every moment today. Where it was lost before, it is found in abundance today. The chip to the zip, but is it the same to have chunks of numbers that are decoded to reveal more chunks of numbers? Could it all be zipped up into one big statement: that we were underprepared to carve the knife as sharp as we did? That man in the owl hat wouldn't think so. He seemed to be enjoying himself without being able to see around him. What about the girl? Ethnic-ambiguity-but-some-kind-of-exotic, Lena; was she being fucked by the Turkish-Chinese movie star? Or was he a Turkish-Armenian music producer? What about the frogposter? Was that himself? There's no wrapping one's mind around the fact that the frogposter had a full life behind him and at least a moment's worth of life ahead of him. He was a frogposter and nothing more. Did he choose to be a frogposter or was he infected by others? The frogposter may have been an innocent victim, a bystander who chose the wrong moment of activity and was forever plagued by obscure disease, a sickness crafted specifically to bask in its own smugness.

What about the blurry small-framed figure that trotted about in a white coat sheepishly as this all started? Before the cat and the blood-letting, but after the DJ. Maybe the only thing that could have made someone believe in a god, this little scurrying figure of narrow shoulders pulled up to his ears but moving so swiftly and surely, some sort of eternal light shining on one's eyes, some merciful being in this very ruthless world reforming treacherous terrain to a new liking, the sharpest of knives being used, these sharpening you up for the night ahead, a night that no eternal light would reach. We wish peace for the dead when the living are suffering. Seventy-two virgins are being used right now and tossed a tissue afterwards for consolation. Seventy-two markers in anuses and ten thousand tissues thrown away in a second; the mass production and consumption of depravity. Demand is at a record high and supply has been corporate-sponsored. We have the means because thou art merciful. LCD pixels shine into pupils stimulating penises everywhere, and the shepherd sleeps soundly at night.

"Flashing upper, now, *go!*"

"You fuckin' flashed me."

"Don't worry about it, oh, you're dead."

"You biffed that flash hard."

"Yeah, I mean—"

"Probably going to blame that round on you."

"Nifty should have been pinching from A at window."

"I called that I was late."

"Don't fucking call; be there."

What you don't realize about being there is that it's ones and zeroes. The bottle isn't a gray area nor is the laundry or the shoe. That's what we never learned about in primary school, that the man is ones and zeroes; for if he was anything but he wouldn't be a part of the formula. He is, and by being is he the most elite of being-in-the-world. He is trained and professional in doing what he does, else he wouldn't be able to make do doing what he did: the unseen and unheard of victim of the day: a monkey is handed to you, the foreigner, by a man that lives with a trained monkey, the native, trained to take pictures for cold-hard cash and to recognize when cold-hard is only warm-soft and let go; the monkey moves on quicker than the human for he has less humanity; the little bastard chews on sunflower seeds, and his little feet feel like human hands on your forearm. Look at his little grin. He's so cute in such a grotesque way, and he's reaching in my pocket for the money that he knows allows him more sunflower seeds. You little son of a bitch. And the man that lives behind the monkey, who knows of his cause? He is the baijiu drinker, I tell you now. He is the man who knows the taste of the grain in its rawest form. He goes to sleep in a closet with a monkey every night hoping only that the next night's sleep is supplemented with a dose of grain alcohol that might allow him the forgettance of the very night he wasn't trying to remember: does he love? His tongue tells only the commands of the monkey jumping back on his arm when it is mutually decided that this foreigner will not pay for the picture with the monkey. The monkey is more ones and zeroes than the man behind the monkey, though he was raised to raise a more ruthless version of himself. He was the beaten step-child that becomes the beating step-father. It's monkeys all the way up and all the way down.

The days, my friends, these are the days, that this monkey-closet-sleeper might be more refined that he might be a video editor, overlaying a simply-recorded audio track right over his own offspring and unintentionally ruining a life as such, and, on the other end of the spectrum, an individual ruining himself and others in the form of an owl mask behind the beat; what you see here is the dichotomy of the present era: influencer and influencee at their most clear divide. Here is he, the boy, reflecting on music and visuals he didn't choose, for he is incapable of choosing in these states. Choosy chooser is what most of them are, those consumers, choosing freely like a bunch of choosers. He had no choices early on, and that's why he loved sock-cake like he did. The under-abundance of choice had chose him and he chose to choose it later. In those very recent times of many choices, he chose to watch the unchoosable: voyeurism in the form of entertainment: someone else being entertained.

And the fact that she would spend her time there and devalue her time there as if it was spent at the convenience shop devalues her time to the cents and paprika-flavored crisps, a decided undernourishment when compared with the similarly-priced döner and especially less cultural. And you go through this routine so many times and suddenly you are a tube of what could hardly be qualified 'potato' crisps. It does, however, seem something natural when compared with a childhood spent hoping for the sun, as one often does in these strange days, hoping more than tongue can tell, more than the tele tells, more than the candies dissolve in the vodka; it's colorful but it still bites. And when do you decide to burn your own throat with alcohol? Is that where the problem lies, in the autonomous individual acting of his own accord, independent and without influence—is that asocietal behavior? Is that the basis of all our beloved mental illness diagnoses? That someone might be themselves in a world of being others? So was he trying to force himself, a döner man, acting independent of time-of-day and the appropriated times of eating, on herself, a paprika-flavored diva? And was he so wrong in being optimistic about her or was she so wrong in being a lesser being by his standard? Is this where his conservatism lay—that he wants to surround himself in people like him, opposed to her own standard of self-devaluation-by-proxy? And, more importantly, was that one of her foundational beliefs—fatalism?

Years. Years of his life believing in the improved and improving human. The first-worlder, a fallacy brought to your mouse clicks and history books by West-fetishism, no left-right but instead red people and people, ideologies for microphones and wet dreams for ideologies, which, in defense of the world at large, was his own personal problem as well in more ways than one; however, in assault of the world at large, he wasn't the ideologue behind the cat and the ball of string bouncing around the screen with a soft jazzy sax holding a note for longer than Dougie Wallace could hold his breath.

"Come with us, with me. The sun's almost done and the lights will come alive soon. The show is about to start and you have nothing to lose. The stars will come out for us! The city itself, living, breathing, wants you to join me tonight. What else would you do? Let's lose ourselves with each other. There's nothing for you here on your computer, nothing new to find and certainly no fun. Look, the sun is hiding over there and next time we see him he'll be over here and he'll show us the sweet rainbow tips on the blades of grass. Would you miss that for the world? I don't want to miss that. Don't make me miss that. Come out with me! It'll just be you and me and our lucid dreams. That's what night is for, isn't it? Dream with me. Don't you dream? Not after a long day? What would you dream about if you could? And don't say anything about your foot bread or the smell of fish. I'm going to be nauseous. Well, Heiko, it's now or never, and never's forever. I was doing fine without you anyway."

"Somebody said you bumped your head and bled the floor, jumped into a pit of flames and burned to coal, drowned inside the lake, outside, away you flow, and that means the world to me. My world, my little grown-up Heiko, my world, what happened? I didn't want to lose you and then I did. When you left you pulled my heart right out. I heard you and you heard me but we couldn't listen to each other and you slipped between my fingers like sand, and you were so passionate that you melted into a pile of glass that that brute stepped on and I kept cutting my hands trying to pick you back up, so it might have been a good thing that you left.

How was I to know? You loved the bakery. A lot of kids love the bakery, especially the chubby ones with the rosy cheeks covered in cake crumbs. It was so cute that I would scold you but only enough to make you feel bad, not change your habits. It wasn't responsible but it was aware. I loved hearing you outside the kitchen window, chewing and mouth-slurping in confectiony delight, *kleine Brötchen für kleine Jungen, keine Brötchen für keine Jungen, und aber doch mehr Brötchen für so suße einen Jungen*. What was the worst that could happen?

It was worse than I could have ever imagined. I've never been one to imagine, unlike you, my sweet Bubchen, with your poetic laugh. You were always off in dream, ever since I held you, a warm bundle, in my arms. You used to look into my eyes, and then you took your first steps and you looked into the eyes of flowers, and then you learned to talk, and you spoke into my eyes, and then you learned to read, and you looked into the eyes of others, but by the time you learned to write, something had changed. It wasn't flowers and sock-cake; no, my Bubchen grew out of the fat in his cheeks and bone appeared, and you wouldn't look into my eyes, and you certainly never went back to sneak something from the baker. Stranger yet when you suddenly stopped going with me to buy bread.

Stranger yet when I went into your room while you were in school and glanced at an open notebook on your desk, I never told you, and saw the pictures of cats and the titles of cats and the histories of cats, and once I even turned a few pages until I saw a dying cat with its red red brain falling out of its little dying head. It was closer and closer and closer and then that was the moment. I could never look into your eyes again, and it was then that the idea came up, who even remembers who suggested it? You could move to the big city, the place where your art meets opportunity, and you could set up a life there on your own that I could maybe visit and be impressed by, maybe some sort of distance could give you a new home, maybe you could even make it big! I know you have it in you, and I know that I can't get it out of you.

But the city! There are so many bright lights there! The city lives on! The city grows every day! You should have seen the city thirty years ago, Bubchen, you should have seen it. Half of the city was completely dark and the other half was blind anyway, and both halves didn't amount to a whole. Your father and I went there once on holiday. It was beautiful and big, the blind side was, and the blue soldiers were big and brave. I knew it was all going to get better, and I want you to show me that it did. Soon you will show me. Will you show me?"

...

"Some men just have bad in their hearts."

Guo Yu was taking a selfie to remind his son that he was still training hard. The Air Quality Index was at a relative low of 107 in December in Chengdu. The trio was posed on a track outside of a gym on the eighth floor of a shopping mall, the perfect training ground for the next Chinese Man. The circumstances for the picture had arisen quite innocently: three Chinese (Sichuan) were performing a circuit of strength, strength-speed, speed-strength, speed workouts followed by several consecutive rounds of sparring with each other. As the outside workout was dying, as the jabs to the jaw took hold of the brain, a petite trainer stepped out with a client, an older Chinese woman who had no place in or around a gym; she offered to take a picture for marketing. Guo Yu was more than proud to include his training partners in the picture.

"We learn so that we can be in control. We have seen situations that tell us that it is always better for us to have the power, for we are better at dealing with difficulty than our adversaries. If we did not have this mentality, then we would never grow above our adversaries, and no one would ever make better the situation. The world would change according to the least growing or the evil. It is our duty to take control and administer power to the best of our ability. There are many who would strike to hurt; there are few who would strike to help."

The trio had a four-hour routine three days a week. This was the first day—a fighter's circuit. In two days was a compound exercise that incorporated strength and endurance, and another two or three days after that was a pure strength exercise. The fighter's circuit left spirits high, the endurance circuit, low, the strength circuit, proud.

Unfortunately, as they walked in to the gym to reset their strength-speed cycle, they saw a trainer and a scrawny figure in the only squat rack doing a slight-knee-bending exercise with a few kilograms on either side of the bar. The trainer was staring at his phone and the little Chinaman's veiny neck was about to explode from the pressure. The weakness of the character was a welcome sign: surely they could convince the trainer to leave the rack for a more gimmicky exercise; anyone new at the gym was either in it or not, and anyone that required a trainer for their first session was definitely not.

The figure turned to face the trainer after resting the bar, who, without looking up from his phone, said "good, you have completed this part of the workout. Grab a five kilogram dumbbell and sit on that bench."

The trio was already advancing on the bar by the time the trainer's words left his mouth. They immediately put two twenties on the bar and sat in the depth of bodyweight squats to stretch. The weakest of the five sat on a bench with a padded plane pressed against his chest. The trainer used the Marvel Fitness Total Physical Representation Method to demonstrate a curl.

The trio never glanced his direction again, but he stared at them climb their way to a hundred and twenty kilograms for five deep reps each. He could see the glory in their eyes as they bounced back up. They commented frequently and dryly on the technical aspects with which the movements were performed. They were dressed in varying combinations of black and gray, sweatpants, hoodies, and basketball shoes. Here he was in past-the-knee cut-off sweatpants and sneakers and a blue t-shirt with a big-titted anime goddess printed across his own deflated chest, struggling to pull four percent of his bodyweight towards himself.

He had never been one for exercise, but, having seen Bahman's precisely-sculpted body over the course of countless roles, he'd convinced himself that even he, a central laborer, industrious as the Chinese, could redefine the physical parameters he thought he'd been given, a break from all the fatalism that flew around in these troubled times.

The trio abandoned the squat rack after a long bout of concentrated effort, carrying with them each a black bag with boxing gloves tied around the straps. Would they beat Zack Damon in a fight? Would they be the good guys or the bad guys? K-pop was blasting in Guo Qu's ears, a song whose music video featured prominent popstars BD Wang and Tapp playfully urinating on each other and whose lyric parade BD Wang's chronic illnesses, which are many, and Guo received this strange blend of influence while he thought over the whole situation. He had to assume that the trio didn't like BD Wang or Tapp or even Zhang Li films, and they might still type with one finger at a time.

His own typing had been slowing after being paid an exorbitant amount recently for a few days' work. This was the advantage of international undermining: a beneficial conversion of currency. He headed back to his little den with a little bowl of noodles and vegetables, for he didn't want to get 'too big.'

He sat down in front of his computer and booted it up, going through the normal process of activating several proxies and a virtual private network and running analytics on his connection. His connection was inexplicably slow, however, so he ran a test to trace the route of his information. It was being diverted through somewhere in the US.

...

"Typical cishet shitlord quack with a BS in sizism," she feverishly typed, backlit screen reflecting on the mayonnaise around her rosé lips. The crunch of corn chips offered some percussive counterpoints to the slopping sounds of macaroni salad gobbing. She had replied to a thread made by the voice himself, Fatty, about how he was told that he was dying. The original post read as follows:

"Attention all of those interested and all of you who are part of the problem: it has recently come to my attention that you all are living in complete denial, that there is a superstructure of refusal that has become a staple of our everyday lives. No, I'm not talking about religion, but instead about SCIENCE. SCIENCE has led us to bombing each other and polluting our only home, and SCIENCE regularly attempts, how DARE they, SCIENCE regularly attempts to ATTACK the very BEAUTIFUL PEOPLE of our COMMUNITY with SLANDERS and LIBELS and LIBERAL AGENDAS. YES, folks, you heard it HERE: the very SOCIALLY-PROGRESSIVE activists we have LOVINGLY supported for years have turned on US and ACCUSED YOURS TRULY of DYING. *But why, Jacob?* you might ask, *why would they accuse YOU of DYING when you're CLEARLY living?!* They've been fed LIES. LIES!! THEY've been fed LIES from a conglomerate of interest groups hell-bent on seeing ME dead, a group of window-licking NERDS who hate to see TRUE HAPPINESS. We didn't eat the LIES they fed to us, instead favoring much more palatable snacks such as the #TACORITODILLA. ATTACHED is a LIST of PEOPLE who you should all SPAM with pictures of your FAVORITE MEAL in order for them to SEE their PATHETIC IDEALS FALL APART. FORCE-FEED them with your LOVE and PASSION. LET THEM SEE CAKE."

Alyssa, close to three months of hermitude and a pitiful amount of erotica later—a more frequent hobby of hers now—was both smiling and tearing up at the idea of her favorite icon falling victim to some vicious campaign wrought against him, and it seemed to be some sort of cruel analogue to her own attacks against her uncle, but that direct implication was long lost on her as she shuffled through folders of pictures of food on her computer, trying to find the perfect fit to spam the overlords of nutrition that had published the falsifications that led to the assumption that her rival and hero was on his way out.

She had gained close to one and a half deca-kilograms, her preferred metric, since she had made her accusation. Despite the strength of her initial support group, she had fallen to the side of the internet's focus after various incidents, namely a controversial and frankly dystopic concussion treatment, China's burgeoning nationalist cyber-crime industry, and

FattyRants' own death spiral. Her own hashtag, #IAmAVictim, had fallen severely in popularity as #DietOfPussy, #GuoWHO, and #FatChance had risen to the top, but her crowdfunded income still had her lifetime left in it, about $30,000.

It may or may not have been for her to decide, but her quality of life had decreased severely since accusing her uncle of molesting her. She had utilized a total blackout of her main blog account, Destroyer_of_Cishet, in favor of any of her burner accounts that she used for her more niche interests, such as FattyRants.

She decided to log back into her main account, hoping to see something that would further bury her spirits. There was a choir of the normal voices of concern, people asking how she had been since the event, making sure she was okay, making sure she had enough to get by, making sure her family was taking care of her in a politically-correct way. One brave soul, a certain GenghisKhan6969, had even asked her out to a date with a strange rationale that he could make sure she would always feel good inside if she were with him, a 'warm feeling through her gutti-wuts attuned to when listening to Liszt's third Liebestraum in A Flat Major.'

Maybe it was the thousands of centigrams she had gained, but something about the offer appealed to her slight desperation. She replied neutrally, certain that nothing would ever come of it:

"Hello GenghisKhan6969. Thanks for reaching out to me. You sound like a gentleman, which is something I'm not used to in my life. I've been subjected to mostly fuckboys and dickheads, which, you might know, have been exemplified by my own uncle who did horrible, unspeakable things to me (which can be found in a video on my homepage). You do sound nice though, and I admit that I would really like to feel warm inside after such cold days.

Please consider the environment before printing this message,

With Warmest Regards,

Destroyer_of_Cishet

P.S. I'm pretty sure I read that story in high school. :)"

9: The Sauce

"WEEEEEOOOOOWEEEEEOOOOOWEEEEEOOOOO **BANGER ALERT. BANGER ALERT.**
WEEEEEOOOOOWEEEEEOOOOOWEEEEEOOOOO **BANGER ALERT. BANGER ALERT.**

We're talking gorilla warfare. Fresh off the press, #DicksOutForBlackLives delivers on all levels. Opening with his signature raspy, unintelligible yelling, Juvenile Ruffian sets a clear tone that he hasn't changed a single thing since last album, and that's exactly what I was hoping for. The first verse opens with an allusion to the content of the rest of the song (and it could be said that the entire mixtape is derivative from this early and only theme): that Juvenile Ruffian is not afraid to use violence in the age of information, and that he might even approve of your social media pleas in that it would feed his ego, juxtaposing his own behavior with the gorilla's but suspending his own parallel death. It is immediately revealed that not only will the Ruffian hurt you, but it will hurt you to see his impressive collection of real estate, cars, and the seduction (sexual and social and perhaps in a violent sense) of your own children and significant others. He also references having arrived at his high school prom in a Rolls Royce, though that is anecdotal and as of yet unconfirmed. The first verse closes with Ruffian's convincing of himself that a second person loves him, which I interpreted to be the internet's reaction to him.

The hook of this song is what makes it in my opinion. Juvenile Ruffian has murdered many African-Americans, generally for money, possibly while driving luxury vehicles. In the only direct reference to his role model, Harambe, he claims that he will defend himself and his property just as the famous ape killed a small, defenseless child. In referencing the primate, Ruffian also alludes to Mothra, a famous Hindu tragic hero in an old Bollywood movie. Strikingly, after this comparison, we immediately see a transition to his more sensual side, talking about how he really cares about the act of coitus more than his violent habits, following this up with an ambiguous line which has been the subject of much debate: it's impossible to hear and Ruffian has declined to clear up whether he says *I just wanna have a baby; I just wanna go crazy about you* or *I ain't wanna have a baby; I ain't wanna go crazy about you*. Regardless, the line supplements Ruffian's unstable mental condition which leads to his ability to intimidate, especially knowing how successful he is (which we heard in the first verse) despite this instability. To finish the hook and segue back into the verse, Ruffian reveals that he's on a pain reliever which can induce contentedness through euphoria and mild sedation, often resulting in sleepiness.

The second and final verse basically annotates his willingness to kill everything and anything in a paranoid rage, much like our beloved gorilla. He will kill your mother and brother definitely, and he'll at least aim at everyone else in your family, including your already-dead mother, your house slave, and your child, regardless of its age. The verse then transitions to a quick but deep ontological discussion of the greater forces pulling at and forming Ruffian, with Satan inside of him and God being tempted to sign a record deal with him, ultimately putting our artist in a unique and stressful position that he admits makes him irrational at times, and he both apologizes and begs the second person—in my opinion, the internet, his true romance—to be patient with him, that this second person might never truly understand him but that he won't change because of them; he'll continue to create art and sell drugs, and that's the most they can ask of him."

Peter, content with the concrete work he had done, returned to his manifesto, the silent response to a world's reflection.

"When the fire finally reaches you, you feel the intimacy of violence, you see that you empathize through pain more than love, and it's the juxtaposition of both of them, fire and ice, that wakes your spirit. No one knows that they like being choked until they are choked, and then a new world opens up, a raw existence without the contracts we generally sign ourselves into. It would be naive to say there aren't pitfalls in this dreamy nightmare world, that wills would never misalign and cause some damage, the thin line between hurt and injury irreversibly crossed, but isn't that again when we are closest to each other? When we have mutually damaged each other, never to be repaired or empathized by anyone else? It is the branding of love, the fires of passion, that has been the subject of all stories, of all history, of every lyric and verse under the sun."

His heartbeat was skipping and doubling down in very strange rhythm, contorting Take Five into Take Seven and the Unsquare Dance into an Unpentagonal Jive at different moments. The gods were speaking through his keyboard strokes and for no one to hear, the only way they could ever speak. It was just a shaking, weak little boy, who forgot how to play the violin, that listened, and his fever was growing as the drop was fast approaching. He was listening to his own sound, something he very seldom did, and his heart anticipated every bump in the ride.

"And it is this very violence that we seek to emulate with these harsher sounds of the young generation. What was transrealist in sound is becoming a realistic interpretation of this crazy world, a science nonfiction. What is at the crossroads of trans and real? Human spirit, historically manifested as occultism sometimes, mysticism others, legend in organized societies and myth in spoken-word, religion in the power-hungry and superstition among the fatalists, and here we are in the technocracy without technocrats praising the machines that we made to worship us! Here be we," he started convulsing, typing in bursts, "who speak again in click-clacks and listen only in wub-wubs, some could say degenerating but I believe transcending the classical impositions on us as a species that have lingered in some post-primal fetishism that has no place in my new world. I am the singularity and if not then I will be!"

He collapsed at his keyboard, heaving, peripherals closing in and closed, *boom, boom, boom, boom*, standard timing the only thing left in his body.

...

"—(restin'!)"

"Glad to hear you're doing well, son," his ever-supportive mother told him over the phone, "I hope they're not pricking you with too many needles." Her voice was home in a faraway land.

His XXXL mint green bed was a remote alien planet, but he was in high spirits as his trap references had been reduced. He heard the uneven pace of the doctor approaching his door, something he was quite familiar with by now, and looked forward to what the little goon had to say.

He opened the door, then knocked, "HELLO—yes, I'm doctor—"

"Hello Dr. Rash."

"—Simon Rash, but you can call me Dr. Rash."

"What are we doing today?"

"Today? Ah, yes! Today! The same thing—well--from your perspective maybe. *Blasé, blasé.*"

"(whippin' Maserati!)" The giant hiccuped, almost catching his outburst. His huge limbs couldn't be covered by the his blanket, so half of one of his log-legs was visible, which he noticed Rash was nervously looking at.

Startled, Rash replied, "Ah, ha! No, no, her name is Marietta, and we shouldn't—"

"Doc, let's just do it."

"Of course, let's get you to the facilities."

"Okay."

"Actually, we have a few minutes—would you like a cup of coffee?"

"That would be excellent, actually."

Dr. Rash left the room to fetch a cup of decaf coffee, his personal ruse to deceive the giant into thinking he wasn't on drugs as the addy took hold. The drugs were to be administerd by IV, but Rash was maintaining his unpredictability. He returned with a coffee stain down the front of his lab coat and an eerie smile on his face, "here you are."

"Aren't you going to have a cup with me?"

Rash, breaking his smile as he thought about this being a test, brought his smile back, "of course!"

He left to get another cup of decaf coffee because he was still shaking from his morning cups and returned shuffling a cup between his coffee-burnt hands. He walked bedside, closer than he had ever been and smelled the Goblin's aura for the first time, a gentle musk. "Cheers."

"Cheers, doctor," the giant toasted, affecting a bit of the Queen's English. They sipped the coffee, Rash looking skeptically at Chris to assure he actually drank, and Chris looking into his coffee, wondering if this cup would make him feel as good as it did yesterday and the day before. He didn't know where he was in the treatment cycle, the whole thing being fairly secretive, but he was sure that his parents, who he had essentially signed himself away to, had made the right decision. He wasn't used to making his own.

After a few minutes of mostly silence, the coffee was gone and Chris was feeling the effects, a narrowing periphery with what remained in a greater clarity, and he began the process of scanning his environment as Nurse Marietta wheeled him down the sanitary hall full of closed doors. There was nothing but an idle IV stand in the entire hallway, and he knew that he would reach the end, take a right, wait for an elevator, go up, exit right, and enter into the seventh door on the right. There he would be fitted with a sort of mask that covered his eyes, and he would be subjected to wholesome videos about family—pets, home-cooked meals, playing outside with his non-existent cousins, everything seeming abnormally familiar, like false memories, like dreams, like things he never always experienced, things with a dew and a residue around the outside of them, much like his own peripheral vision after the coffee, some fringes that weren't always there.

The nurse took him through these exact motions, and, as he entered the room, he saw Rash behind a glass window, nervously smiling at him. The Goblin gave him a thumbs up.

...

"DOCTOR PINCOCK,

Hello , how're you? I'm excited to see you again. I hear that you're going to come check in on the research. It's going excellent other than a few hiccups with some qualitative measures. You will be very impressed, and I'm excited to see you again. You'll be very happy to know that your patient, the famous ogre, is doing fantastic. The rest of the research, which you will get a tour of, is also very exciting.

I want you to know that I'm very strong now, you know, as a person. Please do not reply to this message.

Excited to see you,"

...

"I'll have a spicy chicken sandwich meal with fries and a lemonade."

"What kind of sauce would you like with that?" *Click.* "Seven forty-five." *Click.*

"I'll take one barbecue and one honey mustard."

"Okay," *click*, "and anything else?"

"That'll be it."

"That'll be seven forty-five. Pull up to the second window. Welcome to Chic Gourmet, home of the famous white-meat—"

"I'll have a spicy chicken sandwich meal with fries and a sweet tea."

"What kind of sauce would you like with that?" *Click.* "Seven forty-five." *Click.*

"I'd like one honey mustard and one signature sauce."

"Okay," *click*, "and anything else?

"That's all."

"That'll be seven forty-five. Pull up to the second window. Welcome to Chic Gourmet, home of the famous white-meat—"

"I'll have a spicy chicken sandwich with fries and a lemonade."

"What kind of sauce would you like with that?" *Click.* "Seven forty-five." *Click.*

"I'll have one barbecue and a signature sauce."

"Okay," *click,* "and anything else?"

"No thank you."

"That'll be seven forty-five. Pull up to the second window. Welcome to Chic Gourmet, home of the famous white-meat—"

"a—uhh—one number three, and can I have water to drink?"

"… That's a spicy chicken sandwich, fries, and a bottled water?" *Click.* "Seven forty-five." *Click.*

"Just a cup of water."

Fuck. "What sauce with that?"

"I—uhh—what kinds of sauce do you have?"

Jesus. Reading off the sauces themselves stacked in a dispenser in front of him, "signature, barbecue, honey mustard, sweet and sour, teriyaki, ketchup, yellow mustard, and Szechuan sauce."

"I—uhhh—can I just have one of each?"

Serious? "Sir, you can only have two sauces with each meal."

"Uhh—okay, can I decide when I'm up there?"

"That'll be seven forty-five, pull up to the second window. Welcome to Chic Gourmet, home of the famous white-meat—"

"I'll have a spicy sandwich with fries and a cola."

"What kind of sauce would you like with that?" *Click.* The man in the car was startled when he pulled up and saw Dave. It was probably the gruesome, sort of festering, nose injury that was darkening his whole face "That'll be seven forty-five."*Click.*

"...I don't know, what would you recommend?" The man looked straight into the steering wheel as he spoke, his body retracted somehow onto the arm rest of his seat.

Click. "What? What sauce do you want?"

"A honey mustard and a ketchup."

Click. "Could you repeat that?"

"What do you like?" His entire body shifted and there was genuine curiosity in his voice.

"A honey mustard and a ketchup?" *Click.*

"I don't like ketchup." The cowering grew serious.

"What kind of sauce do you want, SIR?" *Click.* "That'll be seven forty-five, pull up to the second window. Welcome to Chic Gourmet, home of the famous white-meat—"

"What sauces do you have again?" He grew curious again.

Click. "We have signature, barbecue, and honey mustard." *Click.*

"And I only get two?" He held up two fingers.

Click. "Sir, what two sauces do you want?" *Click.* "Could you please repeat your order?"

"I don't know, what's your favorite?" Both grew frantic but for different reasons.

Click. "Sir, do you want sauce?"

A line of cars was forming at the drive-through, and a stack of orders was piling up next to Dave as this gaunt, sweaty man in a beaten-up car was considering his sauce selection.

"Yes, but I don't know which—" This was matter of fact.

"SIR, do you want the SAUCE?"

"Well, which one is THE—?" Pupils dilating.

"SIR, IF YOU DON'T WANT THE SAUCE, COULD YOU KINDLY PULL FORWARD," Dave pleaded, holding a couple of signature sauces in his hand trying to rid himself of this plague.

"NO! I want the—"

Now threatening, "SIR, DO YOU WANT THE SAUCE?"

A moment of silence. "I DON'T WANT THE SAUCE!!!" The man broke out in a sob, and his tires squealed as he sped out of the drive-through, leaving Dave heaving with frustration and confused as to what just happened while people were still talking about spicy chicken sandwiches in his ear.

Who the fuck doesn't want sauce, Dave thought to himself as he considered quitting his job.

...

The pale light from her tablet revealed globs of chocolate, cheese, and sour cream—shrapnel from the Chocoritodilla. It was a certainly a sensual experience, and the whole event had left her feeling rather frisky. She couldn't help but think about GenghisKhan6969's offer. It would be highly unlikely that he would be close enough to make that feasible.

After having exhausted the backlog of old FattyRants videos, Alyssa flirted with curiosity. She image searched the Mongol leader, who was less than satisfying visually but she did appreciate how hardened he looked. She switched to his Wikipedia page. She read that he was a brutal killer who raped and looted, but also that his efforts were responsible for the Silk Road, which probably helped lots of people.

Genghis Khan was a passionate man, a lover and a fighter. Behind that squat face, there was a strong person. Her mind wandered to a fantasy of her entertaining him for an evening, she as some exotic nymph for him to cherish, and how he would. The thought turned her on. *Did he have children? Was he daddy? Oh my god, more than ten wives.*

All the better. He would be professional about it. The thought of it got her warm enough to snap out of it, another sensual experience, and she noticed the various globs on the stained-t-shirt fat titties covering half her tablet's screen. Was it all the better that he had ten wives? An immense self-pity swept over her, and she decided, as rational adults do, to masturbate over it. She googled "genghis khan erotica" and looked forward to where this was going. She hadn't been very keen on erotica until an independent popcorn incest flick based on a book had made it into the clitoris of #ProbablyAllWomen.

The results were generally unfavorable, but she did find a request thread about an erotic author who was known for staging ridiculous sex scenes between giants of different parts of history. Genghis Khan and Joan of Arc was the most popular request. The author, HairyLarry01, had gone viral (as far as niche erotica goes) after he released four stories in one week, all titled simply with the names of the participants: *Machiavelli and Harriet Tubman, Caligula and Schopenhauer, Brad Pitt and Eve*, and *Henry VIII and Anne Boleyn* (before, then after the execution). HairyLarry01 seemed to maintain an open discussion with the fans of his erotica writing, clearly a strong and close-knit community. Alyssa sensed that she had stumbled deep into a culture.

The sexual curiosity subsided as her interest piqued into this character, the erotica writer, yet another invention of the internet. She was in her own world watching this whole new world from a safe distance, looking through the thread. He replied to most posts in larger, well-written texts that answered multiple people. It was clear that he had interacted with many of the other posters before, referring to them his own way and making buddy jokes. She clicked on his profile.

The picture was a pair of wire-frame glasses on a clean white surface that blended into the clean white background. It almost seemed like they were floating. The various sections of information were blank, but he did have a bio written. It was a story, a real chunk of text:

"Boofhole."

It sounded very crude but she had no idea why.

"At the end of the day, the last thing you want to see in the mirror is a crusty boofhole, but Hairy Larry was looking down the barrel at 6:42. A pitifully long session of writing erotica – the caffeine fatiguing your constant, but gentle masturbation – left him squatting over a mirror in a rash turn of events. His best bet was that he had started around 1 pm, but the events that had cascaded the night before were the cause of his current existential dilemma."

The story so far was strangely in line with her mental image of this guy but worded much more eloquently.

"Hairy was on one. There was going to be a gathering at a sort of pixie-landish Chinese party space. The walls were heavy on Borat references, but the general decorum screamed themeless escape room. Regardless, he had started drinking right after breakfast, right before he stumbled into the party. He was greeted by a rhapsody that was highlighted by the lit tip of a cigarette, a dimly distinguishable skinny male body on the shoulders of another, larger gentleman. *Another blood orgy,* he thought to himself."

The specifics of the imagery were lost on her but still kept her entranced.

"He was greeted by sometimes savory characters with a sense of cheeriness among them. People come and go here, so you could tell when the air was specially sentimental. This was one of those nights, and several smallish bottles of Chinese liquor (the Chinese brunch if you will) let him give some very nice hugs to people he'd otherwise been cold to. He was, of course, the subject of much espionage. Hairy used to work with every single person in the room, and now he worked with none of them. He didn't anymore because he was fired. HR had decided it was best not to keep him after several incidents of him being caught reading, writing, and (egregiously) printing bulks of erotic literature at the daycare center he worked at. Mostly novellas and short fiction, but there were two epics, a handful of powerful haikus, and a full season of a podcast show's script."

At this point, Alyssa wondered if this was deeper into the internet than she had ever been.

"The podcast script was edgy even for his work, and he may or may not have (he himself didn't know) left the entire script neatly and intentionally on his manager's manager's desk. *Boofsploof: A Team Effort*. It featured a romantic (and mostly charming) couple on their first few dates, building a relationship, and slowly teasing the idea of exhaling cannabis smoke into each others anuses, but of course that only happened near the end of the narrative (unsatisfactorily)."

Alyssa briefly snapped out of it, almost but not quite putting together that she was reading a third-person story written by the first person about an erotica author writing erotica (including *Boofsploof*). She would have continued reading regardless of how aware she was.

"Anyway, the hugs went well and the liquor went better, and soon he was in that special headspace, the kind where you are constantly and needlessly erect mentally, so to speak. You become hard-headed in some ways and a dickhead in others. He recognized the precursor feelings and was morbidly curious as to where it would take him."

In this moment, Alyssa sympathized with the male condition in a way that she never had, a metaphor that had finally stuck with her, for in some ways it mirrored her in her present state. It was her own morbid curiosity that brought her to reading this story, which had a few levels to it that were also all missed by her.

"The moment arrived when some sort of goddess in the most tasteful dress and playful nature decided to twerk (*tastefully*) to Avril Lavigne.

Hairy thought about how he had recently learned that somewhere on the wide internet there existed a leaked video of the popstar blowing at least one of her large black security staff. The thought of it alone took him back to his den with more bottles of Chinese liquor and a bender of dirty thoughts and dirtier scrawlings until the sun put him to sleep."

And just like that, Alyssa felt for the first time that her balls were blue.

Then she got a private message from the warlord. It read as follows:

"Alyssa, there's a blight in my life, a fire in my groin. Chagrin, angel. *Uh-Liss-Suh*: the tip of the tongue taking a trip of three steps from void to palate, at three, open, a sheath. Uh. Liss. Suh.

I know you're out there, hopefully thinking of me as I am of you, and hopefully not as that sick uncle of yours thought of innocent, young, sweet, ripe Alyssa. The image of him watching those videos of you brings affliction into my heart, and here I am, watching and rewatching the video of you, dirtied, mature, soured, plucked, *Alyssa*, crying in the admission of it all, in the submission of it all, and here I am, blood rushing to and from my head, a whirlwind of feeling, wanting only to comfort you, to make you feel good, to let a light shine down upon you, forever.

I can travel, or I can travel for you, darling. My home is in Knoxville, Tennessee, home of women's basketball and the graveyard of domestic textiles; it's quite beautiful, and I'd love to marry you here some day, but I will travel to meet you, and we can travel the world together, we can conquer it all with love, give this world something great, something unique, a love that will spread like wildfire: a love that they will talk about for generations to come."

The letter went on to discuss potential specifics.

...

Bahman was growing manic in anticipation. Zhang Li was, of course, trying to arrange the next movie, and Bahman's agent was calling relentlessly about the latest project, in which Bahman was supposed to play the protagonist, a first for him and an entire break from his previously-blended identities Daniel Victory and Ichiro, both faces of imperialism. Now he was going to play a Chinese man, a Chongqing native named Ultraman who disregarded generations of Confucianist collectivism in the seeking of his own (legalist) morality. He was, of course, going to have to wear white-face. The move was titled, in English and unclear as to whether there was an error in translation, *Butterface*. Bahman had read the script, and it seemed a little bit off the deep end for Zhang Li films. There were no car chases, less than thirty minutes of simulated sex, and only a single explosion (though, characteristically, it did look like an ejaculation – a prototypical short-fat dictator's rocket fizzling out of its [*his*] silo) that was really more of a pulsing series of sparks. *Butterface* was set in Urumqi.

It was really about the derangement of a totalitarian regime. Ultraman was born into an engineer's family, his father having sold him off to an elite circle from a very young age to be cultivated into the perfect agent of the government. The movie started with Ultraman arriving in Urumqi to visit the Urumqi Domestic Fiscal Diplomacy and Market Market, where his agency, the CDFDMB, or the Chinese Domestic Fiscal Diplomacy and Market Bureau for memory's sake, was conducting espionage on the elite of the minorities in the city, thought to be siphoning money to the poor Uyghurs, Hui, Kazakhs, Mongols, Krygyz, and Uzbeks, a crime punishable by exile. Ultraman was sabotaging all of his goals due to negligence, but it was staged so that it looked like he was a mastermind. The economic treason wasn't the real reason he was there, as it turned out, as was realized in the only sex scene (twenty-five minutes long and the only reference to individualism [he fucked an Uzbek without a condom, presumably mixing their genes] despite the term appearing four times in the summary written by his agent). He was really there because the moisture he inspired in women predicted the geographical regions where the Western press would report critical levels of air pollution. How this all connected to the climax of the movie, where Butterface, the dictator far to the east of Urumqi and outside of the main land, tried to fit his entire population into a rocket designed for zero passengers, ultimately cramming seven women and children into the rocket in a small compartment where the fuels would mix before being consumed, killing all of them by suffocation before the drooling takeoff, would largely be left to the viewer's imagination.

Needless to say, Bahman wasn't thrilled to play the role, but he was thrilled to go to Chongqing, where he had arranged to meet one of the biggest luxury club magnates in the entire world, thanks to David, and hopefully sign a massive promotion that would redirect his life away from these roles.

...

If he was brain-dead before, he was brain-undead now, not that an alive brain could be distinguished with the cocktail of drugs he was being dosed with. He wasn't cognizant enough to put the routine together (or that it was a routine), but he was in and out of the strangest hallucinations all the time, then he just lied in sterility for hours, sometimes when it was dark and sometimes when it was light. His life was a sequence of colored blurs and a lack of (re)cognition that allowed for nothing other than the most basic thoughts — reflections without a mirror. He was reliving his life within a dream narrative, but it wasn't a dream.

What started as baijiu had ended up displaced with too much freedom. His mind raced, but he started to feel the effect of the xans kicking in as the session ended, or maybe he was just a dog. The anxiety would quickly fade, replaced by a dense apathy starting in the back of the neck. His pupils would undilate and his eyelids would droop. He would be pushed to another room, or maybe he was being pushed right then. The dark became peppermint became wintergreen and the possibility of his being pushed closed. He recognized the smell but did not realize that this was the beginning of his reunderstanding of routine. Still, his spirit was high.

There were a number of things on his mind — real things. There was a paprika-flavored diva, a void of memory that he didn't understand, and some troubling experiences that he had relived. It was hard to say what it meant to be *on his mind*. It was a sort of movie playing through his head, far past the three dimensions we see in, flashes of things superimposed over each other in dream-like logics. The baker, for instance, the fat pervert, was smiling at him in the room he was in, but he didn't know where he was and he certainly wasn't with the baker, but Effy was there, or she would be there soon, with certainty, the cats were watching him think, but they weren't very important compared to fear of lights he had all of the sudden. His brother was there, playing video games while Heiko watched. His mom was sighing at the baker, who still smiled, and Heiko looked back and forth between them, trying to figure out if they were with him or not and if she knew. Was Effy here? Had she ever been there? No, it seemed like he was the only one in there, and it was awfully minty. The void of cinnamon, the inability to remember its flavor, the crust of of three-days-old cake, something not sweet and not savory was here. Real things, he thought.

He had heard something, somewhere, that Effy would visit him. Lucidity settled back into him and at some point he noticed that his eyes were open. The room was as minty as he thought it was or maybe he had just been looking at it for a long time, but now he was sure that he was the only one in the room. There was a TV that was off in the corner, perched. He was relieved that it was off, partially because he was tired of screens and partially because he wanted it to just sit there with him.

After a while, the door opened and a small, thin figure came in, walked to the side of the bed, and began moving things outside of Heiko's peripherals. Heiko couldn't move his head, or it didn't feel like he could, or he forgot how. The person seemed to notice Heiko's eyes were open and they made a sudden movement that Heiko felt.

"Oh, hello! Awake, are we?" The voice was American. It continued, "hello friend, my name is Dr. Pancake. I can't believe you're awake. Wow, I can't believe you're awake. We didn't think you would be awake. You probably shouldn't be awake yet. Are you awake? Hey, buddy, how are you? Are you in there? I'm your doctor. Your friend will be here soon. You should get some rest. Are you awake? I can't believe you're awake. Go to sleep, Bubchen. I'm Dr. Pancake. Come on, my friend, go to sleep. You shouldn't be awake. Goodnight, friend, this will put you to sleep."

His peripherals closed in on themselves and he was alone again.

...

"The Chocoritodilla is the best thing that has ever happened to me," he stammered, at a loss for the first time, livestreaming again from his hospital bed and matching gown to a dying fanbase, "...I just can't... Words can't... Nothing can... Where could—"

The phone dropped, feeding mint green to darkness, and the sound of rustling took over the audio, and then, in the background, "MR. WAAL! WHO BROUGHT YOU THAT?" Footsteps, rustle, crinkle of paper.

"No, NO, NO, NOO!!!" The feed flips back over, now looking up at a nurse reaching over Fatty snatching a Chocoritodilla away and ripping another half-eaten one out of his hooves, cream and chocolate dripping, Fatty craning his neck towards his hands to lick up the delicacy, the furrowed brow of the nurse, trying to wipe his hands clean before his tongue can. He reaches one hand away from the camera and she strains across to reach it, but she can't overcome his width and falls on top of him, right over the camera.

"You can't—"

"*Rrghh.*"

"Who gave you—"

"Get off you she-devil!"

And she rolls off, camera exposed again, almost gasping for breath itself, and she leaves the frame, "Jacob, what do you think you're doing?"

"I'm living my life, you cunt," then a fat paw reaches over the camera, hospital ceiling to pink to dark to a dead feed.

"Jacob! You're going into surgery *today*!"

"PSEUDOSCIENCE!"

"Why did you consent?!"

"IT WAS FREEEE!"

He wailed dramatically, sucking on his fingers.

10: Affirmative Action

Chaos is a frame of Alyssa trying to fit into a dress three sizes her junior for a romantic virtual nomadic emperor. She and Teddy, who she knew by name and had repeated to herself to try to make it materialize in her mind, were going to have a date.

Teddy, on the other hand, repeated her virtual name, Destroyer_of_Cishet, in an attempt to realize it, an attempt to align their differences in ideology under one conquering spell. He was, in a way, his own sort of cisgendered heterosexual destroyer. He was driving to her apartment, a short drive, maybe fifteen minutes depending on traffic, though he told her he had woken up very early to make the long drive from out of state, a white lie that he deemed okay (citing *Il Principe, capitolo XVIII* to himself) while he listened to Prokofiev's *Dance of the Knights* to cope with it not being okay, a piece he had long ago determined to be his go-to high-Mach-behavior song, a sort of hype song for the ill-spirited. The thing about his circumstance was that his ends had no moral high-ground; he wasn't seeking justification for a lie but rather the feeling thereof, a contradiction of his most base essence.

Alyssa was just trying to have sex to stave off the lonelies, but she wasn't aware of that. After she had isolated herself from her entire family by creating a false distance, she was the one who had to maintain the distance to maintain the lie. She could not be normal; she couldn't be lonely in the traditional sense; she was supposed to be changed forever, and this duty had left her in an genuinely-distanced place. In some ways, the lie was more powerful than the truth in her personal relations, and somehow she thought that this date would be an exception to that, even though it was the embodiment thereof. There would have been no interaction without the video, and he knew almost nothing else about her.

He parked his car, texted her, a bit nervous, heart beating a little bit heavy, cock and balls itching profusely, which made him more nervous that the secret might secrete before its due time. He fidgeted, waiting for her text, poking holes in a condom. She replied telling him to wait a moment, and she emerged, ripe, ready for the pluck-and-fuck, squeezed into a different dress, two sizes her junior, spaghetti straps turned angel hair and disappearing underneath already-sweaty folds of skin, the teal skirt riding up as she propped the screen door open to lock her door and revealing, tastefully, red underwear peeking out of her crotch, mostly obscured by the incredible volume of thighs bursting with cellulite and bouncing despite being still.

She waddled to his car, nervously picking her dress out of her folds. He got out, closed his car door, and went to give her a hug. "*Alyssa*! My god, you look perfect!"

"Teddy?" She asked sheepishly.

He nuzzled himself into her shoulder in a nod.

"*Teddy*!" She let reserve loose and embraced him, pulling him deep into her flesh, a skinny frame of a man, not that he was skinny, that fit nicely inside her own.

"It's so nice to finally meet you, Alyssa, sweetie," he affected a much stronger Southern accent than she would have assumed from his writing.

"I hope the drive wasn't too bad."

He reassured her that the thought of her ever being alone had made it tolerable, and then further that his first sight of her had far surpassed his wildest thoughts.

She blushed and grew moist.

"I hate to be a burden, but could I get a drink of water before we get on?" The ambiguity of 'get on' left her nervous but excited, and she led him towards her door.

They entered, Alyssa excusing the mess, though the smell was what Teddy noticed, and he was horrified that and while the blood rushed to his green dick. Nonetheless, he was led by his leader as he always was, and he managed to gently rub it against the side of her leg as he shuffled past her, no room between her and the table in her kitchen, to sit down.

The contact excited her considerably, her having been without sexual contact for months now and with considerable esteem issues, and she tried to find an excuse to lean over the sink, surely exposing her backside to him, but she couldn't find one, so she turned the faucet on and drank from the tap.

"Savage," he said, shaking with anticipation and knowing exactly where this was going.

"I try to stay green," she said, turning to look at him without moving her body and alluding to a false social awareness she practiced.

"Me too," he said, alluding to a true infection that he had harbored for over a year now.

Their gazes met, however, and he stood up, clearly erect, and she stood upright and turned to face him, eyelids lowering, and they kissed each other deeply.

Too deeply, in fact, they both realized, as Teddy broke to gasp for air. "Sorry," she sweated.

"No, it's perfect," he kissed her again.

With fumbling grace he tried to lift her a few inches until she could sit on the counter, which really turned into him pitting his body against hers, leaning futilely, repositioning lower, then lift-and-leaning her onto the counter, where she wrapped her legs around him and they kissed deeply, but this time it was the perfect depth.

Her legs squeezed him and he pressed his hips into her. He could feel her heat, and it turned him into an animal. He grabbed one of her breasts with his right hand and began to kiss her neck, and she moaned deeply, and he tasted her extra salty sweat. His left hand reached under the outside of her right leg and began teasing its way up to her panties, where it quickly slipped underneath and began to rub her wet, soft pussy. *Ripe*, he thought. "*Ripe*," he said.

"*Mmm*, what?" She said.

He tried not to hesitate, worrying she thought he said something about rape, "oh, baby, you're perfect."

"I need you inside me," she said.

"I need to fertilize," he said, under his breath and away from her ear.

"Do you have a condom?" She said.

"Yes, of course," he said.

"No, it's so much better without," she said.

And he slipped his shriveled but standing proud mutating dick inside her without her ever having seen the thing thanks to the girth of her thighs, her straddling him between the sink and the fridge.

...

"I'll have a chicken sandwich meal with fries and a cola."

"What kind of sauce would you like with that?" *Click.* "Seven forty-five." *Click.*

"Two barbecues."

"Okay," *click*, "and anything else?"

"That's all."

"That'll be seven forty-five. Pull up to the second window. Welcome to Chic Gourmet, home of the famous white-meat—"

"I'll have a spicy chicken sandwich meal combo with a sweet tea."

"What kind of sauce would you like with that?" *Click.* "Seven forty-five." *Click.*

"I'd like one honey mustard and extra ketchup."

"Okay," *click*, "and anything else?

"That's all."

"That'll be seven forty-five. Pull up to the second window. Welcome to Chic Gourmet, home of the famous white-meat—"

"A classic chicken sandwich with fries and a lemonade."

"What kind of sauce would you like with that?" *Click.* "Seven forty-five." *Click.*

"I'll have one barbecue and a signature sauce."

"Okay," *click,* "and anything else?"

"No thank you."

"That'll be seven forty-five. Pull up to the second window. Welcome to Chic Gourmet, home of the famous white-meat—"

"I want a chicken salad."

"What kind of sauce would you like with that?" *Click.* "Seven forty-five." *Click.*

"I'll have Italian *dressing.*"

"*Okay,*" *click*, "and anything else?"

"No, thank you."

"That'll be seven—excuse me, five seventy-five. Pull up to the second window. Welcome to Chic Gourmet, home of the famous white-meat—"

"I'll have a spicy sandwich combo with a lemonade."

"What kind of sauce would you like with that?" *Click.* He met the eyes of the customer pulling up to his window for the second time since he started the job, and her eyes met his and cowered, just like the last one did, when she saw the depth. He stammered, "*Katie?*"

And at this moment it was clear to her, from some far off and previously unaccessed telepathy, the kinds of messages only despair can communicate through the eyes, his of course being aided by the darkness of the bruises around his eyes, that he truly didn't understand and that she did know him all along.

He had, of course, tried desperately to reach her in the days after she had kicked him out, especially after his rebirth, the pit of his life, but she had equally desperately shunned him. Her world had collapsed just like the knees of the unknowing prostitute whose bloody cunt had smeared Dave's face, and somehow she felt to blame for his broken nose, though she didn't know why or how he broke it, but in this moment she assumed that some altruists, maybe some hashtag warriors, had beaten him in crusade. And now she was here, cowering underneath his pathetic gaze, watching his eyes swell with tears, not knowing how to say sorry, not knowing how to help him or even answer his nominal question.

There was before the both of them a history living itself out, summarizing itself, offering a pittance for a thesis, retracting its statement, then making a judgment, then a proposal, then a retraction, a lifetime ban and an immediate rescinding. And only then, upon the final decision that both of them met at the same moment, a certainty neither of them had felt for weeks, Katie answered, "*yes.*"

"Yes," he confirmed for the last time to himself after a number of similar tweets, comments, posts, texts, calls, forms, and talks between him and fans, believers, contrivers, warriors, activists, dead and alive, and even one or two friends and family. He was going to go under, and who knows where he would emerge? Not as rhetoric, he wouldn't figure out, for he had never done any figuring if the truth were relevant. Instead, he had always chosen the path of the most cream-filling, much like our other invalid, but in more ways were they different:

Jacob Waal lived a childhood, certainly, though it couldn't be said that he had had much room to grow. He grew up in Seattle, where he looked forward to the rain canceling his summer tee ball games so that he could sneak out the fire escape of his building when he was thought to be locked in his room doing God knows what while his father, an obese alcoholic, a special kind of depraved, was booze-glued to the couch. His mother had died in childbirth trying to push out the heavy-set newborn, for she was no XL mother let alone an XXXL or XXXXL. She had been killed by consumption, just as the husband that consumed her would, and just as the consumption itself would grow up and do.

When he left his room, he would climb down to the street, only a leg-breaking fall or five vertical steps and a hop at first, gradually becoming more and more steps as young Jacob began putting on weight and risking his ankles more and more with less and less. At first he would hop down, spry, and make his rounds looking for change that he could fill his belly with. Donuts weren't expensive, but he didn't have a consistent way of making money. When he was agile, he managed to rip off a busker occasionally, a real artist caught up in this mad world. Then, as he became more apparent, he became more creative. When he sensed that his ability to sneak would soon disappear entirely, he used his last haul to buy cheap trinkets, which he would pawn off to tourists at Pike's Place Market in between vendors kicking him out, but he always found new stairwells to hide in as a safer bet. The child was clean cut with a vibrant smile, that of someone successfully getting the only thing in the world they want, and tourists wouldn't hesitate to at least look his way, some of those looks converted to chats converted to sales, and, after a few of these sessions, he even had a customer ask him what he was saving for. The boy wasn't familiar with saving, and he explained the delicacy of the jelly filling, fresh from the morning, combined with the aroma of coffee (he never drank it, but he smelled it), and the customer was moved so much that he walked with the boy to one of the favorite shops and indulged in a delight with the boy. The man did more than treat him: he bought him a small gift card for the shop, telling the boy that he had a talent with words and foods, foods and words, food-words and word-foods.

Needless to say, this arrangement had taught the fattening Jacob a new method of getting what he wanted: talking about it. He became a grassroots marketer for several shops, donuts on Mondays, Wednesdays, and Fridays, tacos every other Thursday, a designer cake shop once or twice in his career, an ice cream shop on the weekends when the sun came out, but when this happened he had to be weary for his drunk father might wake up and check on the empty room. If his father had ever left the house with young Jacob, he might have discovered that the boy had a network of dessert shops and small restaurant managers that knew him by name and would sort of cat-call his services, pitching deals they would give him if he were to work for them that day.

The trinkets took a back seat to being outgoing and eating in public, moaning in delight in public squares as melting peanut-butter-chocolate ice cream dripped down his chin, other children staring in awe at this free boy enjoying every treat under the sun and tugging on their parents shirts and purses until they, too, got to enjoy the treats, but no one enjoyed anything as much as he did, and he soon put together that he was enjoying the spectacle of the flavor almost as much as the flavor itself, and the combination thereof could not be replaced by any single article of flavor.

"*Yes*," he would gasp between licks and moans and especially when the raspberry-cream jelly burst out of the back of a donut, his hand catching the filling and feeding it to his mouth the moment that the *sss* ended.

...

His eyes opened and a dim, decapitated cartoon silhouette appeared on a table across the way, the only dark thing in the entire room, actually. The rest of it was blinding light, each blink bringing color's context into focus. He began to see an orange point emerge, and then two porcelain plates spawned out of the fuzz, then he realized that this cartoon was his own owl mask staring at him ominously from across the room, the only contrast to a sheen of mint-and-white. And then he was startled when he recognized that one of the mint figures was moving, and suddenly it was a person, a small frame, a woman's figure, he hoped.

She moved slightly, back to him, possibly shuffling through papers, then turning to move to his bedside table, and by this point she was in focus enough to reveal a profile. She was ethnically ambiguous at first, of a dark or olive complexion, then a clear Spanish or ruling-class Mexican, and then she confirmed herself as a South American deity with the slightest tinge, a crisping of the *t* and a sliver of a roll on the *r*, "Hello, Peter, glad to see you're awake."

He thought he might open his mouth but it seemed not to work, not for lack of effort but instead some uncontrollable unwillingness to exude that effort, even despite his mounting curiosity. She must have seen him trying to try, something in the eyes certainly, and she seemed to react by making herself bigger, closer, and clearer. She was now close enough to where he imagined he could smell her sweetness, but he couldn't in a similarly-muted way. Her eyes were something yellow, her skin something tan and creamy at the same time, her hair something shiny and curly in the bounciest unmoving locks, her smile deeply genuine. She was the meeting of spirit and beauty, this kind of aesthetic that leaves a sick boy only with the term 'goddess' to try and capture the moment.

"Peter, you had a heart attack."

He thought she was referring to the feeling he just had.

"And you're twenty-five years old."

He thought she was referring to the length of life he had left in front of him.

"Something needs to change."

He thought she was referring to her own situation with him, that she was ready to start something new.

"Doctor Pincock is out of state for another two days."

He thought she was referring to her current lover that she was to abandon in his favor.

"But we've told him about your situation."

This one jarred his process. Who was *we* and what was his situation? At this, he managed to open his mouth, though no voice emerged.

She again reacted to his effort, coming even closer but continuing unaffected, "and he has given us very specific instructions for the meantime."

And at this his curiosity was actually brought out, that this mysterious person had some advice for him, but it dawned on him in just a moment that Pincock had been his doctor for some time, or at least was his doctor until he had informally dismissed him. And then it dawned on him that he had had a heart attack and that these instructions were coming from his cardiologist, the only person more invested in his heart than himself, and his curiosity vanished.

"Try to let yourself rest. I know you're probably feeling confused about what has happened."

At this point, she became a real person again, still beautiful, but it became clear to him that she had concerns, beliefs, a family, and mortality.

"I will be back to check in on you in about forty-five minutes, okay?"

He tried to reach her with an *okay, I'll be okay, that's fine, I know you have things to do, seriously, don't worry about me*, he tried as much as he could. His mouth opened, voice failing to be found for a moment then vibrating in a distorted parallel to what he had attempted, "uh."

...

Right as she neared the most guilty coming of her life, her eyes desperately scanning the screen for the image that would throw her over the edge into who knows what depth, she recoiled at her own picture appearing in a request thread for 3D CGI triple anal penetration between male dragons of various ethnicities and a Scandinavian princess. The majority of the images were from the same source and as such had a signature: each picture was highlighted by various uses of liquid physics, moisture collecting and streaming down her legs and her brow and their backs, and it had the most tasteful shimmer, little rainbows, almost like soap bubbles reflecting light in a spectrum of purple and blue and some sort of invisible yellow. All of these pictures or gifs were from three separate scenes that he had released, three scenes that he had been commissioned to create which spread like wildfire on the Board.

She recoiled because the picture reminded her of the pressure in and around her favorite place, the safe space she had created and destroyed simultaneously, and, now that she thought of it, having come quietly, was a *safe space* what she had intended this whole interaction to be? Wasn't it something opposite of that? What had happened to the beliefs, to the convictions that all of this had started with? How did she end up being nothing more than her body's reduction to a collection of dark pixels, a royal silhouette, something significantly less than a reflection and infinitely less than the intricacies of her more real interactions, intricacies of Dave stalking her, of the fat greasy perverts giggling about shallow sexual puns, about the circumstances of her situation? The Board had no real circumstances, instead consisting entirely of a false history that couldn't begin to justify itself.

Part of this recoil sent her into fantasy of the most real things she had in her life: Flanker's dependency on the inconsistency of her absenteeism, the second waspy manager she had that referenced Black Twitter, and the old people that regularly died right after her watch ended. The last of these thoughts brought vivid images to mind, images of a bus arriving, expected after a history of circumstance, images of a side-loading liftgate coming out of the underside of the white van, a white door opening, and a white-dressed black man with a wide, white smile appearing before her. She shuddered good.

She checked her phone, wondered what day it was and what time she had to go to work, knowing it was during her week but in between the second and the fourth day, and discovered that it was her favorite day, the looking-forward-to of which had previously been long lost with the dissociative effects of Board addiction. It was Thursday, and the senile would come today, which further meant that her unknowing and unknown savior would also visit.

"*Yes,*" she moaned as she considered again masturbating, which she would ultimately do, relying on her imagination and being sorely disappointed in her ability to do so.

...

Among the more uncomfortable moments in his life, he constantly felt the sweat stains of his felt floral shirt on the tail end of this flight to Bumfuck, North Carolina, somewhere so deep in the heart of the research triangle that it had disappeared long ago off the maps of the area, though GPS clearly revealed the village in its entirety. He worried a little that the snoring man on his left would see the moisture under his armpit and inexplicably less so that the gay attendant would notice as he walked past.

He had not been to work the day before, having made a convenient lie about when his flight was. The truth was that he had had a briefing. The lie was also a truth, however, because he was going to have to call and inform the secretary that his stay would be prolonged, though really it was going to last as long as he originally said, he was just leaving early. Regardless, he felt he had to do what he had to do, and now here he was, between drooling men, drooling armpit drool.

The plane landed, and he met another drooler at the gate, a certain paranoid ex-lover that he had bitterly and sweetly anticipated. His personal affairs, as normal, were not in any state, which left him in a perfect situation to visit this mystical and scientific Atlantis.

Rash smiled and then didn't smile, but then he smiled and offered a handshake and alternatively a hug, regardless, a welcome. Pincock chose the former and the latter, which took Rash by surprise and excited him at the possibility of the evening. Their exchanges were curt, which both fueled and depleted Rash's curiosity.

"Jet lag," Pincock reasoned when Rash asked him to have tea at Rash's before turning in, which, after further questioning, was revealed to be a quite committal activity, some forty miles from where Pincock was staying.

"Oh yes, of course, I was planning to go to sleep anyway." Rash's eyes opened wide, standing there in the doorway of room twenty-seven in the pinnacle of Bumfuck lodging, an abandoned motel whose receptionist kept an erect and angry dog and whose only business was between dinner and midnight as the lot lizards slinked around from room to room.

"Okay," Pincock said, not sure what Rash was doing or thinking, "good night."

"Oh, yes, of course," Rash said, turning his head to the ground.

...

Does he want me? Rash waited outside room seventeen, waiting for a door to open and some sort of confirmation to appear, as if it would, in appearance, instantly. It did not, however, when the doctor appeared, opening the door of room twenty-seven, in a floral shirt. The doctor had an air of deliberation, not that he was decidedly decisive but instead that he was in the process thereof.

The doctor descended the stairs, reached the side of the car, and jimmied himself in the passenger door, trying to avoid bumping the car parked adjacent, a feat that required some skill to overcome the ridiculous angle that Rash had chosen.

"How are you?"

"Let's get a coffee," Pincock said.

"Yes, of course," Rash replied.

Pincock seemed distracted with his phone throughout the drive. When asked, he revealed that one of his celebrity patients had suffered a heart attack at a young age; Rash didn't ask who. He also revealed that another of his celebrity patients had died in surgery; Rash didn't ask who.

The time passed, and soon they were pulling onto the research campus. The buildings were medium-sized but spaced very far apart. They were the color of brick, and they featured a modestly-modern design.

"It's that one," Rash said.

"Okay," Pincock said.

They pulled into the parking lot, and Pincock had to tell Rash that his third parking job was even more okay than his second one. They got out and made their way inside, where they were greeted by Katie, who seemed especially cheery.

"Good morning! You must be Doctor Pincock!"

"Yes," he said, "I am."

"Yes," Rash added, "he is."

Jarred already, the receptionist decided not to pursue any semblance of conversation. She smiled at them with wide eyes and then pretended that her phone had given her reason to refocus on it.

"After you," Rash said, gesturing into a door that led into the facility.

"Okay," Pincock said, moving slowly as if he didn't know where he was going.

"Christopher Grant has been responding exceptionally. His cardiac condition is unchanged despite the heavy treatment. He is optimistic and has shown strength in all of this."

"And how about the rest of the subjects?"

"Well, some are responding better than others."

"But how about the one?"

Rash knew he was talking about the celebrity, but he decided not to answer the question, "some are doing better than others, but how are *you*?"

"How is Heiko?" He deliberated.

"Yes, of course."

...

"Yes, Doc, I'm feeling much better."

"Was it difficult to adjust to?"

"Doc, I don't know if I've adjusted yet, but I'll be okay." His smile showed bigger than himself, a decision that he had come to in precisely that moment, that he was okay in this world, something he had never really considered in the past, and he didn't even notice that he hadn't stuttered.

"That's excellent to hear, Chris. Your heart is doing remarkably well."

"It feels good."

"And I'm sure you'd like to talk to your parents."

"Doc, I don't know. I don't know if they can understand what I'll say, so I might wait a bit on that."

"I understand, Chris, but I'm worried for their sake. Can we send a video, maybe of the both of us?"

Rash was still in the room, picking at his nails. Both the giant and the tourist stared at him in silence until he noticed a shift in the feeling of the room, then he looked up and saw them. "Oh, yes, of course."

Pincock and Chris went over what the video would entail, and then they stood there, posing smiles and leaned almost against each other, stuck in stasis for a brief moment as Pincock struggled with his phone.

"Hello Mom and Dad! As you can see, everything is going very well. I've been extremely busy with the treatment, and I'll call you very soon. It's a little too early to bother you right now, and I'll be on a tight schedule of rehabilitation all day."

"Yes, Mr. and Mrs. Grant, it's me, Doctor Pincock, all the way across the country to visit my favorite patient, and you'll be incredibly pleased with his progress. His heart condition is completely nonexistent right now, though we're still watching it, of course, and he seems to be in amazing spirit. Your son's a real role model on our campus, very brave."

"I'm feeling great! Every day is something new, and they all fly by. They keep me occupied, no time to think about the old me."

"Yes, we're staying occupied out here! I will give you all a call later this evening and we can chat a little more about the program."

"Okay, well it's time to get to it, I love you all and thanks for all your support!"

The video ended with the cheesing tourist shuffling to cut the video off his phone, both of their eyes dropping from the camera to something slightly lower, something a little bit more real to them, the screen with the button.

...

"Okay," Dougie took the phone off his ear and looked for the button to hang up. He was anxiously waiting in a coffeeshop, anxiously sipping espresso, anxiously mulling over how the conversation would go. He hadn't actually seen her in some amount of time that he couldn't even place within context. He remembered what she wore, the way her hair bounced, the way her brow showed disapproval, the single grin she let when he made a fatherly jest, lighthearted and self-deprecating. But he didn't remember where or when it was, not even the bigger things that could have happened before or after, holidays, her graduation (which he missed, duly), her mother's reappearance and subsequent disappearance.

The reason for their meeting was simple and vague: Dougie had expressed that he wished to be involved in her life with some certainty, and she said yes but without any regrets for having previously turned him away. Something had changed, but he was not about to try to figure out what it was, and it didn't occur to him that it could have been the trauma that she had just been through.

He gazed out at the sunlit street, not far from his favorite jazz club, on Müllerstraße, looking out at the waves of people exiting the subway station, different peoples speaking bits of the same language to each other. A short observation would reveal the volume of foreigners in the district: Turks, students, artists, unemployed, the loud and proud of Berlin in some ways and in others a battered people looking only for a place to speak bits of their own language, reflective of the free-body culture that was so carefully preserved on the lake, in the cafes, and in the coal-burnt warmth of some war-aged tenements. And then she emerged, wearing purple, just like he was.

She was looking down at her phone, unwilling to break her gaze until someone had held the door for her and she had entered, only then looking up, seeing her father, and smiling with coal-burnt warmth.

"Lena, darling."

She was bright when she wanted to be, "my favorite *Los!er.*"

"Lena, darling," he got up and gestured to hug her.

She hugged him and held on for a moment.

"Lena, darling, do you want a coffee?"

"Yes," she whispered into his shoulder.

"Lena, darling, are you okay?"

"Yes," she whispered into his shoulder."

"Do you need anything?"

"Yes," she whispered into his shoulder."

"What do you need, Lena, darling?"

"A break, some time to think," she said, breaking the embrace and taking a seat, still smiling but looking sweetly sulken.

"A break from what, my darling?"

"I'm tired," she said, lifting her head up just enough scan for her incoming coffee.

"I understand, darling."

"I don't know about my friends, Dad," she said.

"I understand, darling."

"I don't know about people, Dad," she said.

"I understand, darling."

"Dad," she said.

"Yes, darling?"

"I think you do understand."

"That's sweet, darling, but how could I understand your life?"

"How could anyone?"

"I don't know, darling, I don't know."

...

"No, you can't do that! That's not fair!" She was crying, making a scene, her normal condition as of late, steadily growing worse but so steady that it all seemed one situation that had already played out. The journey from the airport to wherever she had been arranged to go had disintegrated under the weight of her mother's situation.

She hung up the phone, exited a black car, and walked into the lobby. The redness of her wet eyes brought a strength into the blue, a contrast that struck deep into the heart of the receptionist, who surely knew that very moment why this girl was here. Effy was on a postwarpath. She asked where she should go, in broken English, and the receptionist told her.

Effy was still being escorted by the driver, but she didn't notice. He was behind her, just an elongated shadow. She tore through the facilities with a Latin-American nurse both chasing and leading her by yelling directions that the German girl mostly understood. Her escort seemed to not break a brisk walk while he tailed both the scrambling women.

The nurse was yelling advice about talking to Heiko in between bits of navigation, though Effy couldn't or wouldn't understand this, and Effy finally burst into a mint-green room and saw him there, eyes just cracking open and revealing a crusted gloss.

"I'm sorry, Heiko!"

The nurse caught up, "he's not fully responsive yet, miss."

"I'm sorry for everything."

"Please speak gently."

At this, the shadow raised a definite tone, "Ma'am, with all due respect, can we give them some privacy?"

The nurse abided and Effy and Heiko were left alone. Heiko blinking occasionally but only opening his eyes a sliver.

She moved close to him and put her hand on his. "Heiko, I don't know what to say. I don't know what to do without you. I'm completely lost. You were the only sure thing in my life, and I just want you to be better again. I need you to be better. I never thought of it, of us, like this, but I love you, Heiko."

Were these the days? And what is this for silence? Or a park bench? Influencer and choosy chooser at their most clear divide. Here is he, the boy, reflecting on words and people he didn't choose, for he is incapable of choosing in this state. Choosy chooser is what she is, having always had the choices that he didn't. Her over-abundance of choice had chosen him and he chose to choose it earlier. In these modern times of no choices, he tried not to watch this choosing: voyeurism in the form of love: someone else being passionate.

And the fact that she would spend his time here and devalue her time as if it was spent at the club devalues her time to the euros and bitter-flavored doses, a decided overstimulation when compared with the similarly-priced wine and especially less romantic. And you go through the routine so many times and suddenly you are a shell of what could hardly be called a functioning neural network. It does, however, seem something natural when compared with a childhood spent waiting for a home, as she often did in those tragic days, hoping for what the tongue could tell, and only as much as the tele could tell, more than the girl dissolved in the club; it's colorful but it still hurts. And when did she decide to swallow a mouthful of stimulants if the music or the people didn't tell her to do so? Is that where her problem lies? Is that societal behavior?

Her eyes welled. "I love you Heiko. I've never been so sure about anything in my life. I love you, from hanging out in the corner store to liking the smell of fish, I love you. You know me more than anyone knows me, more than I know myself. I love you more than I love my family. You are my family. You are me, but I'm not you. You are beautiful, Heiko, and you always know what to do, and I love you."

Years. Years of his life believing in the improved and improving human, shattered by a skull fracture. The first-worlder, a fallacy brought to your mouse clicks and history books, no left-right but instead red people and people, ideologies for microphones and wet dreams for ideologies, which, in defense of the world at large, was his personal problem in this moment; however, in assault of the world at large, he wasn't trying to be the ideologue behind the cat and the ball on the string bouncing around the screen with a soft jazzy sax holding a note for longer than Dougie Wallace could hold his breath.

"Come with me. The sun's almost up and these lights will cut off soon. We can start anew and you can have everything you need. The sweet clouds will come out for us. The countryside, your home and family, is begging for your return. It's been too long. We can find ourselves out there. There's nothing for you in the city, nothing safe and certainly no love. Look, the sun is peeking out at us, and soon he'll be past those low clouds and he'll show us sweet rainbow tips on the blades of grass. Would you miss that for the city? I don't want to miss that anymore. I don't think you want to miss that. Come home. It'll just be you and me and our lucid dream. That's what the lakes and the fields and the orchards are for, aren't they? Dream with me. Can't you dream? Not after laying there for weeks? What do you dream about? Tell me about the cakes you used to steal when you were a chubby little boy, tell me about the things you do on the internet. I'm in love. Heiko, come back to me. I need you now and forever. I'm nothing without you."

At this moment, he saw vividly the red pouring from Effy's head, from the tremendous crack in her own skull that some rock had caused years ago, some insurmountable brain damage that she had never had to address, and the image of her own crying eyes looking into his as she died before him melted deep into his memory. He didn't know if this made them perfect or not.

Part Three

The Mind's True Liberation

You're in a subway, now a monorail, looking down over a gray-green river to the north, heading east. You exit the subway, south, and suddenly you're on an escalator, north, figuratively, still going south, up more than eighty meters, and, at the top, sewage is pouring down the steps from no source, and a busy young man hurries past you, stepping in the puddle to minimal effect and insuring safe passage for your own crossing. He's one of 30 million to you (a billion and a handful to some), and you're one of the rest to him. The sun reaches through the complicated system of structures above you for a moment before you're somehow underneath an overpass, suddenly on something between a street and an alley with hardened faces and crooked backs motioning shoddy trucks half full of cargo to fit in spaces they can't. Choruses of spitting, honking, and frying blur into a unique bustle. It seems the road is a dead end, yet traffic is all going forward. As you wander and wonder whether to turn back, now so deep that no natural light reaches you, you see a metal staircase climbing over an actual hole in the wall, a public toilet, strangely signified and dignified in English, and above the sign hangs a wet pair of underwear and a shirt. Next to the hole, under the stairs, is a wooden box that someone lives in. You walk up the stairs, losing some anxiety when the sun hits your face again, and find yourself in the middle of a square, surrounded on three sides by construction fencing and one side by a highrise in construction with a functional ground floor. You see that there are three tunnels staring at you from each cardinal direction, and the elders of yesteryear, the pained faces of yesteryesteryear, the innocence of yesteryesteryesteryear, eye you curiously albeit without hostile reserve. The heat sets in on you just as the sticky smells of dried hawthorn fill your nose. In a blinding moment of sun reflecting on construction materials, you choose to escape through the middle tunnel, which bends so that you can't see through it, and the tunnel ends up being over a hundred meters of shipping container, blue as the sky hadn't been for a few seasons. At the end is a brief skylight cut short by the entrance to a market, no doubt the blemished face of the cancerous body you just passed through. Inescapable. There are thousands of shoes on the floors of dozens of walled-in vendors. In front, there is an alley made of folded boxes in two lanes, where young workers peddle and push carts stacked ten meters with bags, barrels, and more boxes, pushing you out of the way as well.

There's no hope that you'll find a comfortable place to sleep among all this, but somehow you aren't yet concerned. After all, you're finally at the local peak, only stairs leading down from here. By early afternoon, the shock fades among the endless markets of eyes and ears. It is only then that you become sensitive to it, only when you're stuck on the rooftop's maze and the guard yells at you for trying to use closed stairwells to get back down; after all, you are an illiterate, almost mute alien, the only dysfunctional cell in an incredibly complex organism. You are, in more ways than one, a foreign contaminant, and are viewed more or less as such, depending on the degree that one is obligated to stand in your way. In coming here alone, you wished to get a new perspective on life and create an image of yourself therewith, but then you saw that the image was created for you, branded on your forehead, a fatal birthright, and now you're sweating in the sun and stuck on a rooftop market, a big leap away from the building you were trying to get to, its windows taunting you with solar glare, giving you multiple shadows in the broad daylight. This building is the potential for salvation, brought to you by a Google listing and a complicated system of radionavigation that is the last hope of all your humanity. You miss many things in this moment, but mostly you miss the ground. You're constantly on the verge of satisfaction, a stairwell here, a stairwell there, closed by men shouting things at you that you can't understand.

You make it down to the street, but you still can't find the entrance to the building. The base of the building seems to be half-open-air half-walled-in market as well, much like the rooftop, with nothing other than freight elevators which you know will not take you to the fiftieth floor, heaven. Now that the problem is purely vertical, no radionavigation will help you. You and your destination are on the same coordinate, yet your destination is in some sort of superposition that you are not, both where you are and not where you are. It seems impossible to get around the building between the various construction fences and the many guards that don't seem to want you to get where you want to go. You finally sneak through a dark stairwell, somehow down beyond the ground floor, and exit out on the street of the other side, spatially confused as always. Nevertheless, you seem even closer. There are three entrances to the building. You choose the middle one. The three towers of the high rise are connected until the forty-third floor. There are four elevators. Two go from the first floor to the forty-third floor. Two go from the first floor straight to the forty-third alternate floor and then up to the top, the fifty-second floor. You go up to the fiftieth floor, home and heaven in hope, but the room number is not there, and you put together that you're likely in the wrong tower. In walking around, you notice a magnificent view of the city, breaking through a temporary door jammed shut, clearly restricted for construction, and walk around the patio, breathing in the freshest air of the trip. There is a construction worker sitting with his back against the half-wall, and he looks at you with complete tranquility, one of those stares that you've never seen in any state of alarm or that you've seen once in a man dying, knowing with certainty that he was going to hell. The view is nice, but it's not where you need to be. You go back down to the ground floor, choose the third entrance, and find the elevator doesn't go high enough. You walk back to the first entrance and get in the elevator. The elevator takes you up and you find the room. You can tell all is well by soft smiles and a 'wait here.' A girl notices you, sitting in the sunlight, on the floor, in the corner, and you smile, quickly rotting your own smile with the realization that you hadn't smiled all day, a stiffness in the muscles.

It dawns on you how many smiles you might have missed by coming here, how many you could have had if you were home. Would they hold the same value as this short smile that you desperately offered this beautiful girl? This one tells a story, but stories are based in conflict. Is heaven or hell the home of conflict? A life out of balance is the only story.

You wish, in a dramatic moment, that you could self-medicate, poison your tumorous existence to incapacitate it and keep it from destroying, a sort of redeeming trade you might make with the universe, but you're probably just tired. Sleep it off so it goes away for a while, and hope that you've worked enough to fall asleep again when it comes back.

But then you sleep, and you feel better, and you meet new smiles and fill the air with laughter, and, for a brief moment, the smiles you missed don't concern you.

...

Cierra awkwardly managed to find a date with her white knight, and, though she didn't have sex with him after the first, second, or third date, her viewing of obscure porn tapered off and eventually ceased as they came to have a relationship.

...

"The big black man doesn't like you."

"I've never even seen TRON," and lights had never been so dark. Bahman stood next to a bao an, employed to ensure safety for workers engaged in production, and embraced a soft-pushing hand on his chest as the stage rose.

The big black man clicked something at Bahman from the stage, shirtless, and offered a gesture of fist-to-chin, and Bahman decided he wasn't having fun. "I don't like you either," said the paramilitary-looking guard a full foot shorter than he. Bahman took the hostility as aggression, which he wasn't wrong about, but had to stand down to the volume of potential enemies around him—the muscle dancers on the stage who had noticed him, the line of guards already with their hands on him, the prospect of a dimly-lit room in the back of the club where they take foreign guests who break vases.

And just as he was going to retreat, a Russian, one of many in this little Russian subsection in a Chinese metropolis, a luxury club full of supermodels paid to drink and pour fake liquor and strong weak-jawed Russian men in white t-shirts, this one no exception, put his hand on the shoulder of the guard and said, in English, "it's alright, brother, David knows this guy," turning to Bahman and pulling the guard's hand from his chest, "Bahman, no?"

"Dway," Bahman replied, turning back to the guard and thinking himself clever in appropriating the guard's native tongue, "and she-uh she-uh, shwy-guh."

The look that returned from the Russian suggested that another phoneme from the Turk would submerge Bahman in Siberian waters, but the look didn't get the attention that it wanted and that naturally quelled the Russian, who seemed to be under a profound influence and measuring things carefully. Bahman was lost in the lights and the sounds. He had lied; he had seen TRON, and this large space was a tribute to TRONian aesthetics amplified by Chinese wealth: specifically, a DJ booth that was the front half of a matte black, neon-blue-highlights

Lamborghini Aventador and a German-looking DJ (tall, gaunt, muscular, baby-faced) in a light blue suit-and-tie that reminded you what kind of culture you were consuming.

Regardless of Bahman's inattention, the Russian friendly-unfriendly pulled the taller but spacier Turk away from the stage with the still-staring black muscle dancer, "David told me you would come, and he told them."

"Who's David?"

"You came here for David."

"I came here to get fucked up," the Turk replied certainly, stopping the Russian who was wading him through aisles with tables of rich Chinese on either side, calling out and whoop-whooping this Caucasian and ambiguously-brown-skinned man. The Russian caught his stare and quickly realized that Bahman was on molly, a signature dilution of pupils and modest sheen of sweat combined with a flexing jaw.

"Okay, but we must keep moving." The disembodied, petite hands of the drunken and excited Chinese girls swarmed over their bodies as they made their way through the booths, purple-blue and blue-purple lights of many shapes and movements covering them and obscuring absolutely nothing, for there was no anonymity in being tall, full-framed, and anything other than Han Chinese in black ties.

The Russian assured Bahman that all would go well.

Bahman replied, "is it always like this here?"

"David is upstairs, but, I warn you, they don't want you to meet him."

On hearing this, Bahman was pulled out of his trip in a familiar way—any compromise of logistics affects a drug user similarly, that you might have to reconsider what you've done just as you were ridding yourself of all consideration.

...

Dave became a manager and continued to have his own thing going. He moved back to his home with his wife. Alyssa apologized to Katie with no rationale, though she would never speak to Dave again.

...

The weeks following the short-lived intimacy were, as is often the case, confusing, tiring, and concerning. Alyssa was affected by him.

The original inertia had caused her to reconnect with her family with some zest. She had talked to her parents, ensuring them that she was okay for the first time in months, that she was surviving comfortably from her slowing blog earnings. She was content with being out of the spotlight, a gentle fall from fame that had admittedly bummed her out at first, she told them, but she had recovered and had even found a nice man, she kept telling herself after he failed to get in touch with her again. She tried to reach out to him, but he told her that he was very often on the road.

By the next week, she had already gotten back into reading HairyLarry01's finer works, including the likes of *Crusty Mosquito King*, a short about an infectious human-sized parasite with a talent for cunnilingus, and *gtfo*, a longer work about the changing sexual patterns of an average camwhore who slowly moved from real group sex to virtual bukkake, where thousands of her viewers would cam themselves cumming onto the lenses of their webcams in a fast-cutting polyptych of videos. The erotica sufficed, but she had an itching or a burning deep down to talk to GenghisKhan6969 again, the real statesman of such a virtual empire. In some moments, she fantasized about his own sex life and wrote several odd excerpts of romantic novel with too much writer's voice.

By the week after that, she had had the realization that she was back to where she was before she had met him: addicted to the internet, not getting her fix from the internet, and the internet's frustrating disinterest in her case. She made several posts, hopelessly making up to force the tears and try to earn her stay again, but there wasn't really much going for her, especially as the memes about the death of FattyRants rolled out. Following the memes were the reactionary apologists for his lifestyle. Following the apologists was a wave of social justice about the unhealthy beliefs on SALT's and THALT's agenda. Alyssa had no place to insert herself here, especially after she had put on so much weight.

By the third week after the encounter, she was growing concerned by a lack of a period, by the continued fatigue, and by her inability to imagine the near future. At this point, she broke down and had an honest interaction online, releasing a video in which she didn't make herself up or force the tears but instead let them flow naturally with the confession that her strange internet fame had ruined her, that she wasn't sure what her original intentions were and that she didn't know if they had been realized. She spoke of her weight gain, of her isolation from friends and family, and of a strange romantic encounter she had had. The last point had caused a small schism among the relatively few people that were still keeping up-to-date on her page: there were of course those who vilified the man, just as they would vilify any consensual-sex-turned-nonconsensual one-night-stand, there were those who praised the man for trying to help her (and in doing so made a mockery of her current state, some aware and some unaware of the power of their words), there were those who turned on her and blamed her for her weakness, and there were those who turned on the rest of the community, blaming the entire situation on the affects of fleeting and only impulsive armchair activism.

By the fourth week, she took a pregnancy test and saw two lines emerge, the simplest digital readout of her life. In fact, it was so simple that it brought her joy.

...

The plane ride was troubling. Between three separate giant cat catastrophes of furballs staring in at him menacingly from the wings of a plane above 40,000 feet, a stewardess trying to serve him *hose*-cake, and the pilot's speech being the alternative Sanskrit lyrics to a Katy Perry song, *balagaja dhanayauvanasalin bheda*, one of those bangers that went unbanged. He could feel the xans keeping him strapped in, and he told the stewardess this when she asked him to buckle his seatbelt. "No thanks," he said, "I'm at long," an impossible combination of *First-Strike* jargon and an English expression whose meaning he was trying to convey (which had no relevance regardless), another bad sign; he was fluent, but that offered no comfort.

"Sir, you have to fasten your seatbelt."

"So the dogs of society howl."

"Sir, are you having trouble?"

"Well, it's not nearly as loud as the voice around me," he mumbled.

"I'll help you."

And she did help him, and he offered no resistance, peripherals closed in from the onset of the drug and nerves numbed just as much. The apathy continued into a slumber, deep and warring, full of horror that didn't stir a reaction in him.

He woke to find himself descending into his fatherland. It looked cloudy with a chance of rocks raining from the sky and killing innocent or guilty things everywhere but indiscriminately. And here he rained from the sky with these other travelers, dangerous as they were, not a single sock-cake eater among them. The pilot again spoke in a dead language, this time something tribal largely without subject-object continuity.

The landing happened uneventfully, or there may have been an event that may have been the stimulus to tell him that he landed, to wake him from his slumber, but he still was in no state to be disturbed. He rose only after the same stewardess unbuckled him, something he felt through her hands close to his hips, exciting him slightly, a minor event.

Then he got off the plane, checked in to his home, found his luggage, met someone outside security, possibly Effy but probably not, and sat down in a taxi to go back to a hotel that someone had arranged for him. His only inquisition was about the availability of a laptop. He was reassured that there was a backpack waiting for him with his few but often-used possessions.

He fell out of the taxi, having taken another dose of xans at some point between deboarding and arriving at the hotel marked only in his memory by the difficulty in swallowing a pill with such a dry mouth.

Someone lifted him up and dragged his feet or his arms into a revolving door, and he felt suddenly crisp as the air-conditioned air smacked him in the face, but then he became again numb. His only hangup at the moment was that he thought he would be in a worse state without the drug. This recognition left a bitter flavor on his disabled tongue.

He was leaned against a surface, fairly sharp on his ribs but not enough to warrant a shift, for a while, then he was dragged and eventually carried into a bright room that went dark, and then he was there by himself, molten on the bed. He couldn't feel his shoes but he knew they were on. He also could have been naked. He wasn't in a place to decide.

He was somewhere else because he was fascinated with the idea of standing up or falling off the bed and seeing if they left his bag in the room with him. The question kept him conscious on the least possibly operable level. He also grew curious as to whether the bathroom light was actually on and he was just so barred out that he couldn't see, the periphery enclosed on itself.

He decided that he trusted his eyes, so he rolled off the bed in a fit of confidence. His legs didn't roll as much so he windshield-wiped the bed and off with his head first. He found himself on his stomach on the floor. He could feel a change in his breathing but it seemed to go back to normal. He tried to raise an arm off the ground and place it further out in front of him, but his arm just dragged along the floor. He slinked it back to pull himself a few hairs closer. He proceeded to initiate a rolling maneuver; once forwardish onto his back, then he could use his elbows to lean on and crab backwards. It was risky because it was narrow between the bed and the wall.

He executed. The result left the middle of his back off the ground and a pressure on his shoulder that again changed his breathing. He decided to wait a moment.

His heart returned to what would have been normal, and he drove his elbow off the wall to scoot backwards towards the corner between him and the door. He cleared it after four scoots, saw the bag after three, and two more before he was at the bag. His arm climbed to the zipper.

Despite the low light and his state, a short zip revealed the metallic sheen of the corner of his laptop. His heartbeat changed again. He waited again, trying to recover his focus.

He pulled the bag on top of him and part of the laptop slid out onto his chest. He pawed at it and it fell out and off his chest onto the ground, leaning upright against his side. He leaned his head to the wide and lifted his arm to the side of the computer. He feebly tried to peel it open. Eventually it took.

He tried to prepare to input his password but ended up smathering his keyboard and hitting enter. He took time to recover.

Then he pulled the laptop onto his stomach again and stabilized it. He forced his will above the effects of the drug to lift his hand above the keyboard, index finger pointing down, and prod until his password was typed.

His desktop emerged, a clean space. Like a yuppie's apartment, it was neatly barebones, though not quite as sanitary. It would have been barer if it weren't for a bit of clutter, assorted poems and thoughts he had scribbled on a notepad and saved there, underthought titles always jarring him for a moment or ignored entirely. He thought over the names of a few of them, *Judith Butthurt*, a short realistic satire he had spammed on the Board for a while about an unnamed prominent feminist's public masturbation sprees, *Gehymen*, an uncompleted cross-cultural jest about the taboo of denying the prominence of Nazism through the sexual exploration of a 1970s SS officer's daughter, and other unfulfilled projects that had sometimes (but rarely) haunted him.

The next step was much more rewarding: to open the browser and drag the cursor to the bookmarked tab for his favorite live-streaming platform. It was no small feat of subtlety and coordination to navigate the trackpad, but he did it, and his adrenaline began to flow as he gazed upon the familiar purple logo of the site.

An error message popped, however, removing any hope he had left in his life. He wasn't connected to the hotel's WiFi. His stock in himself depreciated so far in this moment that he resigned to take a nap right there with his laptop open on his belly, and he did.

He fell into a blur about the state of things. In his blur, he was King Heiko the unforgivable, a wretch long isolated by his family without the personal ability to exile them. He faced a condemnation of whimsicality. His impulses had been long dulled by statesmanhood, and, as such, he didn't feel sorry for himself, and every apologetic moment was reacted to irrationally. He was tucked far away within his own kingdom, Wilhelmshaven, in a massive court that was entirely empty other than his throne, himself, a purple rug, and two Sphinxes at his flank who chattered endlessly back and forth, neither realizing the other was a Sphinx and hurling only rhetoric and riddles back and forth at each other, in front of him and all around him at the same time.

"What can burn for a lifetime or be killed with a whim,

Only to revive without a visible dim?"

"Nothing else but that which has clear analogue,

In humanity's greatest vision,

Resulting in a greater fog,

The inaccuracy of precision."

"And clarity's own cousin making friends afar,

The world itself a small bazaar."

"Small in ways, large in this,

That every life can here be stored,

Deep down in this abyss,

Only trouble brings troubles toward."

"But in such as this unnamed case, would we not,

Finally remove this cancerous rot?"

"When does tumor become the host,

And when is life decided?

And how far is this, man's greatest ghost,

Its own life misguided?"

"What kills a spirit, once, for all,

And rids him from this very hall?"

To this, the King spoke, booming, "I have no use for veiled banter. Should not the truth present itself so?"

To which one of the Sphinxes replied, "but what is truth? Is truth unchanging law? We both have truths; are mine the same as yours?"

The crowd chanted, impassioned, "CRUCIFY HIM! CRUCIFY HIM! CRUCIFY HIM!"

And the King's rug was pulled out from under his feet and he fell from his crown, suspended purplish and gold above him, more of a circle from this perspective. The court became a yard, the Sphinxes Romans, cat-like yet but not enough to disregard legality. He was nailed to a circle, the same rim of the crown, spinning and bleeding with concentric trails of red on his body. The blood dried into an alphabet, both runic and phonetic, and the Sphinx-Nazis, dog-like, sniffed him as concrete was poured and set on the courtyard. They began to lick him, erasing thousands of generations of linguistic indices as they lapped the curdled blood. The blood drove them red and sick.

As they lied down and died in front of him, the stakes in his arms loosened from the crown, and he stepped down, closing the dogs' eyelids as they whimpered to death. He looked up into the sun, a mass of gray with red bleeding out and pooling on the horizon, and the red began to spill over the distant mountains. He could see the violence with which it rushed from afar, and knew that it would catch him soon, yet he did not turn his back.

"I got cat," he called out to his teammates.

They called back, "rotate to A, quick quick quick quick."

"I have no smoke to cover me," he argued.

"You're going to die there."

So he found and threw a smoke that came off the tip of a cigarette in the ripe lips of a soft-featured face so close but so soft, an infinitely-sided figure, like the circle of a crown with red eyes. And it was Effy, standing outside her mother's apartment in the snowy street, shivering, slushy, crying into a cigarette by herself.

"I'm rotating—"

"There's no time."

"I'm rotating—"

"You're not going to make it."

"I'm rotating—"

And he died there, shot by a Sphinx, who stood above him.

"What can burn for a lifetime or be killed with a whim,

Only to revive without a visible dim?"

When he awoke, the laptop was still there. His neck felt immobile, but with a bit of easing-in he managed to pull it off the ground and unblur his eyes on the backlit screen in front of him. He still felt his coordination lacking, but he was able to sluggishly reenter his password, several fingers used this time, and remember his dilemma: he had to get up to collect the WiFi password.

...

Deep into the lit, weeks afterward and after weeks of easing into culture that didn't stop his heart, "and if we're looking for examples of an excellent semi-recent post-moralist story, the kind of unique situation of our age's foundation, we need to look no further than the folk-rock sound that was eminent in the honky-tonk *Rocky Raccoon*. In order to properly interpret this surprisingly coherent story, we must assume something about the crime of passion: that there are powers in this world, and that it feels bad to feel weak: we live in a sublime 'do or die' world, so there's an obscurity and depth to our situation, a deep lack of common that can drive the most *reasonable* of individuals to extreme ends."

"In the story, we have Rocky, who begins in the very-deeply obscure flatland that is the Black Mountain Hills of Dakota. The perspective of the narrator is fairly neutral, so I believe it's fair to say that that was an adequate summary of events with little added. There could have been a dramatic brawl that he lost; there could have been a random sucker punch and his woman, Magill, self-proclaimed Lil, popularly known as Nancy, could have run off with the aggressive man. Regardless, Rocky was in a tough place, so he goes to a saloon where he presumably knows they will be."

"He goes into his room and finds Gideon's Bible, but he disregards it because he has a gun. It's a delicious inversion of power that he has power, and, more importantly, that he has the strength of spirit. After all, he had been crushed past existential crisis. Magill, Lil, or Nancy was with her man, Dan, and they showed up to the hoe down. Rocky comes in, challenged Dan in a honorable manner, an imperative that showed the homosocial comradery-of-enemy, a fatalism-in-courtliness. But we are again reminded who had the power, and Daniel pulled his weapon and shot poor old Rocky boy into the corner. What a *great* scene."

"Then the rationalist appears, a defeated will, hunched-over after years of abuse, and offers Rocky the easy way out: *stop*. The democratic answer sways from that of the higher individual occasionally, but it is worth mentioning that these subtle differences of opinion tend to result in great changes. Rocky replies with strength that he will recover and hurt that man; he will be absolved, and his spirit may move to the next trap."

"He goes back to the saloon, where he finds again Gideon's Bible. Gideon had surely left it 'to help with good Rocky's revival,' but Rocky hadn't yet died. In fact, he was stronger now than ever, needing least a morality to strangle his spirit. *Why would Gideon leave his Bible there?*"

"And what is this *revival*? What happened to the *rebirth*? The former surely implies a continuation of sorts, that he would be spawned back again right where he had left off. What perspective changes with mere revival? I'd love to see a premeditated murderer shot-in-the-act being brought back to life, only to go on a small rampage, a very *liberating* experience."

But where did this leave the man frequently under the owl mask? Here he was—destitutely removed from the common of anyone; he was the noman or at least from his perspective, deformed from his first genius, that murderous sawing of the fiddle that he had poured himself into; it was the very hardness of his father, a degree he had long ago exceeded as a result of the fall, that had thrown him into the depth of hardship; he was refined, bred out of a great lineage of spirit and cultivated to a high standard; his father and his father's forefathers were creators, and, like his father's forefathers, his father had inspired in him a lack of pity, a creative situation—writing a post-moralist interpretation of an English-Dakotan folk ballad. Needless to say, he had a drive to create just as he was created.

...

Why was *he* here? Well, he reasoned that he was in this titanic city after being invited to meet the heads, which meant that he might be a head. Why was he *here*? He realized that he had no idea what he was doing in the titanic city, and his few face-saving friends had recommended this club for its luxury.

The logistical operation that stood in his way was a winding staircase lit by the pulse of the music, silhouetted figures holding their faces stumbling down or huddled in a corner they seemed to have created. The walls were pitch black, unnavigable and a gentle reminder of the void that he may be entering, heart racing to the beat. The Russian's back gleamed with sweat; he was quite muscular, clearly a servant of this exact circumstance, in his white shirt, and Bahman's drug stupor had left him unwilling to consider any sort of further hostility by this point.

He managed to climb the first step, and the second, and the third, until a Chinese girl fell on him at the fourth step, both looking at their feet until she hit her head square on his chest and looked up, meeting his eyes, and hers were the darkest thing he had ever seen. Void oceans, uncharted, pitied his shallow existence, simultaneously screamed for help and knew that he couldn't pull her out of there. Her fair cream face clashed like a mask, and he wondered what sort of rite, what depravity of collective psyche he was stumbling into that this soul had been meaninglessly thrust into nothingness, that she was a casualty of bigger things that she had no part of, that this was someone's little girl and now she was someone's little girl, long lost and drowned out in the night that wouldn't end.

He thought about kissing her after she broke his gaze and continued down the steps. He thought he heard her sob before the music took over again. He looked back upwards, now on the sixth step, only a few more to go as he wound blindly and pairs walked past him arm-around-shoulder, head in hands. Pure sorrow in the most joyful place in the world. He felt himself clenching his jaw and the peripherals of feeling closing in around him, a tingling sensation telling him he was happy just as he thought about a single bead of sweat leaving the Russian's armpit headed for his elbow, past a crafted tricep and thinking for the strangest reason that he wanted to taste its saltiness as if that would return him to his own direction.

He lost track of it around the ninth step as the Russian lifted an arm to nonchalantly wave at a Chinese man in a similar white shirt and tall hair, a man whose callousness informed the music itself, changing the beat to something mechanical. The Chinese man flagged back blankly as Bahman climbed the last step, surrounded now by a panorama of new lights, tables, unconscious people and pupils, heads leaning. The energy was low but seemed as if it was returning upon his arrival, a refreshed low-light curiosity, a passive impassive perking up and suppression of the other influences of the night, namely the reorganized beat and the massive multi-tiered chandelier above the dance floor at eye-level to the balcony, something Bahman hadn't noticed when he was under it but quickly lost himself in.

Rows and columns of independently-operating lights formed a grid of swaying energy, pure white and untouched by everything below it, something religious with certainty, something that would inspire hope in a cynic, the arrhythmic motion clashing with every other sound and light in the entire production, a soft wave moving across the floor giving influence from above, or, for those on the balcony, from a wavering eye-to-eye level as the lights rose and fell in perfect non-synchronicity. At his level, the lights appeared two dimensional, forming a complicated pattern of rises and falls that could only be simulated by nature.

...

The routine of it all had set him deep in a rut, a sort of state of permanent reflection because there was nothing new to see anyway. There was, in front of him with mustachioed grins and various background colors, several tins of different-flavored crisps: paprika red (Heiko's favorite), sour cream green (what is sour cream?), barbecue brown (where does this barbecue come from?), classic darkish red (what flavor is classic?), and the off-putting orange of the cheese crisps. Unfortunately, he preferred the off-putting orange.

He had two consecutive unanswered texts from Effy, which never happened, but he was in a special place. He had typed out two drafts and deleted both.

The first was this: "Why are flowers always so tragic?"

The second was this: "I tried to find the appropriate emoji but I couldn't."

He had also an unanswered-for vision, something he couldn't quite respond to, of Heiko standing before him, trying and failing to keep all the meat, grease, and pickled vegetables from falling out of the back of the wrap, his hand pooling the spillage with a tinge of regret, the leaning over the counter, the individual, big bites.

It was the vision that inhibited his ability to answer the texts. It confounded him, to see something that wasn't there so vividly, something that would never be so vivid again, something that had been spoiled by the light, like anything left out in the sun too long or maybe more like those greasy Americans that go into tanning machines and come out orange on reality TV. Maybe they call them 'stars' because of how they lead the rest of us to rot. Maybe there weren't two separate metaphors but instead an interpretation that lays gently above both of them, connecting them in an uncertain and otherwordly way, some reasoning that doesn't work in the real world but applied perfectly to this situation.

There was Heiko, the flower, or maybe the author of the flower, the press that gives attar, the agent that takes the idea of the flower and turns it into some product that is more than accessible, visual to the nose, the essence that we spray on our lives or in our foyers, and some circumstance led to a mishandling of the machinery, the press jammed under its own pressure. It's stuck with an embossed flower somewhere in the middle of it, completely removed of all its precious oil, squeezed dry. And here was this vision of him, a goofy strain on his face as he tries to catch everything backfiring out of his favorite daily treat. Was it his own indulgence that did him in – this tasty treat? The parallels were there, the references to sock-cake in stories of his childhood, and here this dürüm was wrapped in something of a sock, a tubular napkin that is mutually dependent on its contents.

And there he was, dry and compressed, like a sock-cake would be.

...

The sight was one to get lost in as if he wasn't lost already in this neon wilderness. The rail that he was leaning over to gaze out at the lights was invisible except the thin white line on its top, apparently floating like a wire holding his elbows and keeping him from falling into the void of Russian and Chinese strippers below, a fate that he may have wished on himself in times of less serotonin. As such, he retreated from the ledge, knowing that he would soon be depleted into the very state of consideration, the great gray of nightlife.

As he retreated, shocked by his own fear of it all, his arm was grabbed and his attention brought to his rear-left, where he again saw the blond, muscled Russian.

"Here, now," the Russian reassured him. The syntax could have inspired some more fear in him, but its simplicity actually made him feel a little bit better about the plan of it all, as if the Russian wasn't commanding him but simply informing him of a bigger picture.

And there was a bigger picture. At the most distant point of the Russian's extended, open hand was a large booth with two Chinese gentlemen, four Chinese women in full club regalia, a number of Russian high-end prostitutes, one darker-looking man, possibly Middle-Eastern, one square-jawed fair-complexioned dark-haired man in a suit (everyone else was in a suit or equally as formal, but the rest of the whites in the club were dressed very casually, so this one stood out), and what could have the Russian guide's brother, father, or son, equally as weak-chinned, stocky-necked, and hard-browed.

The whole table was its own universe looking down and out on him, clearly caught up in themselves beforehand and interrupted only by his spawning. He was a certain uncertainty that had certainly not been there before, though he was expected, his presence being some sort of break from belief, a judgment of all predispositions and finality to it all.

He saw reflected in the eyes of the whores the same void, the same optical illusions he had seen in the other girl who was stumbling down the steps in his last life, and he wondered if their reflection was his reflection or what his eyes would seem like to them and if they were thinking the exact same thing about infinities in the finite spaces of eyes, those organs of all and nothing at once and never simultaneous, the visual representation of their change in appearance when they looked at him, that very break from belief, judgment of all predispositions and finality to it all.

The Russian pulled him towards them, and his fears were realized. He did know David. In fact, there was David, right there, ethnically-ambiguous but now clearly Mexican, a new finality of identity that he had been looking for and avoiding all night.

...

These things finish just like they start. His pupils looked starrier than they did on that special night, the night of the stars, the night with the star, light leaking from something long ago dead and forming something mystical, something that a lesser-educated man would sacrifice a lamb to. Minutiae to some is eternity to others, getting lost in Babylon's burnt library.

The vision persisted and then became something aural. The memory manifested in the perfect projection of his voice, not a representation but something genuine and new, a structure that he had never used, in English, "bomb down, cat."

Ihsan, stunned by the image in his mind, didn't want to imagine speaking to himself in this solitary shop, so he didn't reply.

Heiko continued, "are you there? I'm watching under, there's nothing here."

Ihsan clenched his jaw, trying to feel if it was real.

"I think he's rotating cat."

Ihsan knew he didn't know enough English to dream with what sounded like fluent English.

"I'm moving cat." At this, Heiko scanned the counter, grabbed a pair of scissors from underneath a pile of receipt papers, turned, and walked out the door.

Ihsan was relieved that it was over, and then it dawned on him.

...

"You must be Mr. Guó."

"Yes. My name is Mr. Guò."

"Nice to meet you, Mr. Guó. My name is Jake."

"Hello Jay-kuh. Nice to see you."

"Very nice to meet you too. Sit down, and we will look at the book."

"Hao-de."

"OKAY. Dickie tells me that you work with computers."

"Yes. My job is a IT."

"Very cool. Do you know what IT stands for?"

"Stands for..."

Jake stands up and writes "stands for..." on the board and then "IT -" below.

"It STANDS FOR information..."

"Information..."

He writes "T E C H..."

"Tetch, techn, techno-"

"Technology! Exactly. Great job, Mr. Guó."

"Information technology."

"Very good job, Mr. Guó, do you like working in IT?"

"Ha ha."

"OKAY, so why do you learn English?"

"I don't use it in work."

"But why do you WANT to learn?"

"I like movies."

"Oh, wow! I love movies too. Do you also like to travel?"

"No."

"Ha ha. Do you like American movies?"

"Yes. Zach Damon."

"Ohhh. That's funny. Those are actually Chinese movies."

"Actually Chinese movies."

"Yes, the director, the man who makes the movies, is a Chinese person."

"Makes the movies. Zhang Li!"

"Yes. He's the director of the movies."

"I love its movies."

"Yes, you love his movies. So at this school, we like to study things that you like. We can talk about movies, music, or traveling!"

"I don't like travel."

"Ha ha, that's okay, too. We can talk about anything with our VIP class. Are you interested in the VIP class?"

"What's mean?"

"VIP classes are one on one. Just you and me, or another foreign teacher. If you like me, you can tell Apple, and then we'll only have class together."

"One and one."

"Yes, exactly!"

...

David is Mendez, he realized, *David Mendez*. The name fell through his consciousness, from on the very top of the spiral bouncing odds and end downward into the widening gaps back and forth, the rainbow road in a cavity tremendous. Profound darkness surrounded him, the helix translucent and upon further inspection transparent, and then nothing at all and he was completely there with the name of a face or a face of a name floating around with him in there, still bouncing off the winding and widening invisible structure.

Out of the space he came, and then he realized he really was in Space. The moment had been particularly chilled, arctic, by some infinity of silence between songs in the set, the limits with which time passes murky in this state. What he realized was realized forever ago, something to undermine our most basic law, that two sounds would never touch, no matter how good the mix. The first beat ended, and the second began, but the nominatives and the conjunction couldn't be hidden. Never the two shall meet. There wasn't a moment that they started or stopped, or there was a moment to him for a moment, but the moment couldn't have been the same for the deep-eyed girl who was surely losing her kidneys in a hotel to organ thieves by now. And this association burned him, fueled his trajectory across the space, and he considered that there was no moment when she died, no moment that the gentle man who called the police in the morning would notice she died, or there was a moment to him but not to her or the rest of us, and this relativity broke the truth of the situation like the two beats sent him into an aimless trip across a starry sky without stars. The very language he was using broke down into a vague attempt to categorize things for convenience, a sort of eternal compromise that could be practiced until the vast majorities would rapture at the ability of a DJ to keep a beat. It was almost a machine, this DJ and his laptop, and his set, but not quite, though the *not quite* wasn't as praised here in this space as others he had been in. His oranger appearances surely were based on some dose of compromise deemed entertaining, some would say ironic, some would say aware, but they weren't. He was, in fact, a bad compromise.

And there the face was, and the name. It undermined everything else. There was no compromise here. What was there was there.

Was there was there.

Was there.

...

"Heiko! HEIKO!" He moved his hips around the corner of the counter, eyes on the door, saw Heiko take an aggressive right, a motivated right, the very right that you don't want to see your friend take with a pair of scissors.

He moved past the crisps and out into the blinding sun, one of those special Berlin days when the men would be naked in the park, and looked right to find Heiko approaching a black man, bent over and petting a street cat. The black man looked up and his eyes opened wide. Ihsan was the only member of the event with the knowledge of every other member. It was clearer than the daylight that the black man saw nothing except what was immediately in front of him and same went for the young German.

"HEIKO NO!" The scissors were at his side, handle against blade, held open and cutting Heiko's hands open under the pressure he was putting on them. It was clear to all.

Heiko moved without hesitation, raising his hand laterally and slashing cross-ways at the man who held his hands up in fearful defense. The hands repelled the first swing, but there was no hope after that.

The second swipe, a quick second, also hit the hands and a bit of the arm of the man, a little bit down the road and spreading wide a seam that had never before been found; then you see how fleshy the body is.

After the second, he had to recover for a moment for another two, pulling his arm back again, and Ihsan was running at him to do something, but he didn't yet know what. The moment was vapor.

Fifteen meters from a collision, Heiko attacked again, this time reaching between the arms to the throat, and fate was immediately wide open on the man's neck. This kind of blow takes the hope right out of a person. The eyes open wider than the wound in some cases, like this one.

The quick second was slowed by Heiko's arm caught between his victim's arm and neck, but sure enough it ripped backwards towards Heiko's body and right back through the same area it had landed the first time, though not on the same path. Resistance was finally over.

And then Ihsan tackled Heiko from behind, who had just pulled the blade towards himself. The pair slammed into the ground and a screaming emerged. It soared briefly before it disappeared, replaced by exasperated agony, the painful sounds of distress.

Ihsan tried to tie up Heiko's arms, but Heiko struggled to keep his arms tucked around his chest and rolled backwards with Ihsan, and then Ihsan saw the bloody handle of the scissors partially lodged in Heiko's chest. The blade was through him and poking out the other side, though modestly.

Ihsan shuffled around his growing-limp friend and set him down gently, perched over him to assess the gravity of the situation. He looked at him.

...

So now there's Bahman, something bad between cooperation and coordination, and there's David, surrounded by nameless and faceless entities in a sea of purple black. David would certainly have something to say, and Bahman certainly had nothing. There was the question of *why was David in China* that could easily be answered with some simple arrangement, but the arrangement didn't quite answer *why* as much as *how* or *what for*, a semantic device he sorely missed in English despite its presence. It was, in effect, lost in space as a term. The spiral had closed back in on itself and nowhere in the free fall did Bahman notice this piece of language, though he hadn't noticed much language at all, but it was dawning on him at the end of the helix that he would have to come out the other side and again show a mastery of mediocre compromise in communication in a dreadfully free language, fluent for him by this point, aphasic even. There would be the introductions of new, informative nominatives, and then a brief bit on the darkness around them, and then the settling of wills, his own of which he was not sure, and insofar as he was uncertain, he was certain that he didn't want to be there. When had that lucid moment crossed the threshold? Was it when the big black man didn't like him? Was it when he first looked at the Russian's white, tightish V? Was it when he looked in her eyes? Was it when he looked into the sea of people under the waves of lights? Was it when he saw David's face?

He tried to avoid looking like he was scurrying over, something more nonchalant than that, but he felt his pace wasn't right. The same snap-out-of-it of logistics were paralleled in thinking about his feet moving one after the other, about where his chest and shoulders were, about where there eyes were, and about what were behind their eyes. He managed what he felt was a cool smile, hiding his flaccidity. The whole trip had taken all of his edge away, and he sorely regretted it all, the orange faces in helicopters, stringy snot rockets not his own, a false intimacy that lent everyone an edge over him, a deep exposure that was made manifest in his unknowing of this situation.

From an objective standpoint, there was on the table a well-lit bottle of cognac, several chrome carafes, an elaborate bouquet of arranged fruits with a watermelon rind for a base, confetti, and golden packs of cigarettes with their golden ashtray counterparts. The entire table was topped with glass, underlit with a smooth and soft white glow.

David subtly waved him over as if to be warm in this vacuum, something human that inspired change in their agent of hope. Bahman's cool smile warmed; he touched the edge of the circle.

"Nice to see you again, David," he affected, booming far under the music.

"Bahman, mi hermano, meet my friends. This is Wallace Stevenson, " in the suit with the jaw, who was perched professional-defensively between a Russian and a Chinese prostitute and reached forward to crush Bahman's hand, "this is Xiao Jinlu," one of the suited Chinese, who now obviously overshadowed the others in presence, gave Bahman the slightest of nods, "and this is Artur Vodovatov," now understood to be the figurative patriarchal figure of the relatively smallish V-necked Russian guide who had led him in here and was yet slightly cowering behind the Turk. "Thank you for joining us tonight."

"The pleasure is mine, comrades, *friends*," though he wasn't quite pleased with this overt charming, this trip he was on was confusing his proportionality, and he recovered quickly, "and all these beautiful women, do they have names?"

At this the Chinaman leaned back, the American's jaw clenched, and the Russian smiled. David laughed, at ease, "you can ask them yourself, perro, take a seat," he gestured at a space that Bahman could now see was waiting for him, a sort of head or tail of the table, a lush chair with two arms that were designed for women to lounge on around the interrogated.

He sat down and smiled at the two women who moved to join him on either end, and, as they sat down to frame him as a sort of mercenary-king, he smiled famously and wide-eyed at the group and reassured all of them of his ability.

"There he is, gentlemen, our man," David looked around for confidence. "Do you know why you're our man, Bahman?"

"I'm afraid don't know what you're talking about, no." His own answer put a pressure on his shoulders that made him pull the women into him defensively.

"Do you like America?"

"It's a nice place, yes." He felt his body heating up in anticipation, maybe heating up as it reentered the atmosphere at an incredible rate.

"We're going to bring you to America," the home of the brave.

...

The inversion of the situation took the fury out of his eyes, now looking like a mortally-wounded puppy rediscovering the most visceral of virtues, that life itself is precious and fragile at that, that everything up until this point had a lack of meaning; a large arch-like structure without a keystone is a pile of bricks.

His friend looked him in the eye, still holding the scissors limply, and saw the sock-cake eater again, a gentle person who couldn't will harm on anyone—the vacuous eyes of a creature without hope. After their eyes broke each other's, they both dropped to the hand on the handle sticking out of Heiko's chest. Not knowing whether to leave the open scissors in or take them out, Ihsan resigned his hand from the handle and put it on his friend's whimpering face. The universe existed within this moment, but, outside of it, police approached on foot and an ambulance was en route. As the men shouted at him to get down and put his hands behind his back, he rolled off of Heiko and onto his back, sobbing and reaching to the sky, his leg resting in the pool of blood that had already asphyxiated the artist, who had stopped choking by now. Where was the cat?

The police cordoned off the scene and the paramedics rushed in, strapping a sedated-dying mostly-bleeding Heiko to a bed wheeling him towards their vehicle, scissors still in his chest. Per the frantic corroboration of a few onlookers, Ihsan was not detained, though a policeman was trying to crowd control his personal crowd. Ihsan broke from the man and caught up to the paramedics and Heiko, who looked empty and emptier by the moment. They raised the bed and slid him into the back of the ambulance. They began the busy work of caring for his wound, pulling a voiced sigh out of him as they removed the scissors, revealing two slit-like punctures, and replaced it with pressure. He heaved, head upright enough to look at Ihsan, eternity, then fell back on the bed, dead. No more döner, night lights, or looking at naked old men in the park with Effy, and certainly no more paprika-flavored chips.

Ihsan had the blood of the other victims on his chest, hands, and face after the struggle. Never had he seen so much spirit, never something so great in humanity as the desire to kill or be killed, never had he been strong enough to imagine he could have killed anyone, much less his crazed, gentle friend. Even given the uncertainty of the recent weeks, he would not have guessed that he would learn so much today. He couldn't go back to the store and work long hours with no customers or the occasional wandering drunk looking for less savory snacks. The thought of it alone took all the blood off him, out of him, and promised to murder him again after he had just barely survived.

And the thought that the others didn't survive struck him, that two of three people were going to die today, and he wasn't one of them, a fantastic logic that belongs only in the most spirited, a fatality. It wasn't that he was going to kill the others, but that the others were going to be killed, and he was the only other in the situation, so it became a sort of choice without a choice that he would decide to kill the others, or that they would be killed, not that he killed both of them, or did he? Was he too slow running after Heiko? Should he have thought to hide the scissors? Or would that have killed him? Would it have killed him to stop this from happening?

Then the charging tone, screeching with familiarity, straight out of the movies, as the paramedics prepared the defibrillator unit. They shocked once, twice, three times, and, on the forth, Heiko sprung back upright, fury returned to his eyes, another delicious inversion, and he freed his arm from its strap in a magnificently-coordinated motion, reaching to a table behind one of the men in blue, grabbed the bloody scissors, and began slashing indiscriminately, a tangle of bodies, screaming, crying, thrashing, then cutting the straps and freeing his upper body after the two attendants collapsed bleeding from their throats, faces, arms, and chests. He sat upright, dislodging much of the gauze that had been carefully pressed into his own wound, starting again to bleed freely, looking vacuous again and staring at Ihsan for a moment, who was frozen between fear and indecision, or maybe a resignation. Heiko's eyes turned sympathetic again as the blood flowed out of him, onto the bed and onto the floor of the ambulance, where it mingled with the blood of his enemies, where it would dry to crust as it spread itself thin, another indiscriminate signature on the metal and pouring now onto the concrete below the van. Heiko died with two paramedics choking on blood next to him, and Ihsan considered whether they were meant to die. He fainted in the shallow red pool, giving his own head a slight bump in the process, as the police surged towards the commotion.

...

After nine months of dwindling or swindling joy, a baby boy was born with swollen eyes crusted shut. The doctors saw the problem coming, dosing him with an antibiotic ointment of erythromycin within minutes, but it had no effect over the next week.

The doctors prescribed a regimen of continued doses for the child, warning of the potential for side effects like pyloric stenosis, a narrowing of the valve at the bottom of the stomach.

The baby spit up or vomited much of the breast milk it was fed, but a system of vitamins and formula seemed to keep the boy healthy enough to be on track to develop somewhat normally.

The boy's eyes didn't open for six weeks. He was named Eric. He was formally diagnosed with the stenosis via ultrasound just before they opened, though they had been treating the disease prior to this with electrolyte correction. They considered surgery.

Epilogue

Twelve weeks later, when the initial depression transitioned into a medium-term slump, Ihsan curiously visited the Board after having a vague knowledge of its existence from all the recent media coverage.

The first Pepe he saw had wings; in the background, which seemed below Pepe, was a decapitated Wojak face glaring upwards. The head was a part of a archipelago of bits of his body in a brown lake.

The second Pepe he saw made him question his limited knowledge of Pepe. It was the same colors for the same features, but the Pepe was done in the spitting image of a bearded young man, more Caucasian than he but a bit ambiguous ethnically.

The third Pepe he saw was labeled 'medium-rare,' and it was both a smaller resolution and an objectively-worse, slightly off-color rendition of the frog.

The fourth Pepe he saw was eating Skittles and drinking Arizona tea, and it was black. The signs called forth something in his memory but he couldn't find an association.

The fifth Pepe he saw was framed inside some sort of trading card, with health and cum levels full. It was a relatively common-looking Pepe, but it had an ability at the bottom: "Deceive: pretend to be a normie, achieve maximum levels of smug."

The sixth Pepe he saw was the first one that faced the left. Its eyes were closed in pleasure. There was a speech bubble that sort of melted into itself. It read: "feels big cum."

The seventh Pepe he saw was not a Pepe in body but rather in spirit. It was a fork with five cuts of steak, labeled and ranged from rare to well-done.

The eighth Pepe he saw was a negative image of the original that had a certain blur of focus around the facial features.

The ninth Pepe he saw was trying unsuccessfully to put his head between his legs and lick himself. The face was strained.

The tenth Pepe he saw was wearing a mask and had a gun.

The eleventh Pepe he saw was paddling a crying Wojak who was bent over with his bruised ass showing. The tears were streaming and the face was in anguish, but Pepe was smug as ever.

The twelfth Pepe he saw was clearly a sketch of him, stabbing Pepe in a blood-covered mint-green hospital gown. He was Wojak, the same crying, anguished Wojak. The Pepe had huge black pupils, and there were also three lifeless bodies bleeding around them, right outside the back of an ambulance. The scene was incorrectly depicted though a likely order—that Heiko stabbed all three before Ihsan intervened instead of the reality that Ihsan stabbed him after he stabbed Dougie but before he stabbed the paramedics.

The thirteenth Pepe he saw was extra smug with the signature Cheese Whiz hairpiece. It was Donald Trump in an ontological or maybe a semiotic sense, but also just directly in appearance. He was at a podium with an American flag behind him. On the front of the podium was a banner with his face on it, similar to the "feels big cum" Pepe he previously saw. It read: "Make America Good Man."

The fourteenth Pepe he saw was a hooded jacket that Wojak was wearing. The jacket was the green of Pepe's face and only his sad eyes at the top of the hood really revealed it as Pepe. The Wojak was distant, face partially covered by his drawn hood.

The fifteenth Pepe he saw was the first one that he really related to. It was actually many screaming Pepe faces blended into a sea of green, which sort of looked like a textured carpet at first, an angsty shag carpet. Below the faces, little Pepe arms stood up indignantly and uniformly.

The sixteenth Pepe he saw was the first one he associated with a self-sustained aesthetic, the first one that had its own sort of association despite it being clearly thematized by an external movement – the '90s. This Pepe had a little propeller on a multicolored bucket-ish hat, and the Pepe was youthful and even cute.

The seventeenth Pepe he saw was a bee, and its face was gray rather than green.

The eighteenth Pepe he saw was himself, walking away from the massacre scene of the ambulance with several bleeding-dying Wojaks.

The nineteenth Pepe he saw was an actual frog, only slightly morphed from what could have been a children's cartoon. The frog had a number of warts, and the face had only been slightly adapted from the original to match the meme. The color scheme was exact, though if it wasn't, the picture could have been mistaken for a non-meme.

The twentieth Pepe he saw was full-framed with an erect penis that seemed mid-throb. It was equally smug, but it seemed to have been drawn by an amateur. The non-copy-pasted part of his head was a little too round for the face. The body was somewhat in the posture of David.

The twenty-first Pepe he saw was Europe, but it wasn't smug. It was a sad Pepe.

The twenty-second Pepe he saw was a dead, fat Pepe on a hospital bed with a wide-open cut bleeding some thick orange substance. Littered around it was various fast food paraphernalia.

The twenty-third Pepe he saw was a hat in the colors of Pepe but without any other distinguishable traits in common. Upon further inspection, however, the white sheet that the hat was on seemed to have a slight discoloration, certainly a dried cum stain left by the proud owner of the hat.

The twenty-fourth Pepe he saw was another part of this internet aesthetic that he felt he was beginning to recognize. The Pepe was transparent, and in its foreground or background was part of a ceramic bust, several Japanese characters, and a grid of staticky pink and purple.

The twenty-fifth Pepe he saw was an intergalactic Pepe, possibly the smuggest of them all, and in his eyes glowed several constellations brighter than anything else in that sky.

The twenty-sixth Pepe was an octopus raping Wojak in his mouth, anus, and down his urethra. Wojak was crying with the same face of anguish.

The twenty-seventh Pepe was a watercolor with shit smeared on for his grin.

The twenty-eighth Pepe was again in the aesthetic, and next to its smile was a well-endowed anime maid who was bursting out the bottom of her skirt as well as out the front of her blouse. In the corner was the logo of Windows 95.

The twenty-ninth Pepe he saw was melted into the face of an American sitcom character, the name of whom and which he could not place. The character was smug and holding a baseball bat in front of a chain link fence. It was more photoshopped than drawn in a a simple, free painting application, a higher quality but not necessarily rare Pepe.

The thirtieth Pepe he saw was Japanese and it was spearing Chinese infants on its bayonet, smug.

The thirty-first Pepe he saw was facing the left, and its body was frumpy at best and featured a limb of some sort extending from its ass cheeks. The limb itself had ass cheeks, and only on looking at these cheeks did he realize that the Pepe had a dick coming out of its butt. The butt had a bit of hair on it as did the shaft of the dick. The Pepe's legs were stubby, significantly shorter than its dick.

The thiry-second Pepe he saw was threatening with a gun and a wig that sat on his head strangely and made his whole head look look lumpy.

The thirty-third Pepe he saw was eating KFC.

The thirty-fourth Pepe he saw was a 3D rendition of an orc fucking a decapitated elven Wojak head. Wojak was, of course, in anguish.

The thirty-fifth Pepe he saw was larger, leaned back, and dressed as a black American gangster. Its gold-frame glasses matched its huge golden chain.

The thirty-sixth Pepe he saw was a shark.

The thirty-seventh Pepe he saw was a Godzilla-sized mass of its own faces and huge, erect dicks. All of the Pepes were spewing shit over a crumbling city.

The thirty-eighth Pepe he saw was on the body of a bent-over girl wearing shorts that hugged her pussy and asshole to a lewd degree. It was sad, but most of its face was cut off in the picture, leaving half a frown and deflated eyes.

The thirty-ninth Pepe he saw was Jesus. Its scene was borrowed directly from a film Heiko had made him watch – *Jesus Christ Superstar*. Pepe's face was in agony, and its throat was inflated like a frog's would. Its arm was outstretched, and it was wearing a white robe. The figure was pleading on top of a rock.

The fortieth Pepe he saw was the Illuminati Pink Floyd jihadist cyclops Pepe, and it was quite smug.

The forty-first Pepe he saw was Dougie Wallace, dressed in violet and sex, playing a smooth black bass guitar, smug as a cat.

The forty-second Pepe he saw was smug with the caption "when your signature strain of gonorrhea hits the mainstream."

The forty-third Pepe he saw was wearing a breathing mask connected to a tank marked 'memes.'

The forty-fourth Pepe he saw was Lena in the leaked interview. It was black, but it was enraged red at the same time. It looked like it was screaming.

The forty-fifth Pepe he saw was Donald Trump, but this rendition was flattering.

The forty-sixth Pepe he saw was Donald Trump, this time in an SS uniform.

The forty-seventh Pepe he saw was Donald Trump standing half-behind a podium with a MAGA poster on it, cumming on the face of a kneeled Barry Sanders.

The forty-eighth Pepe he saw was Osama Bin Laden with a large volume of goat-fucking pornography.

The forty-ninth Pepe he saw was a stitch of Shrek's facial features from various scenes. The textures clashed into a picture that almost seemed to have a smell.

The fiftieth Pepe he saw was a member of ISIS. It was extra smug because it was sitting in a French cafe wearing a black mask with a visible erection.

The fifty-first Pepe he saw was Donald Trump but cartoonish with beautiful blue eyes and blond hair. It playfully glanced towards the viewer and left a natural wave there in a stasis, almost like it was reaching out to you, wanting you to be with him in all this, and it had a warm, deserving smile. The color of its suit jacket did not match Pepe's normal blue.

The fifty-second Pepe he saw was a glance into the future, the condition of being after the meme. It was Pepe, old, pale, withered and weathered, not so smug but certainly not humble. It was gentle. It had seen too many days to fight for any of the remaining ones.

The fifty-third Pepe he saw was a reply to the previous one, and, with the same face and washed-out colors, this one also included a body with a wrinkly, dark, erect dick in a wrinkly, dark hard, and in front of Pepe's gaze was a picture of its younger self fucking a female tadpole, tearing in the eyes but clearly growing callous to the whole thing, which was quite impressive given the ratio of its member to the entire tadpole.

The fifty-fourth Pepe he saw was swiping right on a fat black woman named "Unique Mayo."

The fifty-fifth Pepe he saw was watching himself shit with a shit-eating grin by looking between its legs. The viewer was behind the frog.

The fifty-sixth Pepe he saw was Max Stirner, smug but looking off to the side.

The fifty-seventh Pepe he saw was mostly a silhouette facing the backlight of the computer monitor. On the monitor was the Board, and in its visible post was another Donald Trump Pepe.

The fifty-eighth Pepe he saw was misleadingly smug as it held a double-barrel shotgun to the back of his head, an impossible angle and perspective for its apparently broken arms.

The fifty-ninth Pepe he saw was accompanied by a quote, "Memes were a mistake."

The sixtieth Pepe he saw was a sad native from France.

The sixty-first Pepe he saw was excited for something, a unique expression on its face, and its eyes had color, green, a break from the tradition, and its hands were up next to its open mouth in anticipation.

The sixty-second Pepe he saw was sad and surrounded by other smug Pepes who were out of focus.

The sixty-third Pepe he saw was force-feeding Wojak bleach with an elaborate contraption that appeared to force Wojak's mouth open, much like a dentist's speculum, and Wojak's face was anguished.

The sixty-fourth Pepe he saw was going to sleep, sad, and facing the other direction. Its body was underneath a red blanket and its head on a pillow, and the entire color scheme was a bit darkened.

The sixty-fifth Pepe he saw was dancing, with different proportions, a leg kicked up in the air, a top hat being tipped, a small cane, and a crushing depression visible in its face.

The sixty-sixth Pepe he saw was depressed and staring at a picture in its hand, held up before its face. There was a caption above, slightly overlapping with Pepe's forehead, in a '90s teal with some basic WordArt font. It read: "I still love you."

The sixty-seventh Pepe he saw was wearing a breathing mask connected to a tank marked 'helium.'

The sixty-eighth Pepe he saw was a sexually-ambgiuous Latin-American-looking Pepe with a huge neon-painted sign that had a rainbow dick cumming an ISIS banner. It was smug.

The sixty-ninth Pepe he saw was blowing a kiss to a dead Wojak lying next to a speculum with bleach in a small pool on the ground next to Wojak's face.

The seventieth Pepe he saw was a Godzilla-sized mass of its own faces and huge, erect dicks. All of the Pepes were spewing cum over a crumbling city. A cheap imitation.

The seventy-first Pepe he saw was mostly a silhouette facing the backlight of the computer monitor. It was visibly creating another Pepe on the screen.

The seventy-second Pepe he saw was his own creation, an imagining of Pepe behind the counter, selling crisps, after all of it. The room was dark, and the stock was shanty. Pepe was looking out into the seemingly distant light of the outdoors. He was sad. He posted it several times, but never saw it reposted, and so it drifted safely into obscurity.

A Poem Written by Heiko in English as He Broke Down

...

When I was stuck in years and years of rote,

My mind would walk to distant greens,

And there I'd sing a pleasant note.

There was something blond or dark-haired,

A constant variety of scenes,

Whatever my adolescent fancy dared.

And later in freer or sadder times,

I found a girl of my dreams,

And in her freed my greatest crimes.

What I knew after was refined,

To a number of changing themes,

That my love wasn't blind.

Further that my love was far-sighted,

That it loved extremes,

In distance it was delighted.

And mostly that my heart's vision

Found a lot of in-betweens,

With a most tragic precision.

Kodachrome.

John von Dorf is a straight, white male, an

www.ingramcontent.com/pod-product-compliance
Lightning Source LLC
Chambersburg PA
CBHW022211050726
47590CB00002B/744